VULPI

VULPI

kate GORDON

RANDOM HOUSE AUSTRALIA

A Random House book
Published by Random House Australia Pty Ltd
Level 3, 100 Pacific Highway, North Sydney NSW 2060
www.randomhouse.com.au

First published by Random House Australia in 2012

Addresses for companies within the Random House Group can be found at
www.randomhouse.com.au/offices.

National Library of Australia
Cataloguing-in-Publication Entry

Author: Gordon, Kate
Title: Vulpi / Kate Gordon
ISBN: 978 1 74275 236 5 (pbk.)
Target audience: For young adults
Subjects: Tasmania – Juvenile fiction
Dewey number: A823.4

Cover photograph of girl by Madalina Popa Photography
Other cover photograph © iStockphoto.com/Gago-Image
Cover design by Christabella Designs
Internal design by Christabella Designs
Typeset in Minion 11/17 pt by Midland Typesetters, Australia
Printed in Australia by Griffin Press, an accredited ISO AS/NZS 14001:2004
Environmental Management System printer

This one's just for you, Bear, for teaching me that we're all made of stardust. And because, of all the stars in the sky, for me you shine the brightest.

CHapter
one

'HOW SHOULD I BEGIN?' I ASKED.

Tessa found me sitting alone by the smouldering coals of our dying campfire. I held a pen in my right hand. On my knee was the journal she'd given me after the fight at Cascade Falls school. After she came back to us.

She thought it might help me to have somewhere to put my thoughts but it had been weeks now and the pages were a desert. I just didn't know where to start.

Tessa sat down, fixing me with those eyes that seemed much too old for her young face. *Were* too old. She tilted her head to one side. 'Are you still having trouble, Cat?'

I nodded.

'I suppose . . . Just begin with your name. Or even with one *word*. That is how *everything* starts, isn't it? With one tiny, tentative step into the forest.' She smiled and reached across to squeeze my hand. Then she disappeared into the night, off to patrol.

'Trouble is, you need to know which direction you're meant to walk in,' I muttered. I looked down at the faintly lined pages, stroking them with the tips of my fingers.

I took a deep breath and wrote on the very top line:

Cat.

'Awesome start, Cat,' I whispered. 'You've read a million books and that's the best you can do?'

I closed my eyes. I pictured myself: red hair, pale skin, green eyes, just like my mother. Then I pictured my new self. My real self. Fangs. Claws. Ankles long and bending back. Pointed ears. That Cat was fearless. That Cat wouldn't let some stupid pages beat her.

That Cat was a Thyla.

Once, I ran away. Well, actually it was more like I ran away from running away. It was just after Tessa disappeared. After she left I felt like half of me was gone. The clearing seemed even bigger, my thoughts even louder. I couldn't handle the noise of them. So I made sure the camp was disguised, all evidence of our existence hidden, and I ran.

It wasn't far from the mountain to Mum's new house in Sandy Bay and I knew that she always left one upstairs window around the back open to let the air in. Mum's a cop so of course she made sure it was too high for a human to reach. But I was a Thyla. I could leap. I let myself in and I lay on her bed, smelling the lavender perfume she loved, which seemed to cling to everything.

I missed the smell.

I missed cooking currant pikelets together for brekkie every weekend and dancing around the kitchen singing Willie Nelson songs and the way she always cried when she laughed. I missed being little and falling asleep on her lap and her carrying me to bed. I missed days spent running under the sprinkler and making ourselves into sand mermaids at the beach and how she always stroked my hair when I felt sick.

I missed my mum.

I went through old photo albums and I saw me as a wild-haired, freckle-faced toddler, safely wrapped up in her arms. I flipped past photos of Mum's best friend, Cynthia Hindmarsh and her husband, Raphael, trying to forget what Ms Hindmarsh had done and what he had become. Raphael was a Sarco – half-devil. He was turned not long after he and Ms Hindmarsh married. Then ten years later he disappeared. The Diemens got him. But Mum didn't know that. And she didn't know her best friend had betrayed the Thylas; betrayed *all* of us to the Diemens because they promised to turn Raphael human again. They never fulfilled their promise and Raphael was still missing. Mum didn't know anything about the Thylas then. She still doesn't know that I'm one of them.

There were a couple of photos of Dad with Mum and me. I tried to see it in his eyes – a hint of what was to come.

I sat there for ages.

Just looking at us.

Missing us.

I only sneaked away like that once. It was weak and I felt so guilty about it. Guarding the Thyla camp site might not seem like the most important job but it was still wrong to leave. Whenever I thought about running off now, all I had to do was imagine the look on Tessa's face when she found out and I knew that I'd need a really, *really* good excuse for ever leaving again.

What I needed to find wasn't at Mum's house anyway. What I needed I wouldn't find by going backwards. By being the girl I used to be – Sergeant Connolly's kid. That wasn't what I wanted and I knew it wasn't what my father wanted for me.

He wanted me to find *me*.

I was trying. I was looking. But I was lost. I'd run away from everything, even myself, and along the way I'd shed my former selves like a snake shedding its skin.

I wasn't the policewoman's daughter any more. I wasn't the outcast student any more.

I was a Thyla. That was all I knew. That was a start, though, wasn't it?

I pressed my pen down again and another word sprouted on the page.

Thyla.

I looked at the tiny dark furrows I'd made on the paper. I stared so long that the words stopped making sense. They became just marks, like grooves cut through earth. Like veins under skin. I needed to make more than marks. I needed to make *meaning*. I picked up my pen and spun it around in my fingers. Then I began to write.

> *We are shapeshifters. Our blood is half-human, half-thylacine. We don't grow old but severe wounding can kill us. And we're born through violence – through bite and blood.*
>
> *Before the biting and the blood we're human, just like the rest of you.*

CHapter
two

THE FIRST THING I HAVE TO WRITE ABOUT IS THE DAY we said goodbye to Beagle.

It was two weeks since the Diemens had attacked Cascade Falls. Two weeks since we fought them in the forest. Sarcos, Thylas and humans had died, Rhiannah and Laurel were taken. Tessa had returned.

But we lost Beagle.

I liked Beagle. He was soft where Isaac was hard. He was like a crumpled envelope. You could see bits of words written on the paper. Bits of life. But the creases stopped you from seeing all of it. I liked trying to figure him out.

And he was even more intent on deciphering me.

'Why do you stay here, Cat?' he'd ask over and over.

'Why do *you*?' I'd counter, but I knew his reasons were clearer than mine. Beagle had been doing this for over a century. His family had all died long ago. Our leader Isaac was the closest thing to family he had.

Me? My mum was still alive. And my mum was good. Everybody knew that. Everybody knew Rachel Connolly was the best of the best. Beagle hadn't understood how I could abandon her like I had. Everyone loved Rachel Connolly. And that was part of the problem. Part of the reason I had to leave.

But it wasn't the whole reason. Not even close.

'I do it to protect other girls from the Diemens,' I'd say finally, when Beagle wouldn't give up. 'I do it because I'm a Thyla now and you're my family. And I do it because I want to get rid of Edward Lord. Like all of you do.'

I'd said that before we found out about the Solution. Before the battle in the forest. Before Isaac was kicked out of Lord's circle.

And I meant it. If Beagle could ask me again I'd only mean it more. But Beagle had known that there was something else I was looking for. Something else I hoped being a Thyla would help me to find. And he'd wanted to know what that something else was. He wanted to know *me*. He died still trying.

I was glad. Maybe some secrets should be kept. Maybe some goodbyes should be forever.

I thought again, as I often did, of the words I'd read two years ago, while crouched on the floor of my home back in Campbell Town, before I ran away for the first time. I wondered how my life would be different now if I'd never seen that letter. I thought of the little girl dressed in black, with all the crying adults holding her tight. Of the secrets they'd conspired with her mother to bury along with the man in the coffin. Of the truth they'd kept from her for so many years.

From me.

In the Thyla world we don't have funerals. We don't dress in black. We don't cry. We don't bury bodies in coffins. It's a bit difficult to do that when there's no body left to bury. When the body has already turned to dust and dirt.

Instead we sit around the campfire and tell stories about the Thyla we lost. We throw earth on the fire to release their souls and the souls of all the Thylas who have come before them into the air and the universe. I like it. I like that way of saying goodbye.

I knew my grief was small compared with what some of the other Thylas were going through. I hadn't been a Thyla for long. I looked at Isaac and Tessa and I knew that inside them were hundreds of years of sadness, of love, of fighting, of hope and of loss. I still couldn't imagine what that would be like.

I still didn't understand immortality. I didn't under-stand much about this life at all. But when a clan-mate died it felt like death and life were creatures too, standing in the middle of the clearing with us. Impossible to ignore.

Beagle wasn't the first Thyla who'd died while I'd been in the clan but he was the first one I was close to. We were a small army now: Tessa, Isaac, Delphi, Luda, Boots, Hatch and me; the last of the Thylas. Delphi and I lived here in the clearing full-time. The others came and went. They had jobs. Lives. But when Isaac called they came. Still, we weren't enough, just by ourselves. We weren't enough to fight the Diemens. That much was clear now. Our army needed to grow. And we'd started to, with the treaty.

We'd added Sarcos to our army.

The Sarcos were coming to Beagle's goodbye. Isaac had invited them as a sign of kinship and solidarity. The treaty wasn't final yet but we were well on our way. Rha had come. And Perrin and Harriet and five other Sarcos whose names I didn't know but whose faces I recognised. I was grateful to them for coming when they were still going through so much themselves.

Harriet was still grieving for Sara, her friend at Cascade Falls, and Perrin was still frantic over his sister Rhiannah. I knew the Sarcos had been looking for her all day, like they did every day. Rhiannah had been my roommate back at Cascade Falls. She'd been the closest thing I had to a friend in that place. I hated the thought of what the Diemens might be doing to her. I hated the thought that she was somehow caught up in this whole Solution business. We didn't entirely know what it was yet, or what the Diemens could do with it, but we knew it was scary. We knew the Diemens had been testing the Solution on shapeshifters. Were they using it on her? I didn't trust all the Sarcos but I knew that Rhiannah was good. She'd been good to me.

Many Sarcos didn't believe *any* Thylas could be good. That's why only some of the Sarcos were at Beagle's goodbye. Like Delphi, the rest had chosen to stay away.

Delphi was the only one in our small Thyla family who really disagreed with the treaty. The rest of us could see the necessity of it even though every fibre of our beings told us it was unnatural. But Delphi believed you could never trust a Sarco. Especially if they were acting like a friend.

'It's a farce,' she growled as she packed up her belongings for a night away from camp. 'I'll say my own goodbyes to Beagle. Proper goodbyes. Without Sarco scum there to dirty them.'

I didn't ask Delphi why she hated the Sarcos so much. I had once before and it hadn't gone down too well. I accepted that it was a secret she didn't want to share with me. I was okay with that. Instead I just put my hand on her shoulder. She blushed and tears sparkled in her eyes. 'Cat,' she said, her voice splintering. 'Cat, it's two weeks now and the pain hasn't gone away. Not even a little bit.'

'It will. It does,' I lied. Sometimes the pain of losing someone never goes away. Not even if you didn't really know them. But I couldn't tell Delphi that.

She leaned in, putting her head on my shoulder. 'I'd leave if it wasn't for you,' she whispered. My muscles stiffened. I hated it when Delphi said things like that. I hated being reminded of how she felt about me; feelings I could never return. She pulled away, wiping roughly at her face. 'Gotta run,' she said, flashing a small, plastic smile. 'I hope the goodbye goes well. Beagle deserves . . . he deserved it.'

And then Delphi walked away.

I felt someone at my side. 'Are you all right, Cat?'

I turned around to see Tessa standing next to me. She'd managed to sneak out from Cascade Falls and Charlotte Lord's constant watch for the night. Charlotte had sneaked off herself, to a nightclub, when she thought Tessa was asleep. It wasn't the first time she'd gone out like that at night and it made it easier for Tessa to get away and join us in the clearing. The new acting principal, Mrs Bush, didn't seem to notice any of this. Tessa said she was much less watchful than Ms Hindmarsh had been.

But at least she wasn't making deals with the Diemens.

'I'm doing better than Delph,' I said. I tried a smile but it faltered and fell.

'The relationship between a creator and their created is a strange and intense one, isn't it?' Tessa said solemnly. 'I'm finding that out all over again.'

'With Isaac?' I said.

'And you.'

We were interrupted by a shout. 'Tessa! Cat! Time to start now!' Isaac's voice was gruff and growling but I knew it was hiding worlds of pain. He loved Beagle, perhaps more than any of us had.

Tessa took my hand in hers. 'Come, Cat,' she said. 'Time to say goodbye.'

We were sitting around the fire, dirt on our hands and a weightlessness in our hearts. We'd let Beagle go. We watched the flames flicker and fade, lost in our own thoughts and memories. I remembered Beagle's dusty smell, laced with coffee and tobacco; his black sense of humour; his encyclopaedic knowledge of history. Before I knew Beagle as a Thyla he was just a teacher I saw around the hallways of Cascade Falls. I'd walk past him with a 'don't-mess-with-me' expression on my face, the way I did with all teachers. That's how 'rebels' acted. That's how the *cool* kids acted. The ones people liked. The ones who *shone*. And that's who I'd wanted to be. I was glad I got to know him better, outside of school. Beagle deserved to be looked at and listened to. I was glad I got the opportunity to show him I wasn't that insolent, disrespectful kid. That I wasn't really a rebel. Not even close.

I glanced over at Isaac. His jaw was tense. His eyes were closed. I looked away before they opened. I didn't want him to think I was staring.

Eventually, Rha stood up. 'Well, friends . . .' he began.

We heard it then: a crashing, pounding, smashing noise coming through the bracken and the sound of rasping breaths. My hand flew to my cuff. Next to me, Tessa's hand was on hers. All around the circle, hands grasped cuffs – the only things that stopped us going Thyla and Sarco. Going wild.

'It's me.' I heard his voice before he came out of the trees. Hatch. He pushed through, his face caked in dirt and blood. 'You need to come. The Diemens have attacked. Three girls taken. Three girls dead. One from Cascade Falls. And Charlotte Lord –' Hatch stopped in front of us, panting. He bent over with his hands on his knees.

'What *about* Charlotte?' Tessa asked. I saw her neck muscles tightening, her jaw tensing. I knew why because I felt it too. Charlotte Lord wasn't just the prefect responsible for supervising Tessa at school; she wasn't only the queen bitch of Cascade Falls, she was also the daughter of the worst Diemen of all. Edward Lord.

Hatch straightened and wiped the sweat from his brow with the back of his hand. A fresh streak of blood made a pattern like war paint on his forehead. 'She was there,' he said. 'One of her friends died.'

'But she was spared?' Tessa asked.

'Of course she was!' I cried. 'Her dad's their boss!'

'But she doesn't know that, Cat,' Isaac reminded me tersely. 'To her it will just seem as if one of her friends has been randomly taken.' Isaac turned to Hatch. 'Where did the attack take place?'

'They were out. At a club,' Hatch said. 'I was only meant to be there for a quick drink to steel myself for this. But after what happened I had to stay and try to help. I guess the Diemens didn't realise Charlotte was there. They mustn't have known it was Charlotte's friend they were attacking.'

'Did Charlotte . . . see?' Tessa asked.

Hatch shook his head. 'From what I can tell she was with a boy. But she went looking for her friend after she hadn't seen her for a while. She found her body. And two others.' He looked at Tessa. 'She was pretty messed up. I looked after her. Talked to her. That's how I know what happened. She wasn't coping too well.'

'Poor Charlotte,' Tessa whispered.

'Wait,' I said. 'You said three girls dead and three girls *taken . . .*'

Hatch's eyes snapped up to meet mine. 'Yes,' he said tightly.

'Why would they kill some of the girls there and then but not all of them?' I asked. 'Usually the Diemens take their kills away, don't they? Why would they change their habits like that?'

'Cat, I don't know.' Hatch said. 'Why would you think *I* had any idea?'

'Isaac, do you know –?'

'No,' Isaac snapped. 'Lord's decided he doesn't want me in his circle any more, remember? He's done working with "humans" after what happened with Hindmarsh. Just our luck he kicked me out before I managed to learn anything useful about where they hide or what's actually bloody going on with this Solution.' Isaac shook his head. 'We need to work out what the hell the Diemens are up to. These past couple of weeks have been bullshit. We've found nothing. We need to work harder.' Isaac grabbed his satchel and pulled out his blue police jumper.

'We've been trying, Isaac,' Tessa said. 'We've been out every day. We delayed Beagle's goodbye until now so we could concentrate on –'

'From now, we up the ante.' Isaac looked at Hatch again. 'Are the police there already? Is Connolly there?'

I bristled at the sound of my mum's name.

Hatch nodded. 'Connolly's there. And the other police are trying to make sense of what happened.'

Isaac shook his head. 'The last thing we need is those meat-heads cottoning on to what's really happening.' He sighed. 'Another "incident" I'm going to have to work out how to cover up. We can't let the public know about this. We need to get there before my esteemed colleagues do anything stupid, like tell the media. Or let the Lord girl tell the media. Or *anything*. We need to be in control of this situation. Come with me,' Isaac said to Hatch. 'You can tell me more while we drive.'

As Isaac and Hatch were swallowed by the shadows of the forest, I turned towards Tessa. My mouth was open, ready to talk about what had happened. But Tessa wasn't alone. I was surprised to see Harriet standing next to her. Harriet and Tessa had become friends at Cascade Falls, before either of them knew what Tessa really was. But since they'd both found out, the friendship had withered. Thylas and Sarcos might be able to get along now but they definitely weren't friends.

Across the clearing I could see Rha and Perrin and the rest of the Sarcos standing by the forest edge. Why was Harriet making them wait?

'I have a message for you, Tessa,' she said. My eyes flicked to Tessa. I expected her to look surprised.

Instead, Tessa nodded. 'All right. I'll be back in a moment, Cat.'

I nodded. What was going on?

I watched as Tessa and Harriet walked away. Without Tessa to talk to, my thoughts grew big and heavy inside me. I was bursting with questions about Beagle and Charlotte and dead girls and Diemens and Sarcos and Thylas.

And my mum. She was there, at the scene. She was still living, still working, still carrying on. Without me. I shook my head. I couldn't think about Mum. Not now. No matter how much I wished she was here with me, holding me. I couldn't let the Sarcos see me cry.

Instead, I thought about what Hatch had told us. Three girls dead. Three *taken*. What was going on with the Diemens?

Was it all to do with the Solution?

I looked across the clearing. Harriet walked away from Tessa towards the Sarcos and Tessa moved back towards me.

'What was that?' I asked.

'Nothing you need to worry about,' Tessa said, smiling. 'I'm tired. Harriet and I are going to go back to Cascade together. Will you be quite well here by yourself?' I half-smiled at Tessa's old-fashioned language. Sometimes it was easy to forget she'd been raised a hundred and fifty years ago. Sometimes it was all too obvious. Even though she had her memory back after her fall she still seemed stuck in the nineteenth century.

I shrugged. 'Of course I'll be okay on my own. I'm used to it.'

'If we thought you'd be in danger here we would not leave you,' Tessa said. 'But –'

'The Diemens never come this far up the mountain, I know,' I said.

Tessa squeezed my shoulder. 'I will see you soon,' she said. Then she turned around and walked away, leaving me alone in the forest. The clearing was too quiet now. Beagle's campfire was still smouldering. I approached it and threw one more clump of dirt.

'I don't want to say goodbye, Beagle,' I said. 'I don't want you to go.'

I lay on the ground, looking up at the stars. 'Are you still up there somewhere?' This time I wasn't talking to Beagle. I closed my eyes. 'Are you watching me?' I whispered, before I let the soft hum of the bush sing me to sleep.

CHAPTER

THREE

I HAD THE STRANGEST DREAM THAT NIGHT, BRIGHTLY coloured and solid as the ground I slept on. I felt the dream and smelled it too. It was more real than waking life.

In it, Charlotte was in a dark room. Above her was a bare flickering light globe. The walls were made of sandstone and were lined with shelves of beer and wine. Thudding house music made the room vibrate but despite the noise I could hear it.

A whimpering. A sobbing. Coming from Charlotte.

'Wake up. Wake up, Jenna.'

Cradled in Charlotte's arms was the body of her friend. The dead girl was dressed in a tight white mini-dress, soaked through with wine-coloured blood. And at its chest, a section of fabric had been ripped away.

Beneath the fabric the skin had been ripped away too. And the ribs broken.

Her heart had been stolen. That's what the Diemens did. They stole hearts and ate them. They stole blood and bathed in it. That's how they got their power and how they lived forever. Unless we stopped them.

On the floor next to Charlotte were another two bodies. One of them wore a pink dress and the other wore jeans and a leather jacket. Hers was the only chest that hadn't been ripped apart.

The stone tiles were slick with blood.

Charlotte's whimpers turned into screams. 'Help!' she cried. 'Please! My friend's been murdered!'

The scene changed then. The basement blurred into another location. It was a mansion, high up on a hill overlooking Hobart. It was painted charcoal grey. The windows were tinted black.

And there was Charlotte again, walking up the front steps in a white pants suit. She was carrying a tray covered in a white cloth with scalloped edges.

She pressed the doorbell.

For a moment there was no sound except the distant squalling of seagulls.

'Hello? Daddy, are you home?' Charlotte balanced the tray on her knee, took a key from her pants pocket and opened the door. 'Daddy?' she called out. 'Are you there? I just came to say hello.'

Charlotte walked inside. As she closed the door behind her she looked out into the night and for a moment it seemed as though her icy eyes locked on mine.

Like she saw me.

But then she was gone and my eyes were flying open and I was sitting up from my bed on the forest floor, my heart bursting from my chest. What was that? What had I seen?

I didn't like it. I didn't want it. I was scared. Properly scared. I knew it was only a dream, but I felt more terrified than I had for a long time – and I'd been scared lots of times since I became a Thyla. All of a sudden I felt very lonely. The world seemed so big and I felt so small. I tucked my knees up to my chest. And silently, I started to cry.

CHAPTER
four

DELPHI AND I WERE MEANT TO BE GUARDING THE CAMP
together. We were the only ones who spent our days
here, the only ones without homes or jobs or school
to go to. Tessa used to stay here too, before she went
to Cascade Falls but now it was just me and Delph.
The camp site was mostly used for meetings, and it
was up to Delphi and me to make sure our clearing
wasn't found.

Not that there was much to find. Even though the
Diemens never came this high up the mountain, we still
needed to make ourselves as invisible as possible. We
hadn't built any structures. It wasn't designed to be a
permanent home. Delphi and I didn't have a bathroom
or a kitchen. We washed in the icy stream and we

cooked for everyone on the campfire. We slept under the stars.

Lucky we shapeshifters don't mind the cold.

The clearing was functional. And it was sort of home, I guess. But it could get so quiet.

Delphi didn't like quiet. Delphi liked screaming and yelling and growling. She liked metal music played at full volume. She liked the buzz of a tattoo machine and the *thunk* of a piercer's gun. The quiet made her itch. Sometimes she itched so much she just had to *go*. She'd do it while I was sleeping. We took turns, napping and keeping watch. And sometimes I'd wake up and she'd be gone. There'd always be a note, written in Delphi's crazy huge writing.

Today it said: 'Gone AWOL sleepy little tiger. Back soon I promise. Love Delphi.'

The 'love' was written much bigger than all the other words.

Without Delphi to protect me from them with her noise and chaos, my thoughts seized the opportunity to take me over. They didn't like being pushed aside. They didn't like it when I ignored them. They wanted me to see them. They wanted me to remember.

They wanted to be in charge.

On other days I might have fought them off. I could usually manage to distract myself with petty jobs or with singing or talking to the animals in the forest or trying to retell the story of *Tess of the D'Urbervilles* in my head.

But not today. Today nothing worked and after a while my thoughts grabbed hold of me and led me away. They took me back to the dream, to the hollow chests and screaming. And then they took me to Rhiannah.

They showed me her bruised and bloody and broken, tortured by the Diemens. It made my stomach churn, made acid burn in my throat. And then the image changed. The pictures in my mind grew even darker. I saw blood soaking through hay. My small hands wet with it. And his face. Lifeless. But his eyes still watched me. They were always watching me. Waiting for me to do what he'd asked of me.

I hated my thoughts for leading me to those images.

I hated my memory for keeping them there.

I hated the letter that reminded me of it all.

I hated Isaac for making me stay in the clearing while the others went out and *lived*. I knew I couldn't go back to the human world like they did but surely there was something I could do that *meant* something. Something more than pacing in circles and tidying sticks.

A new scent floated towards me. Wallaby. I looked up. There were three of them. They crept up to the edge of the clearing and watched me curiously, sniffing the air with their shiny black noses.

'Dance with me,' I said to the wallabies. 'Come on.' I stood up. 'It helps. Come and dance with me.' The wallabies cocked their heads, looking at me like I was mad. 'Fine,' I whispered as they bounded back into the bush. 'I'll dance alone. It's fine. I'm used to it.'

Delphi sneaked back into the clearing only moments before Isaac popped in to check up on us. He didn't tell us what – if anything – he'd found today. He rarely did. He looked grumpy. And Delphi – far from being all meek and sheepish about nearly being caught sneaking in – was spoiling for a fight. When Isaac asked grouchily why Delphi wasn't helping me with dinner she found what she was looking for.

'What, do I *look* like Nigella Lawson?' she snapped.

Delphi hated cooking. She thought Isaac made it our job because he was a misogynistic bastard. 'He thinks a woman's place is in the kitchen,' she'd say with a roll of her eyes. 'Comes from being brought up, literally, two hundred years ago.'

I actually enjoyed cooking. I always had, ever since I was a kid and Mum and I would cook together. So I didn't really mind when Delphi left me to it.

She was a crap cook anyway.

But Isaac minded. 'Do I look like I *care*, Delphi?' he growled.

'This isn't fair. It's just another example of your patriarchal approach to this clan. You never ask our opinions. You never ask us what we think of this treaty. You never ask us our thoughts on the Solution or why the Diemens abandoned the girls at the nightclub or –'

'Delphi, do I need to remind you that only a few weeks ago you left your post and allowed Diemens into Cascade Falls? I'm sorry if I don't value your opinion all that highly.' Isaac started to walk away.

'Yeah? As if you've never made mistakes!' Delphi called out after him.

Isaac looked at Delphi over his shoulder. 'Delphi, I may have made mistakes – many of them – but never on purpose. Because of you, a human girl is at the mercy of Lord and his men. And one of our new allies is, quite possibly, being experimented on. Tortured. That's a pretty huge mistake.'

'When am I going to *not* be in trouble for that?' Delphi cried.

'When we find them.' Isaac's eyes flashed amber and furious.

'But so much stuff has gone down since then!' Delphi protested. 'More attacks. And there's so much we still need to do. Why can't we concentrate on that? Seriously,

Isaac, you're the one who's always saying the past is the past!'

Isaac paused and looked at Delphi thoughtfully. 'You're right,' he said. 'It is important to leave things in the past and move on. But it's also important to prove that the mistakes of the past have been learned from. And I don't believe you have learned from your experience at Cascade Falls. You shirked your responsibility and because of that your kin were in danger. I need to know that won't happen again. I need to know that if you are put in a situation like that again you would act as a Thyla should and protect your clan. In the meantime, you will stay here and perform the duties I ask of you, even if you think they're *below* you! It's not really that big an ask, is it? I still have to go to work every day. I don't get a break. And it's not like policing is getting any easier, with all these girls disappearing. Stop complaining. Life could be worse. You could be Rhiannah.' Isaac threw one more volcanic glare at us, then bent down and unclipped his ankle cuff. He shuddered as he turned Thyla, and then whipped around on his paws and sped off into the bush.

'Bastard,' Delphi muttered at his retreating back. She rolled her eyes and turned to me. '*Mon dieu, mon cheri!* What *are* we going to cook this *fine* day? Smoked salmon vol-au-vents? Coq au vin? Slow-cooked beef in red wine and peppercorn jus? *Oui?*' She swaggered towards me, grabbing an armful of kindling for the campfire on the way.

'Did you have a fun little outing?' I asked, raising an eyebrow at her.

Delphi dumped the kindling on the ground and pulled her Zippo from her pocket. It had the Metallica emblem printed on its side. 'Sorry for leaving, chook,' she said. She flopped down on a log, reaching behind her to retrieve the backpack she'd hastily stowed when we heard Isaac approaching. 'I didn't think I'd be gone that long. I promise I won't leave tomorrow.' She looked up at me with expectant eyes. 'Do you *want* me to stay?'

I looked away and changed the subject. 'You know, Nigella Lawson isn't French. She's more like this.' I cleared my throat and then said, in my best version of an upper-crust English accent, 'I was thinking we'd cook some cream with lashings of lard and a dollop of chocolate, baked in a case of lard pastry and then garnished with lard shavings and a light lard gravy. With a generous dollop of cream on top. Doesn't that sound *decadent*?'

Delphi laughed. 'That's hot,' she said. 'Do that voice again.'

'Shut up, Delphi,' I muttered.

The smile toppled from Delphi's face. For a moment there was silence. Then she said, 'You know, I hate them all. I hate that they force me into this "subser-vient woman" role. And I hate that they can't just get over what happened. They're never going to forgive me for that night. You're the only one who's worth giving the time of day.' And then she looked at me with *that* expression. The one that made my stomach lurch. That hungry, *wanting* look. 'If I left would you come with me?'

'What would we do? Join the circus?' I joked, trying to lighten the mood.

'I think we're already there. They're all clowns. This treaty's just a big three-ringed circus. We're the only true, good things left. You and me.' And there it was. That look again. That wanting. I didn't say anything. I never knew what to say when she looked at me like that. Then it was gone, replaced by anger. 'I'm just so *over* this,' Delphi growled, pitching a potato on the dirt. She ran her hand over her stubbly shaven head. 'Potatoes, carrots, beef – same thing every damn night! Ooh, maybe fish stew for a super special treat! Yippee!' She threw her hands up in the air, showing the skull and crossbones tattoo that covered her left forearm and the dagger and rose one that decorated the right. For a while neither of us said anything. Then in a calmer voice, Delphi said, 'Thanks for not dobbing me in to Isaac. I just needed to get away, you know?'

'You're in enough trouble already,' I said, shrugging. 'And it's no big deal. Nothing happens in this clearing anyway. So. How are you at making damper?'

'You want me to crochet you a cardigan while I'm at it?' Delphi sighed. 'Okay, okay. Let's make this stupid damper then.'

We worked in silence for the next hour, kneading bread and chopping vegetables and cooking meat over the hot coals. 'I suppose we have to go off on patrol again with those bloody Sarcos tonight, hey?' Delphi said finally, as she poked at the mound of blackening bread. She'd overcooked it but I didn't want to interfere. 'Seriously, have the others *forgotten* that the Sarcos are our natural enemies? It makes more sense for us to side with the Diemens than it does for us to side with them.'

Now that I *couldn't* agree with. We could never side with the Diemens. The Diemens were murderers. They were cold-blooded psychopaths. They *ate girls' hearts.* Delphi had gone totally bonkers if she thought the Diemens were better than the Sarcos. The Sarcos may have fought us for centuries but it was only instinct making them do that. And they never attacked us without a reason. If we came into their territory, instinct told them to fight us. Our instincts told us to fight them back. I knew that. The first time I saw a Sarco, just after I'd turned Thyla, every instinct in my body told me to kill it. I knew they felt the same about us. It was in our blood. We'd fought the Sarcos for centuries over this territory and some of us had died in the process. But now we'd come together. We were fighting side by side against a common enemy. The Diemens.

Because it *wasn't* instinct that made them do what they did. It was pure evil. The Diemens were horrific creatures. They terrified me. I opened my mouth to disagree with her but the words caught in my throat as I saw a flash of something in the trees that circled the clearing.

At first I thought it was Isaac coming back again. Or one of our other kin. But it was the wrong colour for a Thyla. It was too copper. I grabbed Delphi's arm. She inclined her face towards mine. 'Hey,' she said softly.

'There's something there,' I said.

'What?' Delphi's eyebrows shot up. 'What is it?'

I pushed myself upwards to a crouch and sniffed the air.

'Did you –'

I held a finger to my lips. Delphi nodded and rose quietly to her feet. Together we crept forwards towards the dense forest, neither of us breathing. There was no sign of the copper flash again but I could hear something not far away, darting through the grasses. 'Is it Sarco?' Delphi hissed.

I shook my head. 'No. Wrong colour.'

'Was it just a wallaby or –'

'No.' Even though I'd only seen a glimpse of it and not a whole form, I knew it wasn't a regular creature. It was big like us. It was a shapeshifter. Crap. I tried to think what Tessa or Isaac would do now. I tried to remember the skills I'd learned when Delphi and I had practised fighting. I moved my cuff down a bit so I could use just some of my powers. I sniffed the air. I tried to catch its scent but all I could make out was that it was *foreign*. It wasn't a Thyla. I'd need to take my cuff all the way off to make out more and I didn't want to do that. Not yet. Just in case it was something harmless, maybe just a big dog being walked by a human who'd strayed off the track.

We kept moving forwards. We were out of the clearing now; stalking between the gum trees and Huon pines. I saw Delphi's hand move towards her cuff. I shook my head. 'Not yet,' I mouthed. I couldn't hear it any more. The forest was still. The only noise was the whispering breeze and the 'yack yack' call of the wattlebirds. Delphi looked to me for guidance. I don't know why she thought *I* knew what I was doing. I looked around. I sniffed the air and listened. All I could smell was Thyla. Relief flooded through me. I relaxed my posture and said, still quietly, 'It's okay. I think it's –'

A rustle in the scrub behind us made me jerk. My muscles tensed. I planted my feet, ready to dart away from the creature, out of its path of attack. Why hadn't I smelled it? I reached for my cuff. Just as my claws curled around the rim, a soft hand fell on my shoulder. I took a deep breath inwards. It *was* only Thyla I could smell. And I knew the smell of this Thyla. The tension melted away.

'What are you doing out here?' Tessa asked as I turned around.

'I thought I saw . . .' I started. But then I noticed the look on Tessa's face. 'Tess, what happened? You're early.'

'Isaac just got a call from his station as he was coming into the city. He rang me at Cascade Falls.' Tessa's forehead wrinkled. She looked down at the forest floor. 'I came straight here. A bushwalker found her . . .' She trailed off.

'Found who?' I prompted. Her eyes jerked up to meet mine. They were wet. She blinked back the tears. *Tessa doesn't cry*, I thought. It must be something bad.

'They found . . .' She cleared her throat. 'In the bush. They found a body. They found Laurel.'

CHAPTER
five

after tessa told us her news, we'd gone out on patrol, even Delphi and me. I didn't tell anyone about the copper flash I'd seen. Everyone was too busy and preoccupied.

In the end the patrol was a failure. No evidence of Diemens. No sign of any further attacks. Which was good and bad. We had two goals on every patrol: protect the girls, and find the Diemens and kill them.

We'd only succeeded on the first goal tonight. And too late for Laurel.

By the time we got back, Delphi's damper was horrible but my stew was still pretty tasty. I was glad I could give the Thylas something nice when everybody was so sad.

And it was good to have the job of being cook and waitress to focus on. It made me forget for a little while about the funny, crazy girl with the ginger curls. The girl they'd found in the bush today, her body mangled. Killed by Diemens.

'The stew is lovely,' Tessa said and I felt my chest puff up a bit. But then it deflated when, after only managing a few bites, Tessa stood and said, 'I'm sorry, Delphi and Cat. It *is* very nice, but I need to get back to Cascade. Charlotte will be wondering where I am soon.'

'How is she?' I said.

I could almost *feel* Delphi rolling her eyes.

I knew she was wondering why I was so concerned about Charlotte. I'd told Delphi all about her; how much she hated me. I said it was because Charlotte thought I was 'wild'. I didn't tell her that Charlotte knew my wildness was only an act and that really she hated me for being so pathetic as to pull that act in the first place.

I'd also told Delphi about that day in the forest – the day I fell. I told her about Charlotte chasing me. Helping her father to catch his prey. She might not have known what he was after – why he wanted to catch me – but she had still chased. Because of her I'd nearly died. I could understand Delphi wondering why I cared how Charlotte was feeling.

So did I, to be honest. But I knew that Charlotte was hurting. Tessa said Charlotte had been as shocked as all the other girls at Cascade Falls when Ms Hindmarsh and Sara died, and Rhiannah and Laurel went missing. And now not only had she lost her friend Jenna, she'd been the one to find her body. I knew what a trauma like that could do to a person.

Tessa shook her head. 'I don't know, really. She still snaps at me sometimes, but it seems almost . . . half-hearted. She is still going to most of her classes. She is still avidly completing her prefect duties but something in the way she is behaving is . . . *off*. It is as though she is going through the motions. She seems almost . . . robotic when she is in class. The tragedies at the school and the nightclub are affecting her, of course, but I think there is something more. I can't put my finger on it. There was one night, about a week ago, when Charlotte came back to our dorm and she seemed as though she had seen a ghost. I asked her what was wrong and she told me to "piss off".'

'Charlotte never talks like that,' I said. 'She's never "uncouth".'

'And she is still going out, but now she goes alone.'

I bit my lip. I didn't like the sound of that.

'And, just sometimes, I see a *kindness* in her eyes that was never there before. An understanding. She will come to check in on me before I go to sleep and, only once or twice, she has asked how I am. And she seems to genuinely care about my answer.'

'Really?' I asked, hearing the disbelief in my voice. I couldn't imagine Charlotte Lord being kind to anyone.

Next to me, Delphi snorted. 'So the ice princess is gone for good, you reckon? I never met the girl but from what I've heard I wouldn't be too quick to believe it.'

Tessa shook her head. 'No, she is still an "icy princess". But something has changed. I do not know how long this change will last. I'm not certain if this metamorphosis will continue, or if she will revert to her old ways.' Tessa picked up her satchel and slung it over her shoulder. 'So much of these times seems bizarre to me,' she said quietly. 'It seems as though the more I know and remember, the less I understand. And just as I grasp something, it all changes once more.' She shook her head. 'I must go now.'

'Bye, Tessa,' I said.

'Goodbye, Cat.' Tessa smiled at me but her voice was flat. Her eyes had dark shadows under them and she moved more slowly than usual. Laurel was her friend. She must be aching inside. I knew how she felt. I felt like my insides were full of stones. Laurel and I had never been close but I'd liked her a lot. It didn't make sense that she was gone. It didn't feel real. Or fair.

'Are you okay?' Delphi put a hand on my shoulder. 'You knew her too. The girl they found.'

'Yeah,' I said. 'She was one of the good ones.'

I went off to clean the dinner things. When I came back, Delphi was still sitting by the fire. Her face was hard and she was examining the potato in her hand as though it had done something to offend her. 'What's up?' I asked.

Her head snapped up. She was grimacing. 'Nothing,' she growled.

I raised my eyebrows. 'Um, it doesn't look like nothing, Delph.'

Delphi shook her head roughly. She hurled the potato into the fire, where it sizzled and blackened. I bit my tongue. I'd worked hard on that potato. 'Forget it,' Delphi said. 'I don't want to talk about it.'

'Is it what happened to Laurel?' I asked. 'Do you feel guilty about what happened at Cascade? Or is it the Diemens? Are you worried about them getting more power or –'

Delphi's expression darkened even more. 'It's not the bloody Diemens, okay? Why do you think I'd be worried about the Diemens?'

I shrugged. 'You get a bit funny whenever people talk about them. It's okay to be scared of them. I know I am.'

'I'm not scared,' Delphi growled. 'And I'm not *guilty*. Yeah, so the Laurel girl was taken from Cascade Falls when *I* was meant to be patrolling there and now I'm probably going to get blamed for her *dying*, too. Hell! They're never gonna stop blaming me. But, you know, why doesn't anybody ever stop to ask me why I wasn't at my post that night, hey? Nobody gives a crap about what's going on with me!'

'So why *did* you leave, Delph?' I asked.

'Sometimes I just don't want to fight Diemens, okay? Don't be mad at me, please, Cat.' Delphi's eyes were on my face again, searching.

'It's okay,' I said.

Delphi smiled. Then in a quiet voice she said, 'You know, the Sarcos could be helping them.'

'What? *Delphi* –'

'I mean, I wasn't there. At my post. So it could have been Sarcos sneaking in to Cascade Falls. We already know they had people on the inside. Harriet, Sara, Rhiannah, Ms Hindmarsh –'

'Delphi, you're demented,' I said. 'Ms Hindmarsh was working with the Diemens –'

'And her husband was a Sarco! And Laurel's body was *left out,* wasn't it? Same as some of those girls at the nightclub. The Diemens don't leave bodies out.'

'Just eat your stew, doofus,' I said, jabbing her in the shoulder. 'You're talking crazy. You're overtired. You need to get some shut-eye.'

'I don't want to sleep,' Delphi whined.

I punched her on the arm. 'Don't plead "nocturnal" on me, Delphi.'

'But I *am* –'

'Shut up,' I said, smiling. Delphi was pretty good at playing the 'Thyla' card whenever she wanted to get out of doing something. In this case it was the *We're nocturnal so we don't sleep at night* card. Which is total crap. Our powers are stronger at night-time and we find it easier to turn when the moon is on us but we still turn during the day if we have to. And yeah, we don't necessarily have to sleep the *whole* night, but we still sleep when we're tired. And I was zonked.

'All right, all right!' Delphi groaned. 'You're such a bossy boots! I'm going to have to start calling you Mini Tessa if you keep being such a goody-goody.'

'I'm not a goody-goody.'

'Oh yeah, I forgot. You're a rebel.' Delphi started singing, *'You're a real wild child . . .'*

I put my fingers in my ears. Delphi had learned how to sing by listening to death metal. It wasn't pretty. 'I'm going to sleep now, Delphi!' I said, curling up on the ground. 'If you're so awake you can take first watch.'

Delphi stopped singing and I heard her rustling around in the leaves and dirt, getting comfortable. 'What do you think that thing was? Out in the bush?' she asked.

I rolled onto my back. 'I don't know,' I said. 'It could have been anything. It could have been my mind playing tricks on me. I mean *you* didn't see anything, did you?'

'No. But still, should we tell Isaac, you reckon?'

I thought for a moment. 'Not yet. I think he has enough to deal with. And after all, it *might* just be me going mental. I don't want Isaac and Tessa to think I'm crazy.'

'Yeah, we can't have that,' Delphi said, dryly. 'Can't have Tessa The Wonderful thinking you're not perfect. Gotta be just like Tessa, don't you?'

'Sleeping now, Delphi,' I said, rolling over. She didn't reply.

For a while everything was quiet and I started to drift off.

But just as I sank into sleep I heard Delphi's whisper, 'Don't turn out like Tessa. We're the same, you and me.'

CHapter

SIX

I DIDN'T KNOW WHY DELPHI WAS THE WAY SHE WAS. Maybe she'd always been wild. Or maybe something had happened to make her that way. I knew she'd been in trouble before she became a Thyla. She'd been in detention, at Ashford, which is where she met Beagle and where he turned her Thyla. Beagle volunteered at Ashford as a teacher. He turned Delphi after a brawl left her badly injured. He saw something in her that no one else at Ashford saw. A strength, an intelligence and a loyalty. He told me that. He never told me why Delphi was in Ashford in the first place and neither did she. I didn't push her.

Beagle was the only authority figure I ever saw Delphi show real respect. He was like a father to her. When he died Isaac didn't tell her straight away. She was at the school so she didn't see the battle. Isaac decided to wait until we were away from humans before he told her.

In case she did something crazy.

As it turned out, Isaac didn't have anything to worry about. When he did tell her, back at camp, she didn't turn wild. She just sat there nodding silently and reached out to hold my hand. 'You're all I've got now, Cat,' she whispered to me through gritted teeth.

I liked being friends with Delphi. It was just nice to have a *friend*, since I'd never had many before. It was good to have someone to talk to, especially another young Thyla still coming to grips with all of this. We had long talks about life and politics and all the messy, wonderful things that fascinated us about living.

We talked about what we missed about being human. I missed hot showers. And books. Especially books. Isaac and Tessa brought me as many as they could, when they remembered, but my appetite was huge and I devoured them so quickly they could never keep up. And, besides, Isaac kept bringing me Clive Cussler and James Bond and Tessa brought me whatever she could scrounge from the library at Cascade Falls without drawing attention. So mostly ancient Nancy Drews and Sweet Valley High books from the 1980s. I appreciated them bringing me anything but I would have given my right arm for a Thomas Hardy or a new release YA. Delphi was the same with new metal music. She had hundreds of songs on her MP3 player but she would have given anything for the new Opeth or Pain of Salvation. And she missed McDonald's. Sometimes, in her sleep, I heard her saying 'Big Mac and fries please, extra salt.'

We both knew we were better off here than in the human world, even with the lack of books and processed food. But it was impossible not to miss some things. I wondered if we'd always be like this. If we'd miss those things forever.

Delphi and I talked about forever too. About immortality. Neither of us could get our heads around that.

We talked about what we'd wanted for our futures before we turned Thyla. I'd have guessed Delphi would want to be a tattooist or a guitarist in a metal band but she surprised me by telling me she wanted to be a naturopath. She'd been studying natural medicine at the detention centre. She told me she wanted to help people get better.

I told her I hadn't known what I wanted to be back when I was human. Now I knew: I wanted to keep being a Thyla. And I wanted to help people too. I wanted to help all those girls the Diemens wanted to kill. Every death I stopped made up in some way for the one death I had helped to cause.

Delphi was off looking for potatoes. I'd sent her on the mission. Even though I didn't much like being alone in the clearing, I could tell she needed to get away. She was wound tight and fidgety, full of an anger I didn't know the cause of and was almost frightened to ask about. It could have been something to do with the treaty or it could have been deeper than that. Whatever the case, I knew she'd feel better after she had a march through the bush. Delphi liked walking. She'd take her MP3 player with her, which Hatch charged for her at work because he knew she'd be even crazier without her music. She'd plug in her headphones and get lost in the beats. Time became elastic. It was her way of blocking out the bad stuff. I knew she needed the escape. But I did hate being alone.

I tried to keep busy. But after half an hour of pacing and tidying things that really didn't need tidying (we were in the middle of a *forest*, for heaven's sake), I gave up.

I sat down on a log and closed my eyes and gave in to it.

I saw his face. This time he was smiling at me.

I didn't look like him. I had Mum's features. His hair was sandy, like Tessa's. His eyes were hazel and his skin was the same ruddy brown skin all farmers have. I don't remember much about him but laughter and dancing to Steve Earle and warm nights on the deck bouncing on his knee as he drank a stubby of Boag's and told Mum how he loved sunsets. 'So sad,' they said later. 'We didn't see it coming.' I never understood what they meant by that.

I opened my eyes again and let my sighs merge with the gentle wind that whispered through the trees. I didn't want to think any more; I knew what thoughts would come after the happy ones. His face would change. He wouldn't be smiling. I didn't want to see that.

I'd told myself I wouldn't run away again. Or at least, not without a good reason.

But I was getting sick of being stuck up here. What good could I do in the clearing? The Diemens never came this far up the mountain and if they did, the worst that might happen was them finding our sleeping bags stuffed into the logs. I couldn't make any difference to anything staying here. I'd be a speck of dust forever if Isaac had his way.

A thought struck me: the others only patrolled at night but why *shouldn't* we patrol during the day too? The Diemens hunted at night but they were behaving so strangely at the moment, wasn't there a *possibility* they'd attack during the day? And that thing I'd seen – that flash of copper – that was in the daytime too. Of course it was still probable that I hadn't seen anything at all and my mind was just going screwy after all that time alone in the bush . . . But even so, I could still watch out for Diemens. I could still fight one if I saw one. It was true that Thylas were more powerful at night but we *could* still change during the day. We could still use the daytime hours to patrol. I could still be useful. I was surprised nobody had thought of it before!

Delphi was gone but she'd be back soon. And even if she wasn't the clearing had never had blood spilt on its dirt before. I doubted it ever would. There was no harm in me leaving.

'Dad,' I whispered, letting my words be carried away into the forest, into the mouths of birds, the holes in the logs, the dirt, the leaves. 'Dad, I'm going to do a daytime patrol. I'm going to make sure no Diemens come near the girls. I'm going to make sure what happened to Laurel and Jenna doesn't happen again. Isaac thinks I can't do this but I can. I can be a good Thyla. I'll prove it to you. I won't let you down.'

I made sure all of our stuff was safely hidden away and started off down the mountain.

In shadowy trees I changed into a Thyla. My canines got longer and razor-sharp. My ankles bent backwards and extended. My fingers grew inch-long claws. My whole body stretched taller and its muscles tautened. Without looking I knew that the stripes on my back were darkening and moving forwards to tickle my ribs. My eyes were getting bigger and turning the colour of sandstone. I didn't look animal. I didn't look human. I was somewhere in between. The others might prefer changing at night but I actually loved changing in the daylight. I loved the feeling of the sun on my Thyla skin. I loved the feeling of being lit up.

I moved quickly. The terrain was rough and risky but I was so thrilled at being Thyla I didn't dwell much on the danger. I concentrated instead on the sun bouncing off the small clumps of snow that slowly melted in the midday sun and the clean, medicinal scent of the eucalyptus. I passed bandicoots skittering through the scrubby under-growth and above me I heard possums rustling the tree leaves. Soon I was at the edge of the bush, pulling on my cuff and throwing on the crop top and light t-shirt I'd stuffed in my trouser pocket when I started to change. I tried to stifle the grunts of pain I always made when changing back to human form, and moved into the bushy suburbia of South Hobart, past the Female Factory and the Cascade Brewery where a yummy hop and malt smell made my stomach growl.

I could've been any ordinary girl in South Hobart. Just a normal teenager on an afternoon stroll. An old man weeding in his front yard gave me a wave and a smile. I smiled back, hoping there wasn't too much dirt on my face or too many twigs in my hair. But then, giggling, I reasoned that if I did look like a wild thing the old guy would probably just think it was some 'newfangled' teenage fashion.

Soon I was *there*. I ran past the front gate, where you had to push a button to be let in by the secretary, Miss Bloom. I went around the back way, through the sports oval, where there was a gap in the fence the grounds-keeper never got around to fixing up. Once I was through, I looked quickly from right to left to check that the coast was clear. I knew it would be; I knew the Cascade schedule back to front. The girls went into period one at 8.45 and they weren't released again until recess at 11.00.

It was 10.45. I had plenty of time for one lap of the school. But still, there was always the off-chance that a girl might be wagging history and having a smoke by the equipment shed. If there was a girl there I'd watch them. A girl alone was prime Diemen prey.

The girls most likely to be ditching class back when I was at Cascade were Laurel Simpson and Erin Mijak. They were best friends and the wildest girls at school. Laurel was gone now so there was only one girl I had to watch out for behind the woodshed. And just as I left my hiding place behind the tree, that exact girl rounded the shed's corner – and began moving quickly towards me.

My heart did a little breakdance in my chest and in seconds I was on the ground, instinct telling me to get down low. I needed to watch out for the girls but I couldn't let them see me. I was dead, or at least missing, as far as the students at this school were concerned.

I watched from the cover of the long grass as Erin slumped against the tin wall of the equipment shed and slid down to the ground. She brought her knees up to her chin and rested her cheek on them. As I watched, Erin's shoulders began to shake up and down and I saw her swipe roughly at tears that puddled on her cheeks. My heart ached for her. I wanted to hold her and comfort her. Something deep within me – something *primal* – wanted to run to her and wipe her tears away and tell her everything would be okay. To be her friend. But I couldn't and I felt the space between us stretch painfully.

I kept one eye on Erin as I ran, hunched low. My best chance of patrolling without being seen was to creep quickly along the hedge-lined walls that surrounded the grounds. I made myself as flat as I could against the prickly leaves and edged away. One of the little timber outbuildings was close by. They were built a few years ago, when student numbers surged and the main building was nearly splitting its seams. I always felt a bit sorry for those new little buildings. They were looking up at the big building like they wished they were as cool as it was; like they were trying to work out what they'd have to do to grow up like that, not realising they were stuck being little and puny and overlooked forever. I knew how that felt.

I took one last look around to make sure I wouldn't be seen and bolted for the first demountable. I couldn't move as silently as Tessa but I was fast. Even Isaac acknowledged that. I used to run, back in Campbell Town. I could never do team sports because none of the other kids wanted the local cop's kid on their teams but I could run like the wind. Being Thyla made me even quicker. I made it to the demountable in a few long strides. Once I was safely leaning against the wall of the outbuilding I placed my hand flat against my chest and breathed out slowly, trying to make all the jittery things inside me steady again. I looked around for Erin. She was gone. For a moment my heart fluttered. Where was she? Was she all right?

But then I saw her, shoulders hunched, walking towards the main building. I watched her skinny legs loping slowly. Erin never used to move slowly. Erin used to bounce and dart and race.

The sound of voices close by distracted me from my watching. At first I couldn't tell where they were coming from. There was nobody else outside the classroom except me and Erin. Then I saw the open window just to my left.

The voices were muffled. The people inside the room didn't want to be heard. My heart quickened again. Who was hiding in the room? One voice was female. The other was male.

A Diemen? A Diemen and a young girl?

I shook my cuff just a little bit lower to let some of my Thyla self loose. It might help me hear what they were saying.

'Why are you still fighting this?' I knew straight away the male wasn't a Diemen. Their voices sound like scraping metal. This voice was hard and a little bit angry but not like a Diemen's. I bit my lip to stop from giggling. It *had* to be a teacher. Cascade Falls was an all-girls school . . . Oh, wow! Had I stumbled upon a secret romance between two teachers, or even a teacher and a student? This was brilliant! It was just like my books. A forbidden love affair.

The girl spoke again. And as soon as she did my giggles were replaced by a jolt of recognition. I wasn't eavesdropping on a meeting between just *any* two people. It was Tessa in that room, having that whispered conversation. Tessa had a *boyfriend*, a secret boyfriend! But who was he? Why hadn't she told me about him? How had I not noticed something going on with her?

'I still don't know if it is *right*,' she whispered.

'What does *right* matter?' the man growled in reply, his voice rising. 'What about how it makes you *feel?*'

'Well, that's different.' Tessa's voice was less anxious now. It sounded . . . *flirty*. I'd never heard her talk like *that* before. Suddenly, I pictured us whispering together by the campfire, as she told me all about him. It'd be a secret we could share. I could be her *confidante*. I could show her what a good listener I can be. I could be *useful* to her for once. 'When you and I are *together*, I am so happy,' Tessa continued. 'I feel as though I am finally free. And yet I am always fearful as well. If Isaac found out, he would be so unhappy. Treaty or not.'

It was like a slap. The hairs on my bare arms stood on end. Tessa had called our leader by his Thyla name. In the human world Isaac was 'Vinnie'. Only the shapeshifters knew him as Isaac. *And* she'd mentioned the treaty too. It wasn't a human Tessa was talking to.

The stripes on my back began to prickle and burn, the way they always did when I felt angry or scared. I felt both now. Who was in that room with Tessa?

I wished that I could straighten up and peek through the window. But Tessa would spot me in an instant. She'd been watching out for enemies and infiltrators for a hundred and sixty years. If I got any closer, even if she didn't see me, she'd probably smell me. 'I wish we could be in love in the open; that people would understand,' she whispered.

'I wish it too, little girl. You know I do. I don't understand why we can't show off how we feel about each other, the way we could if we were both Thylas.'

The breath was sucked from my lungs. He *wasn't a Thyla*. Then who or *what* was he?

I pushed my cuff down more. And I could smell it.

Sarco.

'We've loved each other for so long,' he said. 'We deserve to have that love acknowledged.'

'Oh, Perrin,' Tessa whispered. 'I love you.'

My hands flew to my face. I could feel the claws extending. I was still wearing my cuff but my body was fighting it. It wanted to be Thyla. It wanted to burst into that room and tear him away from her.

There was a Sarco in that room with Tessa.

Treaty or no treaty, Perrin's instincts should be telling him to bite, to gouge, to *kill*.

Tessa was in danger.

CHapter
seven

THE HAND OVER MY MOUTH WAS ALL THAT STOPPED ME
from screaming.

'What are you doing here?' Delphi hissed, pushing her
palm against my lips so roughly I thought my teeth would
break. I took advantage of my new Thyla rage. I let my
fangs grow. I bared them and dug them into the flesh of
her palm.

Delphi sucked in her breath and I saw tears well in
her eyes. 'Now, that was just *mean*,' she whispered. She
grabbed me by the arm and dragged me around the other
side of the building, away from the open window. She
cradled her oozing hand in her uninjured one. When we
were far enough away Delphi raised her voice slightly. 'So,
little vampire, I'll ask again. What are you doing here?'

'I could ask you the same thing,' I said, aware I sounded like a grumpy little kid.

'I asked first.' Delphi raised her pierced eyebrow.

'Delphi, you are such a *doofus*,' I groaned. 'You tell *me* first. It's *weirder* that *you're* here. You never even went to Cascade Falls.'

'I was . . . looking for you.' Delphi's cheeks flamed.

'What if I don't *want* you to look for me?' I snapped, and immediately regretted it. I opened my mouth again, this time to apologise, but Delphi started talking first.

'Thanks, Cat. Real nice. Listen, don't worry about answering, hey? I know why you're here. You're spying on your girlfriend again.'

'She's not my girlfriend,' I protested. *I'm not like* you, I thought. *I don't like girls, not the way that you do.* I bit my tongue this time. I didn't want her to think I thought there was anything wrong with liking girls like that. I didn't. It just wasn't for me. I may not have had a boyfriend before but I knew I wanted one. I'd just never met a boy who lived up to the image I had in my head. The boy I wanted was nothing like the bogans in Campbell Town. He was strong and handsome and smart and *manly*. I knew that the boy for me wasn't wearing a trucker cap and jeans that showed his undies and whose biggest dream was owning a Holden V8. He was classic. Like Mr Darcy. 'Tessa and I are just friends,' I said.

'Well, *that* much is obvious,' Delphi said, her face a mixture of smugness and relief. She jerked her head at the building. 'Looks like our Tessa only has eyes for Sarco skin.'

'I need to go in there,' I hissed. 'Delph, what if he hurts her? I can't let him hurt her.'

'I don't think she's in danger,' Delphi growled. 'I think she wants to be there. I think she's a traitor.' Delphi paused for a moment, looking thoughtful. 'Maybe we all are. Maybe this treaty is making traitors of all of us.'

'You can't tell anyone about this. Isaac would kill her.' I looked at Delphi pleadingly and she rolled her eyes.

'Fine, I promise I won't. But not for Tessa. For you. Isaac would kill *you* if he knew you were here.'

A thump and then a creak told us the door to the building was opening. My reflexes pushed me back against the wall, pulling Delphi with me. I tried to ignore the way her breathing sped up when she was close to me. 'You need to leave now,' I heard Tessa say. Her voice was low and intense. 'Quickly.'

'Can I –'

'No,' Tessa interrupted and I imagined what the rest of Perrin's sentence would have been:

'. . . *kiss you* . . .'

'. . . *hold you* . . .'

'. . . *devour you* . . .'

My hackles rose. Every instinct in Perrin's body *should* be telling him to slash Tessa's throat. She was his natural enemy. Why was he being so tender? It didn't make sense and it scared me.

'We'll be seen,' Tessa went on. 'You know what will happen if I am seen with a boy on school grounds.'

'I'm not a boy,' Perrin chuckled. 'I'm a devil.'

'I don't think the punishment for devils is any less,' Tessa replied. She was flirty again now. A growl rumbled in my throat.

'When will I see you again?'

'We will be going on patrol again together. Has Rha discovered more about Rin –?'

'No,' Perrin said sharply. 'And if you think that doesn't cut me up inside every single moment of every day, you're crazy, convict.'

'I'm sorry.' Tessa sounded miserable.

Perrin sighed. 'I'm sorry too. It's just . . . you and me . . . it's the only thing keeping me going. And you know I meant when will I see you *alone.*'

'I will send a message with Harriet,' Tessa said. 'She's still not sure what to think about us, but despite the muscles and superior javelin skills, deep down she is a romantic. She trusts you and I think perhaps she is coming to trust me. I hope so.'

'Harriet knows how short life can be, even for us. Losing her friends has hit her hard.'

'I know,' Tessa said. 'It is difficult for all of us. But we will find Rhiannah. We have to. I can't lose another friend.'

'I wish I could hold you every night. Make everything all right for you,' Perrin said. The thought of Perrin holding Tessa made my fingers itch. My claws wanted to cut through.

I had to calm down. I had the uneasy thought that even with my cuff on there was a real danger I could go fully Thyla.

'Um, Cat?' Delphi's unusually timid voice punctured through my thoughts. I turned. My mouth fell open. Delphi wasn't alone. Standing behind her was a girl. A human girl. With long white-blonde hair.

CHapter
eight

CHARLOTTE LORD'S eyes were as icy as ever but they were ringed with dark circles. She hadn't even bothered to try to cover them. That wasn't like the Charlotte I knew. Charlotte Lord never left her room without full makeup.

This Charlotte's face was bare. Her hair was tied back carelessly. There were no accessories adorning her uniform. But those eyes were as cold as ever. And full of fury.

'What the hell are you doing here?' she spat.

'Charlotte,' I pleaded, my voice hushed. 'Can you please just . . . just be quiet.'

Charlotte looked at me suspiciously but she lowered her voice. 'Why are we whispering?' she snapped.

'That's the girl, isn't it?' Delphi hissed. 'That's the girl who tried to kill you.'

Charlotte looked genuinely shocked. 'What?' she gasped, looking from Delphi to me.

'Sshhh!' I whispered. 'Please. Just trust me. We need to be quiet.'

Charlotte nodded. 'Fine,' she said, glowering. 'But I still don't –'

'Shut the hell up,' Delphi snarled. She leaned over Charlotte, her eyes flashing. 'Can't you just understand that it's important that we stay bloody –'

'Delphi!' I whispered warningly.

'Okay.' Charlotte's voice trembled slightly. I'd never seen her look nervous before. I guess Delphi could look pretty scary if you didn't know her. Or sometimes even if you did.

'We need to get out of here,' I repeated. I looked at Charlotte, silently begging her to be on my side for once. If only for a moment. 'Please, Charlotte. Just let us go. Please.'

Charlotte shook her head fiercely. My stomach sank. 'No,' she said firmly. 'You're coming with me. I want to know everything.'

I'd forgotten. Charlotte Lord was the queen of gossip at Cascade Falls. Of course she wasn't going to let me go without knowing exactly where I'd been for the past two years.

I jumped as I heard footsteps on the stairs of the outbuilding. I saw Delphi looking at Charlotte. She held a finger to her lips, her eyes menacing. Charlotte nodded. A few seconds later, heavier footsteps sounded on the sandstone stairs and onto the soft, swishy grass. Then there was nothing. We were safe. Delphi lowered her finger.

Just then, the bell rang. A few moments later a flock of grey-uniformed girls spilled out of the doors of Cascade like pigeons being let out of a cage.

'Crap,' Delphi cursed. 'We're stuffed.'

'No, you're not,' whispered Charlotte. 'I know somewhere we can go. It's safe. Private.'

Of course I was suspicious. I'm not an idiot. This was a girl who had treated me like scum the entire time I was at Cascade Falls. And even if she didn't know it, her daddy was an immortal serial killer. There was definitely cause for proceeding with caution as far as Charlotte Lord was concerned. I could tell Delphi was wary too. Her eyes were narrowed and her hand was hovering above her cuff.

I shook my head at her. Charlotte didn't know about our world. When she'd seen Tessa's markings she'd screamed and called her a freak. She'd be terrified if Delphi and I were suddenly to turn into Thylas in front of her. She'd most likely scream her lungs out and then we'd be *totally* screwed. 'Delphi, we have to go. We have to trust her. We don't have a choice.'

Delphi hesitated, her eyes narrowed. I held my breath. Then she shrugged. 'Good point.' She turned to Charlotte. 'Lead the way, princess.'

Charlotte unlocked the padlock on the side of the shed beneath the wattle trees.

'I always thought this was just an equipment shed,' I said as I followed her through the narrow door into the darkness inside.

'Yes, well, it is. Except it's –' I heard a loud 'click' behind me as Charlotte flicked a switch. The room flickered into light – '*my* equipment.'

'Holy crap!' Delphi exclaimed.

'Whoa . . .' I breathed, as I looked around me. I was totally gobsmacked. I don't know what I'd been expecting inside the shed but this *definitely* wasn't it.

It was how I imagined the inside of the Lord Mansion, only in miniature and put inside a shed. The walls were painted stark white and hanging on them were prints (I assumed they were only prints but who knew?), of famous artworks. I recognised a few from art class: John Everett Millais, John Constable, Joseph Turner – British artists from the eighteenth and nineteenth centuries. I was surprised to see them hanging on the walls of Charlotte's lair. I didn't think Charlotte even *liked* art. She definitely didn't like *artists*. Her harem called the arty types at school 'freaks'. Jenna, the girl who'd died, once 'accident-ally' spilled nail polish on the finalist paintings in the Cascade Falls art competition and Bridget was forever loudly making fun of the girls who took creative electives. At Cascade Falls you either liked what the princesses liked and believed what they believed or you were an untouch-able and were never allowed anywhere near the inner sanctum.

And now I, formerly one of the most hated untouch-ables, was in the hideout of the most powerful of the princesses. I felt like Alice in Wonderland. Except Charlotte was more like Alice with her long blonde hair. And her ignorance about the strangeness that hid just below the surface of the world she lived in.

So what did that make me? The Cheshire Cat?

No. Despite my name I wasn't interesting enough to be the Cat. I was the Dormouse.

As I thought about the stories I loved, my eyes were drawn to Charlotte's bookshelf. It was crammed with books. Somehow that didn't seem fair. I'd bet my life Charlotte never even opened them. She wasn't into books, just like she wasn't into art.

I would read those books. I'd love them. My fingers itched to touch them. To smell them. There was nothing

I wanted more than to be able to just pick whatever book I wanted, whenever I wanted, instead of waiting for Isaac and Tessa to remember to bring me one (and hoping to the universe it wasn't another Sweet Valley High). Books had always been my escape. I could hide in them when the bullies in Campbell Town called me names. I could run away to them in my dorm room at Cascade when the harem painted 'untouchable' on my desk and locker. I missed being able to do that; to run away into a world of imagination whenever I wanted to. I forced myself to look away.

In the right-hand corner of the room was an antique maroon velvet couch scattered with sausage-shaped purple velvet cushions with gold tassels. Next to the couch was a nightstand made of polished wood and a porcelain lamp with a frosted glass shade. Dangling off the shade were shards of crystal that made it look like a mini-chandelier. In the other corner of the room was a tiny silver refrigerator and next to that was a cabinet made of the same dark wood as the nightstand. Through its glass doors I could see tumblers and goblets and white porcelain plates. A little sink with gold taps was beside the cabinet. In the middle of the room was a round dining table and three wooden chairs.

I walked a couple of steps forward and my feet sank into fluffy carpet. It was a silvery colour and obviously expensive but most of it was covered up by a large, elaborately patterned maroon and gold rug. The pictures woven into the rug were of dark-clothed men on white horses. They were trailed by lines of smaller creatures – dogs, maybe? The men held spears and javelins, which they were plunging into the chests of strange copper-coloured creatures. They were like foxes but they were much too *big* to be foxes. I remembered, jarringly, the flash of copper-coloured flesh that I'd glimpsed back up the mountain. It had to be a coincidence. Didn't it?

I gulped and looked away. My eyes found their way to the only part of Charlotte's hideout that didn't seem perfectly organised and *deliberate*. Above the dining table was a cork board covered with newspaper articles and photographs. I couldn't make out what the articles were about from this distance but I could see that all of the photographs were of Jenna.

Charlotte walked past me and pulled a black piece of cloth over the board. 'Like my pad?' she asked coldly.

'How did you *score* this?' asked Delphi. She walked over to us with her hands on her hips as she gazed disbelievingly around the room.

'Friends in high places,' Charlotte said flatly. But I could make out the hint of a curl in her upper lip, a suggestion of something like bitterness in her voice.

'I never saw you come out here,' I said, straining to remember. 'You were always with your friends. You had your table in the cafeteria and your space outside in the courtyard –'

'Watching me, were you?' Charlotte crossed her arms over her chest and strode around the room, straightening already-straight ornaments as she did so.

'No,' I said, feebly. 'I just . . . noticed things.'

'Well, I suppose you had no friends to occupy your time,' Charlotte said snidely. 'But then, you were a rebel without a cause, weren't you? You never needed friends.'

'I wasn't really a rebel,' I mumbled.

'Duh,' Charlotte spat. 'Any fool could see that. You were so pathetic.'

'Hey,' Delphi growled, stepping in front of me. 'Don't you call Cat pathetic.'

'It's fine, Delph,' I said quickly. The last thing I needed was for Delphi to start a fight with Charlotte and have Charlotte kick us out right in the middle of recess. 'So, how did you get this place? Was it from – from your dad?'

Charlotte nodded curtly. 'Yes. He arranged it with Ms Hindmarsh.' She didn't elaborate any further. Instead, she looked away. Her eyes flicked over to the covered board and I saw her forehead crinkle. When she turned back to us, her face was unreadable again. 'So, you're going to tell me your story,' she said. It wasn't a request. 'But I suppose I should be a hostess. Do you want food? I have some Turkish delight. Something to drink?' Charlotte strode over to the fridge.

I glanced at Delphi. She shrugged and gave me a 'what do we have to lose?' look. 'Thanks,' I said. 'That'd be great.'

Charlotte bustled about putting the sweets on a platter and preparing a jug of hot chocolate. In a voice like crackling ice, she asked, 'So what did you mean, Delphi, when you said I tried to kill Cat?'

For a moment there was silence. Charlotte kept pouring. I looked at Delphi.

'Talk,' Charlotte said finally. 'Or I'll talk. There's a school full of girls who'd just *love* to know I've found Cat Connolly. Not to mention a certain policewoman.'

'You did try to kill her,' Delphi said. 'You chased after her. You and your . . . father.'

Charlotte went still. The room seemed to frost over.

'Delphi, it's fine,' I said quickly. 'We talked about this. Remember? Charlotte was just chasing me to get me in trouble. I might've overreacted at first. After it happened. But I never *really* thought she was trying to kill me.' I saw Charlotte's fingers grip the side of the sink like she was trying to steady herself. I heard her breathe out heavily.

'I was trying to get you in trouble,' she said quietly. 'I thought you deserved it. Coming to Cascade Falls and acting like some big-shot wild child? You deserved to be punished. I never thought it would end up with . . . well, how *did* it end up, Cat?' Charlotte turned around and laid the big platter of Turkish delight and silver pot of hot chocolate on the table. She slid into a chair. 'You just disappeared.'

I reached over and took a piece of Turkish delight. I popped it in my mouth, giving myself time to think of an answer. Charlotte stared at me. Waiting. I looked over at Delphi. She just shrugged. Fat lot of help she was. 'Yeah. I . . . just ran away,' I said. 'I got fed up with Cascade Falls. I saw an opportunity to get lost and I took it. I've been living with Delph. She's a runaway too.'

It wasn't a lie really. Delphi and I *were* runaways and I *had* hated Cascade Falls. The only part of the story that was missing was, '*Oh, and we're both powerful beasts, the sort you only read about in books and only see in your nightmares.*'

Charlotte smiled tightly. 'I thought it must have been something like that. You really were an outcast at Cascade, weren't you? The other *untouchables* all seemed to band together but you never really found your place.'

The words hovered on my lips: *You never let me.* But for some reason I couldn't make them come out. Even though I knew I should argue with Charlotte; even though I knew I should be angry at how she treated me, I didn't feel angry at all. Instead, I felt . . . happy. Oddly, giddily happy. And relaxed. Too relaxed to be crabby. Too relaxed to argue. So instead I said, 'I . . . wasn't really wild. I just pretended. I wanted you all . . . to like me but you never . . . never did.'

In my hazy, dream-like state, the memories of my time at Cascade Falls floated back into my brain like a series of paintings projected on a wall.

Me in Campbell Town, surrounded by kids teasing me because of my mum; because I was mousy and shy; because I read and I liked art. Because I didn't like football or beer. Because I wasn't a rough, tough country kid like they were. Because my dad was dead and that made me different and scary.

Me crouched on the floor of my mother's room back in Campbell Town, my face wet with tears, holding the letter that changed everything; the letter that told me that it was my fault. The letter that told me who I was wasn't okay, that I needed to find a new Cat Connolly. That I needed to make what happened to my father mean something. I needed to make it *worth* something.

Me on my first day at Cascade Falls, my skirt rolled up so it was short, my hair hacked off, a defiant, sneering mask on my face. I wasn't Rachel Connolly's daughter any more. I was a leader. A winner. I'd rule the school. I would make him proud.

Me telling the other kids stories of nights outside Zeps, smoking and drinking and swearing, stealing garden gnomes and riding around on the backs of utes and spraying graffiti and harassing chickens. Not my stories but I told them like they were.

Laurel and Erin and the rest of the 'outsiders' and 'untouchables' rolling their eyes, spotting the fear in mine. Knowing I was a fraud. Ignoring me. And finally, Charlotte Lord standing over me as I sat alone in the Cascade Falls cafeteria. 'You know you're pitiful, don't you? Your stories are stupid. As if we care about utes or *chickens*. You're a reject. You're an *untouchable*. You're nothing.' And I *was* nothing. I was nobody. I was a speck of dust again.

Charlotte raised an eyebrow. 'Did it matter then? Does it matter now? Who cares about stupid high school? It's all a big game. Didn't you know that?'

'I didn't know how to play the game,' I said slowly. My tongue felt too big in my mouth. 'I never knew. It's hard. It's hard being . . . at a new school. It's hard being the sergeant's daughter in a small . . . country town.' The words leaked out of me. I didn't bother trying to stop them. I felt like I had no boundaries. No inhibitions.

Something in Charlotte's face changed. She looked away from me. 'I know all about being "somebody's daughter",' she said tightly.

I registered dimly, through my fog, a feeling of surprise. I felt my eyebrows rise. I'd never thought that Charlotte might feel anything negative about being Ted Lord's daughter. I thought she was proud of it. But Ted Lord did cast a pretty big shadow. He was the head of the biggest company in Tassie. He was in the paper almost every week. At least once a year there was a push for him to run for Premier. He always politely declined, saying he was busy enough with his business and his family. What he didn't mention was that his hobby – eating the hearts of virgins and bathing in their blood – also took up quite a bit of his time.

'It's hard, isn't it?' I said, trying to reach out to her. My hand seemed bigger than usual. Charlotte seemed very far away. But I needed to reach out. I remembered what Tessa said, about her being sad about Jenna. I saw her tired eyes and trembling hands.

'You don't know a thing about *hard*,' Charlotte spat, her eyes fierce. Then her face crumpled. And she said the words I never expected to hear from Charlotte Lord. 'I'm sorry,' she whispered.

'It's . . . okay,' I said. Because I couldn't think of any other words. When Charlotte didn't reply I added, 'You've had a hard time too lately. Jenna . . .'

Charlotte looked up at me. There were tears like a sheet of glass coating her pale blue eyes. So Charlotte Lord did cry. 'Yes,' she said. 'I found her. And the other girls – my friends – they don't care. They don't understand. They pretend to, but they don't. Nobody understands.'

'I do,' I said simply. 'I know what it's like to lose people.'

Charlotte nodded. Her chin shook. 'She had blood everywhere. I couldn't . . . I tried to clean it. And the other girls were . . . And her chest. They made a hole in her *chest*. I'm not allowed to talk to anyone about it. The police say they don't want me to tell people what I saw. And so everyone's talking. They're saying it was suicide . . .'

A coldness spread over me when Charlotte said the word. Suicide. Even through the swaddling cotton wool that seemed to be filling my head the word still had the power to stab at me and hurt me. I swallowed and tried to concentrate on what Charlotte was saying. 'It wasn't. It couldn't have been.'

She looked up at me. 'It was murder, Cat.' She shook her head. 'I should have been there. I was with some guy. I don't even remember his name. He said his friend had told him to come up to me. That he thought I was pretty. Why did I care? Why did I let Jenna walk away, Cat?'

'Charlotte, what happened was awful,' I said softly, faintly noting that my words were slurred.

'It's my fault,' Charlotte whispered.

'No, it's not. Trust me. You couldn't have done –'

'It is,' Charlotte growled. 'You don't know. You don't know anything. You don't care about me. All you care about is that I won't tell.'

'Will you?' Delphi said. I jolted. I'd almost forgotten she was there.

'No,' Charlotte said bitterly. 'I won't. I have secrets. I know what that's like. I won't tell.'

'Thanks,' I said. 'Because . . . it's important that we're not found. I can't tell you why but it is important. There are . . . things you don't know about. Going on. We need to – it's just important.'

Charlotte looked at me curiously. 'Okay,' she said, her voice small. And then she said something else I never expected Charlotte Lord to say. 'Will you come back?' she asked. 'I can help you, if you need it. With anything. I'd – I'd like it if you came back.'

'Um . . . okay,' I said. I looked at Delphi. She looked just as bemused as I felt.

'You understand,' Charlotte said, her voice shuddering. 'Don't you? How it feels.'

I nodded. 'Yeah. I do.'

'I need that,' Charlotte said. She sniffed loudly and blinked her eyes. Then in her usual crisp voice she said, 'You'd better go now, though. I'm meant to be in class.

I'm a prefect. I can't be late. Everyone else will be inside. You'll be safe.'

'Yeah, we're gonna be late too.' Delphi stood up. She lurched sideways as she did so, hanging onto the back of the chair for balance. 'And . . . um, you know we'll be in deep doo-doo if we're late. Gods, I must be more tired than I thought,' she said.

I rose unsteadily to my feet. 'Me too,' I said, giggling.

'Are you all right?' Charlotte asked.

I shook myself. 'Fine,' I said. 'I think.'

Her eyes narrowed. 'Okay,' she said slowly. 'It's just your eyes. They've gone . . . funny.'

'I'm like Delphi,' I said. 'Tired. It's a hard knock life being runaways.' I laughed far too loudly at my own joke.

'You're still really strange, Cat Connolly,' Charlotte said, not unkindly.

Something in her words sobered me up a bit. 'Yeah,' I said. 'But maybe we all are.'

'Come on, Cat.' Delphi tugged at my sleeve. 'Need to go now.'

'Bye, Charlotte,' I said.

'Bye,' she said.

And then as Delphi and I left Charlotte's hideout, looking furtively around us as we did, I heard Charlotte Lord's quiet voice. 'You understand.'

CHAPTER

NINE

'cat? are you with us?'

'Huh?' I snapped back into reality to find Isaac and the rest of the Thylas staring at me, none of them all that kindly. Delphi and I were back at the clearing. I could barely remember how we got there. 'Sorry, I was . . . um . . . just thinking,' I murmured. 'About – about what you were talking about?' This was a lie and Isaac knew it. My head was still hazy. It felt like it was full of clouds. And Charlotte Lord.

What had happened in that shed? Why was my enemy now my friend? Could I trust her? And what had made my head go so flipping cloudy?

'Oh, really? And what exactly *was* I talking about?' Isaac said mockingly. When I didn't answer, my cheeks burning, he went on. 'Can't remember? Do I take that to mean you don't *care* about the major problems we are facing? The ones we need *your* help to combat? Saving the lives of countless young women? Working out what this Solution is, exactly, and finding out a way to stop it before the Diemens become more powerful? Do you not care about Rhiannah still being at their mercy? Or that they killed Laurel Simpson and Jenna Barnes? Because if you really don't care about any of this, I know a woman who would be very glad to have you *return home to her*!' Isaac's voice grew louder as he ranted and his face more and more like a purple cabbage. When he finally stopped, the silence echoed around the clearing even more loudly than his words.

I cleared my throat. 'I'm sorry, Isaac,' I said sheepishly. 'I promise I'm fully committed to this. It's just . . .' I trailed off. What I wanted to tell Isaac was that I'd come up with the idea of daytime patrols; that I'd gone on my first that day. But I'd lost confidence in myself. Especially since my patrol ended with me eating lollies with Edward Lord's daughter.

'All I can say is it's a good thing you are turning out to be such a good little cook, Cat,' Isaac spat. 'Otherwise there'd be no use for you at all.'

My eyes stung. Is that what he thought? That I was useless? I wasn't! That was the reason behind all of this.

To *prove* I wasn't. To find – to find a Cat that was *worth* something. To find a Cat *he* would have been proud of. I wasn't useless. I was –

'She makes a mean beef stew, doesn't she?' Delphi said, elbowing me in the ribs. I looked at her sceptically, wondering where this was going and hoping it wouldn't lead to more trouble for me. 'But she's also a fantastic fighter. She's fast and she's tough and adaptable and she doesn't give up. Ever. No matter how you beat her down. You should respect that, Isaac.'

Isaac looked shocked. I was too. Why on Earth would Delphi tell Isaac he had to respect *me?* Isaac had been doing this – fighting the Diemens, leading a pack – for hundreds or years. I'd been a Thyla for a blink of an eye compared with Isaac's long shapeshifter life. And in the time I'd been here I hadn't exactly distinguished myself. 'Delphi,' I groaned. For a few moments there was silence.

I waited, the palms of my hands starting to sweat. Finally, Isaac cleared his throat. 'We'll have fish tonight,' he said gruffly. 'Boots caught us some very impressive flathead earlier today. It's in the Esky. You could do something with that, couldn't you?' My jaw hit the dirt and bark. Where was the lecture? Where was the furious rant? Why wasn't Isaac angry? It couldn't be that he'd actually taken on board what Delphi had said. Could it?

'Fish,' I said feebly. 'Okay.'

'Chuck 'em in some foil and give 'em a roasting on the coals with that native pepper Luda found. They'll come up a treat,' said Boots in his laid-back ocker drawl. Boots was a farmer down the Huon and he was about as country as you could get. He was never seen without his flannie, or his Blunnies (hence the nickname). He was also one of my favourite Thylas. He never got angry. He never growled at me. He was always calm and jovial. And right now I appreciated that.

'I'll do my best, Boots,' I replied.

'Can we get back to business, now our culinary prospects have been sorted?' Isaac asked. I nodded in a way I hoped looked humble and obedient. Isaac nodded back curtly and looked away. 'Right, so, to recap for those of us who were snoozing, our leads on the Diemen hideout are getting stronger. The last three bodies we found –'

'Wait, there have been *more* killings?' I interrupted.

'If you hadn't been comatose for the last half an hour, Cat, you would know that. Yes, three more bodies have been found. One was near Copping, the next in bushland behind Dunalley, and the last girl was found – Where did you say you found her, Luda?'

I looked over at Luda, who was sitting with her legs crossed primly on the cleanest of the logs. Luda was the most un-Thyla-like Thyla of all of us. She looked a bit like a younger Catherine Zeta Jones, except her hair was now the straw-like colour that all Thyla hair went eventually. And not one strand of it was ever out of place.

Luda was turned around 1900 and before that she was the twenty-year-old daughter of a rich merchant, engaged to a Duke and about to move back to England. Her coach was mugged one night by bushrangers and the Thylas saved her. The people who'd known her down here were long dead. It was assumed she died in the raid too. She lived with the Thylas full-time for about twenty years but she hated it, so once she was sure it was safe for her to move back to the city, she did. She lived a low-key life, never staying in a job for very long, never making friends. She changed her hairstyle every decade or so. Nobody realised she'd stayed alive – and young – far longer than she should have. Nowadays, she worked in the State Archives. She'd been there for the longest of any of her jobs. Nobody in the archives seemed to notice her at all. She reckoned she could stay there *forever* and nobody would notice.

Luda seemed pretty nice but, to be honest, I didn't know her all that well. She always kept herself at a bit of a distance. That's how she'd managed to live for so long in the city with nobody realising she should have been dead long ago.

She cleared her throat and smoothed an imaginary stray hair around her face. 'Ah, just on the outskirts of Murdunna, Isaac,' she said.

'You've been walking all the way down there?' I asked. Murdunna was kilometres away.

'I took a work car,' Isaac answered for her. 'An unmarked one. We went down together. Hatch has been coming along, too. He also searched Kingston Beach.'

Hatch nodded. 'Yeah, all over there. Scoured the place.'

I looked over at him. He flashed me a shiny smile and I smiled back but I could tell the smile probably looked uncomfortable. Hatch did that to me.

Nathan Hatcher was a bit of a charmer and a ladies' man. He was good-looking and he knew it, with his long strawberry-blond hair and sparkly eyes. He was skinny but he wore it well. He made it look rakish instead of weedy. From what I heard he had a different girl every week. When he wasn't here with us or working as an ambo he was working his charm down the pub. It wasn't surprising he was at a nightclub the night of Beagle's goodbye. He was always on the prowl.

One night he even tried to chat *me* up. He came up to me by the campfire and asked if I'd had a boyfriend back home, before I was turned. When I replied that I hadn't, he said, 'Would you like to go out with me sometime?' I was flattered – after all I'd never had a boy show any interest in me back home – but I could tell early on that

Hatch was more Mr Wickham than Mr Darcy. There was something predatory about him that made me wary. A look in his eyes as he gazed at me by the light of the fire. I told him I didn't think I was ready to go out with anyone; that this whole Thyla thing was too new and I needed to concentrate on that for now. It wasn't the whole truth but it seemed to work. 'Well, keep me in mind,' he said. 'When you're ready. I think we could be good together, Cat Connolly.'

He'd left me alone since then and I was relieved. Hatch might be very handsome but he definitely wasn't the man for me.

His smiles still made me blush, though.

Apart from his reputation, I didn't know much about Hatch. When I first became a Thyla I tried to make conversation with Isaac about the others so I could get to know my new family. I asked him about Hatch but he cut me off pretty sharply. 'We all have pasts,' he said. 'They don't make us who we are and, really, they're no business of anybody else.'

I figured from what Isaac said that Hatch hadn't had the easiest time before he was turned. Delphi reckoned there'd been a problem with a girl – that didn't surprise me – and that he'd been attacked a couple of times on the job. I didn't ask how she knew. I didn't try to find out if it was true. Isaac was right. What all of us did in the past didn't matter. Hatch was a good Thyla now. He worked hard and he was smart and ambitious. We needed people like that.

And it sounded like he'd had a difficult few days. 'It's not exactly been the most enjoyable experience, I'll admit,' he was saying. 'These patrols have been . . . weird. All those girls just left out on display. It's not right. It's not what the Diemens do.'

'It has been strange and, you are right, Hatch, quite horrible,' Tessa agreed. My stomach dropped as I looked over at her. I'd been so caught up thinking about Charlotte that I'd almost *forgotten*. Now it came back to me with a sickening thud.

'Oh, Perrin. I love you . . .'

I felt my eyes flash and burn. My belly twisted and my heart felt as if it was shrivelling and turning black. I knew it was only instinct that was making me feel what I did – a centuries-old distrust of Sarcos that flowed through our veins – but that didn't stop me feeling it. I tried to be sensible. Perrin *might* be lovely. Every rational part of me said that I shouldn't judge him based on his species and yet . . . it still felt like a betrayal. And it still scared me. Maybe Tessa knew what she was doing. Or maybe this Sarco had bewitched her in some way. Maybe his intentions for her were good.

Or maybe he meant to kill my best friend.

No. I shook myself. That was Delphi talk. The Sarco wouldn't kill her. Tessa knew what she was doing. She always did the right thing.

But I still couldn't get my head around it. Not really. A Thyla and a Sarco. In love. It wasn't right. That wasn't the way our world worked.

'Why?' Delphi asked, breaking me out of my trance. 'Why was it more horrible than usual?'

'They were butchered,' Isaac said.

Tessa nodded. 'The other corpses we found just had the hole in their chest, and deep gashes where the Diemens drained them of blood. These girls had chunks taken from their bodies, and they were a strange colour. They barely looked human. I know it sounds queer but my first thought was that it looked like they had been *experimented* on somehow.'

Isaac nodded. 'I thought so, too.'

'Is it something to do with the Solution?' I asked, pushing all my other thoughts aside. For now, this was more important. 'Are they experimenting on these girls?'

'If they are, the Solution is bigger than we thought,' Isaac said. 'If it involves humans too . . .' He shook his head. 'It's odd that we found them at all. These bodies were left out on the forest floor for anyone to come across. The others were always concealed. Apart from the girls at the nightclub, but I'm convinced what happened there was a slip-up on the part of the Diemens. They must have been interrupted – warned that someone was coming. They didn't leave the bodies intentionally. They wouldn't have. We're just lucky I've been able to convince my unit that it's in the public interest to keep things quiet, otherwise the whole town would be panicking about serial killers.' Isaac rubbed his forehead. 'Yeah, I'm pretty sure what happened at the nightclub was a mistake. But these bodies? They were left there on purpose. They were meant to be found.'

'It doesn't make *sense*,' Hatch murmured.

'What doesn't make sense?' I asked, ignoring the churning in my stomach and the sweat on my palms. The image from my dream – the party dresses stained with blood – merged with the image of blood-soaked hay. I swallowed, forcing myself to focus. I couldn't let this affect me so much. I had to be strong.

Hatch looked up sharply. 'Well, it's just not like something the Diemens would do. The bodies seemed so deliberately arranged. Really *showy*. I know it seems like the Diemens are taking more girls and being less careful about where they're taking them from but they still wouldn't do anything to deliberately lead people to them. They'd still try to cover it up.'

'Perhaps it was not the Diemens who left the bodies,' Tessa said. 'The way they were arranged . . . it was like they were *markers*. They were meant to lead us somewhere, like the crumbs in "Hansel and Gretel".'

'Where are they leading us?' I asked.

'Copping, Murdunna, Dunally . . . They're taking us right down south,' said Delphi. 'Eaglehawk Neck.'

'Taranna,' said Isaac, nodding.

'But hang on. Taranna?' My heart sped up. 'That's –'

Isaac finished for me. 'Sarco territory,' he said.

'But it doesn't mean anything,' Tessa said quickly.

Isaac nodded. 'It's just a coincidence.'

'Of course it is,' said Delphi. Nobody but me heard the sarcasm in her voice.

CHAPTER
ten

tessa was in my dreams again.

We were wandering through the bushland of Taranna. I remembered it from the one time she and Isaac took me there. The terrain was hard and windswept. Scrub and ferns hung on for dear life to jagged rocks, as if praying not to fall into the fathomless ocean below. There was an ever-present smell of salt and danger. Taranna was an untamed place. It was deathly quiet, like the land was holding its breath, keeping secret thousands of years of wildness and blood. Every bird call ricocheted off the rocks and transformed into the cries of a whole flock. Every crack of a twig seemed to echo out into eternity.

It felt like the moors of Heathcliff and Cathy. It felt like the fiercest of places.

But Tessa had been the one soft thing in all of it. She smiled at me and made me feel safe. In my dream Tessa didn't smile. Her face was hard and determined as she marched through the scrub ahead of me. I had to run to catch up. I called out to her to wait. I tried to tell her I was tired and I couldn't go as quickly as she could but she just kept on marching, getting further and further away. I looked in the direction she was walking. Towards the sea. There was a boat bobbing on the water. I wondered if that was where she was going. I wondered who was waiting for her there.

Finally, when she was just a blurry, grey shape near the shore, she turned around. She called out to me, 'He is good, Cat. He loves me. These boundaries between us . . . they are the way of the past. The way of the future is us together, united. Those who cannot accept that will be left behind. Or worse. And you . . . you will come to understand this more than most. You'll see.'

And then, as those final warning words echoed out into the nothingness, three dark-suited men ran from the sea.

Diemens.

I screamed, 'No! Tessa!' But it was too late. Tessa disappeared. I ran towards the space she'd left in the sky. But no matter how hard I ran or how fast, I stayed in exactly the same spot.

'*Tessa's gone. Tessa's gone. Tessa's gone.*'

The voice echoed in my head. And then there was another voice whispering in my ear: '*Come with me. Trust me. I'll help you find your friends.*'

But when I turned around there was nobody there.

I let my head fall to my hands.

There was nobody there.

I was alone. Again.

But then I felt a hand on my shoulder. Patting me. Shaking me. 'Wake up, Cat,' someone called.

And then there was a shuddering and quaking. My dream self and my woken self blurred and merged and melted into one. I opened my eyes. Tessa was sitting over me, her hand on my shoulder. Her face was grim. 'Wake up now, Cat.'

'What's happening?' I heard my woken self ask. I still felt like we weren't quite the same person. Part of me felt as if my dream had seeped into the waking world. I blinked, wiping my bleary eyes and looking around the clearing. The light was still silvery and dim. Delphi was meant to be on last watch. Where was she? And what on Earth was Tessa doing in the clearing this early?

'You need to get up, Cat.' Even through my sleepy fug I could hear the urgency in her voice. I sat up and ran my hand through my matted hair, raking out the twigs and leaves. I looked at Tessa and again the memory of her and Perrin slammed into me. I was too distracted by it to reply.

'Everyone else is already up,' Tessa said. 'Delphi also. We need to get going.'

'I actually get to *go* somewhere?' I asked, my tongue finally able to move again. 'It's daytime . . .'

'Yes, you get to go,' she said. 'We all do. Isaac needs as many men as he can rally – and that includes women.'

'Was that a joke?' I asked, forgetting my anger for a moment. Tessa didn't often tell jokes.

'I didn't mean it to be,' she replied.

I rolled my eyes. 'Of course not. I think you left your sense of humour behind in 1860.'

'Not at all.' Tessa shook her head. 'It's just that now is not the time for laughing.'

'What *is* it the time for, then?' I groaned. 'What's happened? Where are we going?'

'We're going to Taranna,' Tessa said, throwing me my satchel. 'They found more bodies.'

'Bodies? How many?' I felt a cold sweat beading on my forehead. My heart was trembling.

'Four. In the bush behind Mason's Cottages. They were all together, in a clump. And they were *arranged* again.'

'Arranged? What do you mean?'

'Like an arrow. An arrow pointing south towards the Norfolk Bay Hotel. Isaac thinks perhaps the Diemens are not arranging the bodies. He thinks someone else did it. And they are trying to tell us something. Trying to show us something.'

'Where the Diemens are hiding?'

'Exactly.'

Tessa and I walked quickly towards the road, where Boots and Delphi were waiting for us in Boots's ute. I'd scraped myself together. Sort of. I'd got the worst of the night-time grit off my skin but I still felt groggy and scratchy. I was trying to concentrate but it was difficult. My dream world and the real world were bleeding into each other. My dream haunted my waking.

Tessa's words still echoed on every rock and hissed in the wind through the trees around us. I tried to silence them. Instead they just quietened. That would have to be enough for now.

I needed to do well today. I needed to show them all.

'So, tell me more about the mission,' I said. 'Isaac thinks the bodies are a message, right? Does he think the hotel is the Diemens' hideout?'

'No. Not the hotel. Not now, anyway. Isaac thinks perhaps it once was. The same family ran it for a very long time and Isaac thinks they may have been Diemens, or Diemen sympathisers. But it's in different hands now.'

'How do we know this isn't a trap?' I said. 'How do we know the Diemens aren't leaving the bodies out to lure us down there so they can kill us? Or take us like they did Rhiannah?'

'That's why the Sarcos are not joining us,' Tessa said. 'They are holding back and waiting. If they haven't heard from Isaac by this afternoon, they'll come too. But Isaac doesn't think it's a trap. We smelled a scent on the bodies. It wasn't Diemen.'

'What kind of scent?'

'Isaac could not identify it. There *was* Diemen scent on them but it was older. The Diemens had not touched those girls for days. They were put there by something else. That's what convinced Isaac this was not a trap.'

I thought again of the orange creature in the forest. Of the *foreign* smell.

'There's something else out there. In the bush,' I said.

'I know,' Tessa said quietly. 'I can feel it too.'

I shivered. 'Is Isaac already down there?'

Tessa nodded. 'And Hatch. They stayed down there. Luda too. There is a jetty there. Isaac made some quick telephone calls and he has arranged a boat for us to use as a base.' Tessa shook her head. 'You know, Cat, I do not understand this at all. We've checked that area in the past. We combed every mile of land from Oatlands to Stormlea, and we have found nothing. Hatch based himself in Kingston for three entire days and saw nothing. But I suppose we never really had a clue to go on before now.' More quietly, she said, 'I wish the Sarcos were coming with us.'

I could have asked her then. I could have told her I saw her and Perrin. That I *knew*. I could have told her I didn't understand but I was trying to. The words hovered in my mouth like moths, their feathery wings tickling my tongue. *'And you ... you will come to understand this more than most. You'll see ...'*

'Cat, are you quite right?' Tessa asked.

'Fine,' I said, shaking myself. I *would* talk to Tessa. But when we had more time. Tonight. When this was all over. 'So, what's our plan?'

'If the clues are correct, this is our best opportunity yet to find the Diemens. We can base ourselves on the boat Isaac has arranged and locate their camp. If we find the Diemens, we will call on the Sarcos. Attack the camp. Whatever this Solution is, it is clear that it will increase the power of the Diemens. This may be our best chance to attack before that happens. Our best chance to defeat the Diemens.'

I spotted Boots's dirt-smeared Hilux perched like a dirty seagull on the cliff-side road. Tessa saw it too. 'Nearly there,' she said, speeding up. 'Are you well?'

'Yeah, I'm good,' I said. And I was. Much as I was terrified by what could happen, I was excited too. A mission. A real chance to stop the Diemens.

As we walked I saw them, floating in the breeze. Specks of dust. Catching the sun and, if only for a moment, shining.

CHAPTER

eLeven

my DAD LoveD couNTRY music.

He loved Johnny Cash, Willie Nelson, Steve Earle and Guy Clark. He'd dance around on the deck with me on his hip. He'd teach me the words to his favourite songs.

My third word was 'Willie'. Mum had a hard time explaining that to her friends.

When Dad was alive, Mum used to call the music 'Hillbilly Opera'. After he died she played nothing else. I liked it too. Listening to it made me feel closer to Dad. And those singers . . . their lyrics were like poetry. Their voices were so flawed and broken and bitter-sweet.

Boots didn't like *that* sort of country music. Boots liked Kenny Rogers.

Delph was smart. She'd been given a bit more time to get ready for our trip and had a heads-up that we were travelling with Boots. She had her MP3 player plugged into her ears and the sound turned up *loud*. Even over the top of all the slide guitar and tears in beer and broken-hearted warbling I could hear that she was playing something hard and fast and furious.

Meanwhile, I wasn't saying anything but I thought I might just hurl myself out of the car if I heard one more song about somebody's damn dog.

I tried to distract myself by watching the scenery. We were passing through another one of the small towns that seemed to pop up out of nowhere down this way, after kilometres of green and trees and nothing. It looked so ordinary. A school. A pub. A Baker's Dozen. So *normal*. And here we were, a car full of shapeshifters whizzing through on our way, hopefully, to find some Diemens. And maybe save one of our new kin. If Rhiannah was still alive this was our best chance yet of finding out where she was. That was big.

I reached over and tapped Delphi on the shoulder, wanting to share with somebody how strange and exciting and scary this all felt. 'What?' she yelled. I pulled out one of her ear buds. 'Gah! What do you think you're doing?' she snapped, her face contorting in what seemed to be actual physical pain as 'The Gambler' broke through her metal barrier.

'What's going on back there?' Boots called out.

'We're dying from a redneck infection,' Delphi yelled. 'Can you just give Kenny a rest?'

Boots laughed. 'I'll have you know this is the music of the gods, mate!'

'Yeah, well, I believe in the gods of metal, and they think the gods of country suck,' Delphi spat. 'Hey, I could plug my MP3 player into the stereo. We could listen to some Ensiferum. They're Viking metal. Much better music for going into battle with Diemens and Sarcos.'

'We are not fighting Sarcos,' Tessa said sharply from the front seat.

'We might be,' Delphi retorted, her eyes suddenly blazing. 'We can't rule it out. It's like you said: the dead bodies point south. They *could* be pointing at the jetty but they could just as easily be pointing to Taranna. The Sarcos could have masked their scent by planting another one on the girls. They could have mixed together wombat scent and potoroo and rubbed it all over them for all we know. It could be the Sarcos laying a trap for us.'

'I would know,' Tessa snapped.

'*How* would you know?' asked Delphi. 'How would *any* of us know, really? We're all just going on trust, and the creatures we're putting our trust in are the same creatures we've been fighting for hundreds of years. The same creatures who've been *murdering* us for hundreds of years.'

'But they're not *now*!' Tessa growled, whipping around to face us. I could see a flicker of fire in her eyes and a hint of sharpness in her teeth. She was fighting to stay in control, like I had been back at the school. But that wasn't like Tessa. Tessa always had full command over her powers. *Always.* 'Rha and Isaac are negotiating. We are close to an official treaty. We can trust them. They will not hurt us again.'

'Says who?' Delphi spat back, her own eyes flashing. 'Sorry, I missed the part where Isaac died and made you the leader. Oh, and I must've also missed the part where you became omniscient, too. You think you know everything, do you? Did you see what happened to those girls? Were you there in the basement of that nightclub?'

'I was,' I said quietly. At least, in my dream I had been. But it had felt real. It had felt like I was really there. Goosebumps danced along my arms. Nobody heard me.

'I know more than you do!' Tessa yelled. 'You are an ignorant child!'

'Hey, fellas –' Boots said, but the girls ignored him.

'You're a bitch!' Delphi growled. 'And you're a traitor. Sucking up to that stupid bitch copper; cosying up to Edward Lord's daughter –' The roar that erupted from Tessa's mouth made me press my hands to my ears.

Jagged fangs ripped through her gums and her fingernails stretched into dagger-sharp claws. She tore at her seatbelt, ripping it apart, and then she pushed at the side of her chair and launched herself into the back seat. At Delphi. Boots almost skidded over to the opposite side of the road.

'Hey! Hey, you two! What the blazes –'

Tessa didn't react at all to Boots. She was too wrapped up in her fury. Too focused on hurting Delphi. She straddled her, muscular Thyla legs squeezing hard on Delphi's still-human thighs. Delphi cried out in pain as Tessa gouged at her arms, pinning them to her sides.

I'd never seen Tessa like this before. She was always in control. What was going *on* with her?

'Don't you *ever* say *anything* like that about Connolly again,' Tessa snarled.

'Get *off* me, you psycho convict!' Delphi cried.

Tessa bellowed and swiped at Delphi's face, taking a chunk out of Boots's seat cover as Delphi ducked to one side.

I found myself curling up and away from them, my hands on my face. I didn't like this. I didn't like it at all. *'Stop it,'* I whispered. *'Stop fighting. Don't hurt each other. Please. I need you.'*

'Hey! Hey! Watch what you're doing to me car!' Boots swerved sharply off to the side of the road. He grabbed

Tessa by the hair and pulled her hard, back to the front seat. 'What are you two *doing?*' Boots exclaimed.

I looked through my fingers at Delphi. She had three dark, angry scratches on her face but she wasn't showing any pain. There were no tears in her eyes. Only sizzling rage.

'Calm down, Tessa,' Boots said, as he struggled to contain the writhing, growling Thyla. I'd never seen Tessa so angry. Seeing her like this was *terrifying*. 'Tessa! Mate!' he said again sharply. 'I said *calm down*. We've got a job to do. We gotta get down south and find those bloody Diemens. It's them we're meant to be fighting. Not each other.'

Slowly, Tessa's struggling became less intense. Her grunts grew quieter and her breathing slowed. I took my hands away from my face. They were shaking. Finally I saw Tessa shudder in pain as her fangs retracted and her claws changed back into stubby human fingernails. Then there was the inevitable agonised gasp as her Thyla legs snapped back into human ones. 'Sorry, Boots,' she said. She looked confused. And guilty. 'I don't know what . . . I don't know why I did that. I'm not quite . . .' She trailed off, her eyes huge and terrified.

'Delphi, say sorry too.' Boots said tersely.

'Why? I didn't do anything! She's the mental one! Geez, talk about going postal!'

'You slagged off Tessa's friend,' Boots interrupted matter-of-factly. 'Cat's mum. You called her a bitch. That's not on, Delphi. We know you're not a fan of coppers, but it's still not on, yeah?'

Delphi looked over at me, horrified. 'Oh, Cat! I'm so sorry.' Her chin wobbled. She reached for my arm. 'Cat, I really am. I forget sometimes that Connolly is . . . Hey! Don't cry!'

My hands flew to my face. Sure enough it was slick with tears. I didn't really know what had made me cry – whether it was Delphi being mean about Mum or her saying bad things about Tessa or just seeing two of my own kind fight like that. My *family*.

'It's okay,' I said quietly, rubbing at my face with my sleeve. Delphi's fingers reached over and gently wiped the last stray tears away. Her face was so tender it nearly made me cry again.

'Sorry to Tessa too,' Boots reminded her.

'Sorry,' Delphi said, her eyes never leaving mine. And I knew she wasn't apologising to Tessa. She was trying again to get me to forgive her. Boots didn't notice though.

'Righto,' he said. His voice was as laid-back as ever but I noticed his arms were covered in painful-looking scratches that were only just starting to heal. 'We need to get back on the road. We're running late now. *And* we're just about at me favourite song!'

None of us said anything as Boots turned the key in the ignition and the Hilux rumbled back into life. Tessa looked shamefaced. Delphi looked murderous. I just felt numb. But when Kenny Rogers's voice twanged its way through Boots's speakers once again the three of us gave a collective, synchronised groan.

CHAPTER
twelve

THE HOTEL ITSELF WAS INCONSPICUOUS. IT LOOKED OLD but once you get that far south lots of buildings looked old. This was real colonial Tasmania. Most of the families who lived here could trace their ancestors to the settlers and convicts. This was a place where time had frozen.

With its bright red roof, the hotel stood out from the dark hills around it like a tomato in a salad but apart from that it just looked like a hotel. It didn't look like the hideout for a clan of nasty immortals.

Boots parked his ute in the small, muddy car park out the front.

'Are we meeting Isaac here?' I asked.

'Are we meeting him for *Devonshire tea*?' Delphi said dryly, craning her neck to get a good look at the building in front of us. It did look like the sort of place where scones and clotted cream would be on the menu. 'I still don't see the point of this,' she muttered. I looked at her warningly and she rolled her eyes. She rubbed a hand absently over her cheek. The scratches were just puffy, shining lines now but they obviously still hurt her.

'You do not have to be here, Delphi,' Tessa said. Her voice was bitter. She was still angry with Delphi. 'If you think this is all pointless, why don't you just go?'

Delphi looked at me. 'No, I want to stay,' she said. I bit my lip and looked away.

'We're not meeting him here,' said Boots. 'We're meeting him down there.' He pointed at the deep blue water lapping at a rickety-looking wooden jetty not far from where we were parked. He swung his Blunnies out of the ute door and jumped down to the muddy ground. I looked over at Delphi. She shrugged and opened her door. In the front, Tessa did the same and I followed, springing down with a squelch in the mud.

'How'd Isaac get a boat anyway?' I asked as we walked towards the jetty. 'How'd he arrange it so quickly?'

'Actually, it's more like a yacht – big bugger and all, from what I hear. One of his rich mates lent it to him,' Boots said, grinning.

I looked at him curiously. A rich friend? Isaac used to have 'rich friends': Lord and his Diemens. But after what happened with Ms Hindmarsh, Lord stopped inviting Isaac to his meetings. It seemed that Lord didn't trust humans any more. Isaac never was a human, really, but Lord didn't know that.

Isaac had been so close to finding out where the Diemens hid and what the Solution was. But the day after the fight in the bush, he got an email at work from Lord's offices thanking him for his services but informing him they were no longer required. There was a postscript too, he told us. It said if Isaac attempted to attend another meeting or inform any authorities of any of the activities undertaken by Van Diemen Industries 'it would not be looked upon favourably by the board'.

Lord hadn't changed his mind, had he? He wasn't the 'rich mate' Boots was talking about? Boots cleared up my confusion. 'Some copper who done good on Lotto or something. I think Isaac called in a favour. Spun some story about a romantic weekend and a plan that had fallen through at the last minute. Said he was desperate so the mate gave him the boat quick smart. It was moored here already so that worked out real well. It'll make a good base.'

When we got to the edge of the jetty, Boots pointed to an enormous white schooner moored to the dock. 'Geez! That's a bit obvious!' I said. 'Wouldn't a little motorboat have done?'

'In summer, there are many yachts here,' said Tessa. 'It is a popular place for sailors. It is quieter now because it is the off-season but look – there are some other yachts moored down that way, although they are probably unin- habited just now. Ours is almost identical to them. And there is even a replica brigantine just along the coast, you see? So we are not the biggest boat here by far! Isaac knows what he is doing.'

'Isaac said he'd check the other yachts while we were on our way,' Boots said. 'Go on in copper mode. But Tessa's right. Reckon they're abandoned. Reckon their owners are at work. Probably won't use 'em till summer. As long as we keep a pretty low profile, I reckon anybody'd think our yacht's abandoned too.'

'Are the others on the yacht already?' Tessa asked.

'Yep. And we'd better get there too. We're late, thanks to you barmy sheilas.'

Tessa's face blushed bright red. Delphi jutted her chin out and glared at her feet. 'Are you ever going to let us hear the end of that?' she growled.

'Nah. Probably not!' Boots smirked playfully. Delphi punched him on his flannie-clad arm. 'Think yer tough, do ya, love?' he said, whacking her back. 'Think you'll find there's not many tougher than me. Hey! You wanna fight? Do ya?' He held up his fists like an old-fashioned boxer.

'Piss off! You got my funny bone!' Delphi rubbed at her elbow.

'You two are like naughty puppies,' Tessa said, a smile finally creeping back to her face. She bounded up to join them, leaving me trailing behind.

Something in my bones told me this place wasn't quite right. It made my skin prickle. I kept looking over my shoulder, expecting monsters to leap from every shadow.

The others sprinted forwards and then began to skitter down the rocky banks of the river. I pulled my jumper tightly around me against the biting wind and took one last sneaky look behind me, back at the hotel. What I saw made my heart leap to my throat.

On the white-painted porch were three tall, black-clad men standing completely motionless in a row. Staring straight at me.

CHαpter
thirteen

'are you *certain* they were diemens?' isaac leaned forward. He was looking at me intently, his hands were clasped in front of him so tightly his knuckles had gone white.

I made myself nod. 'I'm pretty sure –'

'Are you *pretty sure*, Cat, or are you *certain*?'

'Yes,' I said, trying to make my voice sound firm.

'I think we should listen to her, Isaac,' Tessa said. She put her hand lightly on my arm. I was grateful. *She's still Tessa*, I realised. I still loved her. My dream voice echoed again: *'You will come to understand this more than most. You'll see.'*

The anger I'd felt while at the school was faded now. Watercolour. And I felt guilty for all the bad things I'd thought. Tessa deserved better from me. She'd always heard me out and forgiven me, even after I almost got her killed when I was monkeying around up the mountain and she fell. She was good and brave and kind and she'd been through such a lot – not just lately but over the last hundred and sixty years. She'd grown up in a *prison*, for pity's sake. And she'd lost her mother when she was really young. That was enough to screw anyone up totally and yet Tessa had come out of it stronger than anybody I'd ever known. And then she'd fallen in love with a Sarco.

So what?

Tessa might look like a teenager but she'd been doing this for a long time. She *wouldn't* let herself fall for someone she thought might hurt her. Tessa was too sensible for that. She wasn't like the people in my books. She wouldn't be a fool for love.

I brushed my arm where Tessa had touched me. With a jolt I remembered Mum. I remembered how she always used to hold me so tightly when I cried.

After I made my discovery I stopped hugging Mum as much. I wished now that I'd taken every opportunity to hold her.

I wanted her holding me now. But I had to be strong. If there were Diemens at the hotel I had to be bloody strong. 'It *was* Diemens,' I said again.

'We'll go up there. Check it out,' Isaac said.

'You guys should all go,' Hatch said. 'I can stay here. Watch the boat.'

'By yourself? I don't think so –' said Isaac.

'I'll be fine, mate,' Hatch said. 'Promise.'

Isaac narrowed his eyes and nodded slowly. 'All right. Hatch, you stay here. The rest of you, let's go check out this hotel.'

Tessa looked over at me. 'Are you sure you want to come?' she asked.

'Of course,' I said. 'All hands on deck, right?' Tessa grimaced at my stupid joke.

'This could become a big battle, Cat,' she said. 'You realise that.'

'I know,' I said. 'I can do this.'

'Of course you can,' she said, smiling. My heart soared. I turned to Delphi. 'Are you coming?' I asked.

'Wouldn't miss it for the world,' she said.

'Right then, let's go,' Isaac said. He looked at me. 'If it *was* Diemens you saw, we could be in for an interesting afternoon.'

'Closed for renovations,' Delphi said. 'That'd be right.'

The five of us stood looking at the front door of the hotel. The sign was painted in red. The curtains were drawn. 'That'd be why there's nobody else around,' I said, looking from side to side. *Except the men I saw on the porch,* I thought. I was more convinced than ever now that they weren't holiday-makers.

'Should we break in?' Boots asked Isaac.

'I think we need back-up,' Isaac said. 'If Cat did see Diemens, we're going to need the Sarcos earlier than planned.'

'Of course we are,' Delphi said sarcastically. 'Gotta get the Sarcos.'

'Luda, will you go down to Sarco territory? Get a message to Rha? Boots, is she okay to take the ute?' Boots nodded and threw Luda his car keys. Isaac shook his head. 'After this I am making that backwards Luddite get a mobile phone.'

'You know there's no coverage in Taranna anyway,' I reminded him. Isaac rolled his eyes.

Luda nodded. 'I'll be as fast as I can.' She looked down at the car keys and then back up to Isaac. 'You do remember I have no licence?'

'I'm choosing to forget it,' Isaac said.

Luda nodded. 'Yes, boss.'

'Okay, Tess and I will go in. Delphi and Cat, you go back to the boat. Tell Hatch what's going on, okay? We might need him here after all.'

Delphi and I walked away from the hotel. I looked back over my shoulder and saw Isaac knocking on the door. *That won't work, Isaac,* I thought. Something told me that if somebody was in there, they wouldn't respond to knocking.

Back at the boat, Hatch was nowhere to be seen. 'That's weird,' said Delphi. 'He was just here a minute ago. Hatch!' she called out.

I stuck my head down into the boat's sleeping quarters. 'Hatch!' I cried. He wasn't there. I straightened. 'Delphi, this is really –' I looked around. Delphi was gone. She'd disappeared. My heart started to thump. What the hell was going on? I ran to the front of the yacht. 'Delphi? Hatch?' I cried out. Where were they?

As I stood at the front of the yacht a strong smell hit my nostrils. A *floral* scent. What was it? I turned around.

Something dark obscured my vision. Something soft.

Roses, I thought. *It smells of roses.*

And then everything went black.

CHAPTER
fourteen

I WAS DEEP IN THE FOREST. ALL AROUND ME WERE BODIES. Black and white bodies. Sarcos turning to dust. 'You did this,' a voice called from the darkness. Eyes glinted and reflected light. 'It's your fault.'

'No,' I said. 'I didn't do anything!'

'You let it happen!' the Sarco growled, moving towards me with his claws extended. 'You deserve to die.' Just as I thought I was done for, as the Sarco bore down on me, I heard something: a voice calling out to me through the trees. 'Cat! Over here! Come this way. We'll look after you.'

I whipped around to see Charlotte Lord standing behind me. And behind *her* stood three men. I began to walk towards them, my feet moving even though

I wasn't sure I wanted them to. I was drawn to the men as if they were magnetised. As I got closer I saw that each of the three men had silver hair. And their eyes were the colour of the sea on a winter day. When they opened their mouths to smile at me – sickly, cold-eyed smiles – instead of teeth their mouths were crammed with needle-sharp silver fangs.

Diemens.

Charlotte walked towards me. 'What's wrong?' she said. 'What's wrong, Cat? It's okay. I'm here to help you. I'll protect you from the Sarco.' I turned around and, sure enough, the Sarco was behind me, fangs bared. Closing in. I turned back to Charlotte. She was smiling and her hand was held out. 'Come with me, Cat,' she said. 'You can trust me.'

'But what about the Diemens?' I said.

Charlotte's forehead creased. 'What Diemens?' she said. 'What are Diemens?'

I moved forward, holding my hand out to her. As I walked, the men behind Charlotte stopped smiling and in creepy unison they reached down to their pockets. Each of them pulled out a perfect pale pink rosebud. The smell of the roses was so strong it hit my nostrils from metres away. And it was incredible. The rosebuds smelled of hot tea and shortbread biscuits and polished wood and roast lamb and the forest after rain. When I reached Charlotte,

I saw her hands were now holding roses too. 'What are they?' I breathed.

'They're Tudor roses,' said Charlotte, still smiling kindly.

'What are they for?' I asked.

'I don't know,' she said. She looked confused all of a sudden. 'He just gave them to me.'

'Who?' I asked.

'Daddy,' Charlotte whispered.

As she said it the heads of the men snapped down towards me. Their mouths opened again in sneers. 'Vulpis,' they said. Their voices sounded like rasps scraping on steel.

'What –' I began, but before I could finish they said the word again.

'Vulpis,' they said. 'Vulpis. Vulpis. Vulpis. Vulpis.' The word was now a hellish chant.

'What are they saying?' I screamed to Charlotte as the voices grew louder and louder. 'What are they saying? What is –'

'Who?' Charlotte said.

'The men! They're saying –'

'Vulpis,' the Diemens chanted. 'Vulpis. Vulpis. Vulpis.'

Charlotte turned around again. And finally she saw them.

And she screamed.

The world was plunged into darkness.

And then I saw him, standing in a sunbeam. A man with sandy hair and ruddy skin. 'Dad!' I cried. 'Dad, help me!'

'I can't help you, Cat,' he said. 'Nobody can help you. You're on your own.'

A loud thud woke me up. My eyes snapped open. The air was thick with dust and smoke.

I'd been sleeping. I'd been dreaming. How had that happened?

And then it all came back to me. Delphi and Hatch disappearing. The darkness. The roses.

There was no smell of roses now. There was the thick acrid stench of smoke and sweat and blood.

And then there was the screaming.

I leapt to my feet and threw my cuff to the ground. What was going on? All about me was the crunch and clang and hiss of battle and somehow I'd just kept sleeping. I'd been so deep in my dream world nothing could have pulled me out.

And now here in the real world . . .

There was a Diemen in front of me.

'Hello, sleepyhead,' the Diemen hissed.

'Piss off,' I said and clawed him in the neck. I never was a morning person.

As the Diemen slumped to the deck I looked around me.

I coughed as smoke flowed into my throat and nose. 'Delphi!' I yelled. I couldn't see anything through the dust and grit. 'Tessa!'

'Cat! Help!' It was Delphi.

She was about ten metres away, towards the front of the boat. It wasn't far but I could hear fighting all around me, even if I couldn't see it. I could run straight into a Diemen. I could be killed.

But Delphi was in danger.

I steeled myself. I breathed out steadily.

And then I bolted. I nearly tripped and fell as I spotted Isaac fighting a Diemen ahead of me. 'Cat!' he yelled. I ignored him. He could take care of himself.

I saw Tessa too, in my peripheral vision, twisting a Diemen's skull. I willed her to be safe. To keep fighting. To win. She would. She was recovered. She was strong. Delphi was a new Thyla. She wasn't as strong as Tessa.

I leapt over crates and benches and piles of coiled rope. I ducked under a boom and side-stepped a ladder. As I raced I saw flashes of black, of silver, of Thyla yellow and one small flicker of burnt orange. The flash of orange made my heart jolt but I couldn't let it distract me. I had to keep going. And besides, there were so many colours all around me, merging into each other on a crazy, messed-up artist's palette. The colours of battle.

And then I was there.

I could see them. Just. The smoke made them hazy, unreal, an impressionist's painting of life.

Delphi was lying on her back. A Diemen was standing above her. In his hand was a glossy metal pipe with a spike on its end, like something from an operating theatre. He held it above his head, ready to bring it down on Delphi. Ready to kill her. Or worse. I'd never seen a Diemen with one of those devices before. I didn't know what it meant. I didn't wait to find out.

I kicked the Diemen hard in the back. He fell to the deck with a clunk. 'What the –' he began, twisting around. I didn't give him time to finish. I leapt on him, punching and biting. Out of the corner of my eye I saw another Diemen advancing.

'Delphi, watch out!' I screamed. Delphi jumped to her feet and tripped the Diemen. He toppled too and Delphi stamped on his head. I heard it break apart. She ran off. I looked back down at my Diemen. He was covered in dark blood. His face was bent in ways it shouldn't have been. His nose was turned sideways. His eyes streamed blood. He was nearly dead.

Nearly.

All it needed was one last blow.

I always hated this part. I didn't like killing. None of us did. The only way to do it was to think of the girls we were saving by doing it; the lives that would continue because this evil monster was no longer in the world.

And in my case, to think of my dad. Because every Diemen I killed could mean another young girl got to wake up tomorrow happy. Another family who wouldn't lose someone they loved. That'd make Dad proud, wouldn't it? That'd make him see that I'd done as he asked.

I raised my claws above my head and then I slashed them through the air. As the Diemen's eyes widened I sliced his throat. His eyes went dull.

Another one gone.

But there was no time to revel in my achievement. I pushed myself up, wiping away the black liquid on my jeans. And I turned around, poised to race back towards the others.

Delphi was standing in front of me. Her face was caked in dust. Through the dust, tears made tiny rivers. 'Cat, don't bother running,' she said.

'What?' Relief flooded through me. 'Is it over?' Another tear rolled out of Delphi's Thyla eye and splashed on the deck. 'What's wrong, Delph?' I said, grabbing hold of her arm.

'Everything,' said Delphi. 'Everything's wrong.'

cHapter
fifteen

'HOLY CRAP,' I SAID, my HAND flying to my mouTH.
'It's all . . . they're all . . .' I looked around the boat's deck
– what was left of it – through hot tears. The dust was
settling. I could see more now. It was like a bomb had gone
off. The boat was completely smashed to pieces. There
was wood and fabric and chunks of bent metal strewn all
about. And blood, splattered over everything. Black blood
and red. 'Is anyone still here?' I called out to Delphi. 'I saw
Tessa and Isaac before. Are they . . . Is anyone still . . .'
I didn't want to say the last word. *Alive.* I didn't want any
of this to be real. I wanted to still be dreaming.

'Boots is dead,' Delphi said flatly. She walked towards
me through the smoke and took hold of my hand. 'He's
over there.' She pointed to the boat's prow. 'He's . . .'

She didn't need to finish. I could see, through the haze, a flash of tartan flannel.

And a man, bent and broken and floppy, draped over the wheel of the yacht.

'Oh, no. Oh, no. Oh, no,' I mumbled, my whole body shaking. A wave of nausea overtook me and I bent over double, retching and vomiting on the deck.

'He's got scratches all over him,' Delphi said as she continued to pace about among the rubble. 'Big gouges. Like they were made by claws.'

'Diemens don't have claws,' I barked, clearing my throat and spitting out the last of the bile on the ground.

'It wasn't Diemens,' said a voice from behind me. I swung around. A familiar face emerged from the smoke. Hatch.

'Hatch, where were you? And Delphi? You disappeared.'

'Someone drugged me,' Delphi said. 'When I woke up there was a Diemen coming at me with a pipe.'

'Did you get drugged too?' I said to Hatch. 'Is that why you think it wasn't Diemens? Because it *was*. I just *killed* a Diemen. Two of them, actually.' A horrible thought crept up on me. 'I'm not still dreaming, am I?'

'It wasn't only Diemens,' Hatch said. 'That's what I mean. There was something else.' Hatch sounded exhausted and as he got closer I noticed a deep gash and an angry purple bruise on his forehead. 'Whatever it was, it knocked me out pretty much straight away.'

'Wait. It hit you on the head?' I said. 'You weren't drugged?'

Something passed over Hatch's face. 'Oh, no. I was drugged too. We all were. I don't know why it hit me as well.'

'But did you see it? Before they got you?' asked Delphi. 'The – the other thing.'

Hatch shook his head and sat down gingerly on a half-destroyed chair. 'Not really,' he admitted. 'Not properly. But I could *definitely* see that it wasn't a Diemen. They didn't look human. Or *super*human. They looked like a *creature*. They looked like us.'

'Like a Sarco?' Delphi asked.

'Maybe.' Hatch shrugged. 'Can't say for sure. They came at me from the side. I just heard a thump as they dropped something. On the deck. And then . . .' He clicked his fingers. 'Black.'

'So you didn't see what happened to the others? To Isaac and Tessa?' The smoke was starting to clear on the deck and I looked around, trying to make out any other Thylas. Trying to make out *bodies*. 'I saw them here, fighting Diemens. They must've come back from the hotel. I – I ran straight past them.'

'To save me,' Delphi said, squeezing my arm. 'I'd be dead if it wasn't for you.'

'And Isaac and Tessa might be safe if it wasn't for me!' I cried. I turned on Hatch. 'You were here,' I said. 'You must have seen *something*. Something coming.'

Hatch shook his head. 'Sorry, Cat. I just saw a shape. A figure. And then it clubbed me from behind.'

'They must have been planning to take us,' I said. 'To *experiment* on. They probably would've if Isaac and Tessa and Boots hadn't come back and fought them. Oh, God. Where are they now? They must be close to here still.' I moved over to the edge of the boat. I scanned the horizon. The yachts bobbing around in the water nearby had been here when we arrived and they still looked totally empty.

Then there was just the tall replica brigantine that Tessa had pointed out. I'd seen one just like it – the *Windeward Bound* – moored at the docks in Hobart, tourists all over it like ants. 'What about that boat?' I asked. 'The big one. They could be there. Why don't we look there?' I could feel panic rising in my chest.

Tessa's gone.

'It's just a replica,' Hatch said. 'I've been on it before. It's run by students and it's only operated in summer. And besides, the Diemens would never hide somewhere so obvious.'

I nodded. 'You're right.' I ran to the other side of the boat and looked up towards the land. I couldn't see any clues around the hotel but what if they were *inside* it? Isaac and Tessa had checked the hotel, though. They wouldn't have come back to the boat if there had been any sign of Diemens living there. Still, I *had* seen Diemens on the hotel's porch. 'We need to check the hotel again,' I said.

'It's closed,' Hatch said. 'For renovations. Remember?'

'How do you know that?' I asked. 'You got knocked out before Isaac and Tessa came back.'

Hatch pointed. 'There's a sign on the road. Dunno why we didn't notice it before. I'll check if you want but it's . . . hang on. I can smell something. Boots? Guys, I can smell Boots!'

Delphi and I looked at each other. Neither of us knew what to say. For a few moments there was silence. Then finally Delphi got up the guts to talk. 'So, you haven't seen . . .' Delphi looked over to Boots' crumpled body, his tartan shirt flapping in the wind. Tears sprang to her eyes again and she turned quickly around and marched away. She didn't want us to see she was crying.

'That's not . . . awww, *Boots*,' Hatch moaned. 'No! They shouldn't have . . .'

'I know, Hatch,' I said. 'They shouldn't have done any of –'

I was interrupted by a loud bang and Delphi's voice crying out, 'Guys! Guys, come here. Come here *now*!'

Hatch and I clambered over pieces of broken boat to get to her. 'What?' I called out. 'Is it them? Is it Tessa and –'

'Ah . . . No, mate.' Delphi popped her head up from behind a pile of debris. 'But it is someone we've been looking for.'

CHapter

sixteen

RHiannaH's skin had faded to a sickly greenish grey. Her lips were cracked and caked with scabs. Beneath her eyes were bags so dark they looked like bruises. Maybe they *were* bruises. It was hard to tell. The rest of her face was a mess of scratches and grazes and raw-looking cuts. Some of them were almost definitely infected. Her gorgeous black hair – the hair I'd always envied when my own crazy curls were misbehaving – was short and jaggedly cut, like someone had hacked at it with a knife. Her breathing was shallow and her eyes were rolling back in her head. She looked close to death.

For an immortal that's a big deal.

'How the hell did she get there?' Delphi pulled away the torn sail that had been hiding Rhiannah's body from view. 'If her foot wasn't poking out from under that sail I never would have spotted her.'

'She must have been *put* here sometime during the battle,' Hatch said, rubbing at his forehead. He looked completely confused. He wasn't the only one.

My chest was tight and my belly was churning. Tessa was gone. Isaac was gone. And now Rhiannah was *here*. I was struggling to keep it together.

'Someone must have left her here and covered her up,' Delphi said. 'It definitely looks like the sail was put there on purpose.'

'Who would do that?' I swallowed down my nausea and my fear as I bent over Rhiannah's battered body. 'And *why*?' I shook my head. Those questions could wait for later. I could hear the breath catch in her chest and again in her throat. It was like her body was too tired to breathe but Rhiannah was damn well making it. She was tough. She'd always been tough. Even after I'd found out she was a Sarco – after I was turned Thyla – I'd always admired how tough she was.

As I looked down at Rhiannah's crumpled body I wasn't thinking of her as a Sarco. Rhiannah was sick. She'd been mistreated and she needed us. 'What should we do?' I asked Hatch. His face was nearly as pale as Rhiannah's. 'Come on, Hatch!' I insisted. 'You're the ambo. What should we do?'

'Right. Sorry. Okay, so we need to get her on her side. To make sure she doesn't choke. Carefully though. We don't know the extent of her injuries. Can you help me?'

I nodded. 'Yep.'

Hatch bent over Rhiannah and together we moved her on to her side. 'Cool,' said Hatch. 'Now we need to assess her level of consciousness.' He leaned over and spoke in Rhiannah's ear. 'Rhiannah, are you awake? Can you hear me? If you can, open your eyes.'

There was no response. 'Rhiannah?' I said. 'Are you okay? Can you hear me?'

'Stuff this,' growled Delphi, crouching down. 'Oi! Sarco scum! Wake up you piece of –'

'Delphi!' I gasped. 'You can't –'

But just then Rhiannah began to shift slightly. Her eyes focused and she started coughing. 'Roomie?' she murmured. She winced, as if speaking hurt her. It probably did. I saw a trickle of blood ooze from her blistered lips. 'What am I . . . hell . . . where . . .?'

'How do you feel?' asked Hatch, placing a hand on her chest to stop her sitting up too quickly. 'Does it hurt anywhere?'

A wheezy laugh flew out of Rhiannah's mouth. 'Apart from everywhere? How did I get here?' Hatch helped her to sit up slowly. 'Whoa. Dizzy,' she grunted. 'Hey, where are . . . Tessa and Isaac? They were –'

'You saw them?' I asked, my heart racing. A thin ribbon of hope curled around me. 'When? What was happening to them?'

'Just then. Being carried. Or I *thought* . . . time's been a bit funny lately. Maybe it was days ago. Who knows? Where am I? Wait . . . I'm on a boat?' Rhiannah tried to look around her but winced again.

'Geez. Okay, *helping the Sarco*,' Delphi muttered. She reached into her backpack and scooped out a bag of some sort of dried, powdered plant. She pulled out a flask and dropped some of the powder into it. 'Drink this,' she said. Rhiannah looked at her suspiciously. 'It's not poison, you Sarco idiot. It'll ease the pain.'

'I'll help,' I said, taking the flask from Delphi and tipping it up to Rhiannah's mouth.

My hand was shaking.

Tessa's gone. Tessa's gone. Tessa's gone. The voice in my head reminded me of the records Mum sometimes played back home. Records from when she and Dad were young. Sometimes they caught and skipped and repeated the same line over and over. *Tessa's gone. Tessa's gone. Tessa's gone.* I shook myself. I had to focus. I had to focus on Rhiannah.

That's what Tessa would do.

Rhiannah swallowed. 'I'm on a boat?' she repeated.

'Yes, Rhiannah, you're on a boat,' Delphi snapped. 'We – being the Thylas – were here to check out this theory

Isaac had that the Diemens were hiding out somewhere down this way. Girls have been dying. Isaac reckons it's the Diemens but who knows? Maybe your lot are helping. Maybe they're working together. Or maybe it was the Sarcos all along and the Diemens were just trying to stop them. There was a fight. Boots is dead and Isaac and Tessa are missing and *you're here* and Hatch saw a creature that didn't look like a Diemen so, obviously, something pretty messed up went on.'

Something niggled at my memory. Something from the boat. The flash of burnt orange.

'I saw orange,' I whispered. Nobody heard me.

'It's not the Sarcos taking girls!' Rhiannah cried. 'Why would you think that?'

'Evidence is pointing that way.'

'What evidence?'

'Oh, you know. Corpses arranged like an arrow pointing towards Sarco territory. Hatch seeing a creature – not a Diemen, but a *creature* – on the boat. That sort of thing.'

'I saw *orange*,' I said louder. 'On the boat.'

'Yeah, I saw all the colours of the rainbow,' Delphi said, shrugging. 'We were drugged. Oh . . . You saw orange in the bush too, hey?' Delphi shook her head. 'You said it yourself – it was just your mind playing tricks on you.'

I was confused. Delphi had seemed to believe me before. Why had she changed her mind? Was she so determined the Sarcos must be at fault that she'd decided I must have been seeing things?

'Cat, there are no orange creatures out here. There are Thylas and Sarcos and we know it wasn't *Thylas* who put Rhiannah on our boat.' Delphi put her hand lightly on my cheek. 'You just went a bit brain-screwed out there. Like I did.'

I moved my head away from Delphi's hand. I *wasn't* so sure it had just been the drugs that made me see that flash of copper. I hadn't been drugged that day at the clearing. I shook my head. 'I'm pretty sure I –'

'We need to get Rhiannah patched up,' said Hatch. He'd been checking Rhiannah's pulse, flexing her joints and feeling her forehead for a temperature. Rhiannah winced and hissed and moaned. 'Pretty quickly. She's not good. Not good at all.'

'What about finding the Diemens?' I hissed. I stood up and faced Hatch. 'Tessa and Isaac. They've been taken by Diemens, remember? Hatch, we have to find them!'

'You take Rhiannah to the car,' Hatch said. 'I'll check the hotel but I don't expect to find much. The Diemens are probably long gone by now. Rhiannah's in a really bad way, Cat.'

'What are we going to do? Take her to a hospital?' Delphi asked. 'She's a missing person! How would we explain the way she looks? They'd call the cops.'

'Can't we just take her to the clearing?' I said. 'Try to get in touch with Rha? Or we could just wait here. Luda's gone to get the Sarcos. When they come back we can go and find Tessa and Isaac and the Sarcos can look after Rin. She'll be fixed in no time anyway. She's a Sarco. She'll heal.'

Delphi gave me a funny look. 'I'm not sure she is healing, Cat,' she said softly. 'Some of the bruises look kind of old.'

I wanted to ask Delphi what that could mean but a voice from behind me got in first. 'Oh, no. What's happened?'

Luda.

But where were the Sarcos?

'I am so sorry.' Luda's thin, pale hand floated to her face. 'I could not find the Sarcos. They were all gone from their lair. I do not know where they . . . What's happened here?'

'Tessa and Isaac have been taken.' I grabbed Luda's shoulder. 'There was a fight. The Diemens drugged us and they took Tessa and Isaac. But we've also got another problem. We need your help, Luda.'

Luda looked down at Rhiannah and gasped. 'The young Sarco who was taken,' she whispered. She looked back up. 'What will you do with her?'

'She needs proper treatment,' Hatch said. 'More than we can give her. We need drugs and bandages and we don't have those at the clearing. We've never needed proper medical supplies before. We either heal or we die. Rhiannah is not healing properly. She needs painkillers at least and –' He gestured at the sky, which was beginning to drizzle with rain. 'She needs to be kept out of the weather. We can't take her to a hospital. We just need to get her somewhere warm and dry, and with good access to medical supplies.'

'The Sarcos *might* have such supplies,' said Luda. 'But I believe they would be in the same situation as we are. And they're all gone from their hideout.'

'Cascade Falls has medical supplies,' I said, an idea – possibly crazy – forming in my head.

Delphi snorted. 'Oh, yeah. Let's walk into Cascade Falls with Rhiannah looking like this. They'll just let us do that, no questions asked. Sorry, Cat, but that's not the smartest –'

'I wasn't *thinking* of going to the Cascade Falls staff,' I interrupted. 'I was just thinking of somewhere on the *grounds* of Cascade Falls. Somewhere warm and dry where there's a *student* who could maybe sneak into the sick bay for us to get the supplies!'

Delphi's eyebrows shot up. Her mouth fell open. 'No, Cat –' she began.

'That sounds ideal,' Hatch interrupted. He looked up at Luda. 'Luda, can you go and try to find the Sarcos again? Let them know what's going on. Tell them Rhiannah has been found. Tell them to turn their attention to finding Isaac and Tessa.'

'But Hatch, you thought that it might be the Sarcos who —' Delphi protested.

'If the Sarcos *were* involved in all of this then Tessa and Isaac will be there, won't they?' said Hatch bluntly. 'Either way we have to go to them.'

'I want to go too!' I cried. My whole body felt rigid with tension. 'I need to go with Luda. I need to find Tessa!'

Tessa's gone.

'Stay with me, Cat?' Rhiannah's voice was small. She looked up at me with huge dark eyes. 'I'm scared, roomie. Stay with me?'

I heard my voice speaking. It didn't feel as though it was connected to my brain. 'Okay, roomie,' I said.

'Good. Now, enough arguing,' Hatch said. 'We're wasting time and we need to get out of here. Luda, as soon as I've got Rhiannah stabilised I'll come to find you, okay? Now go.'

Luda nodded and ran back to the car park.

Delphi turned to me. 'I'm not buying it,' she said. 'Your plan. Cat, she's evil. And she's *his daughter*!'

'She said to come back any time and that she'd help us . . .'

'Do you really think we can trust her?' said Delphi.

'I don't know,' I replied honestly. Again my dream came back to me: *'Come with me, Cat,'* she'd said. *'You can trust me.'* 'I – I think so. And we don't have any other ideas, so –'

Delphi rolled her eyes. 'Great. So here am I. A Thyla. About to take a Sarco to the hideout of a human who is the daughter of a Diemen. Is there any potential possibility my life could get any screwier than this?'

CHAPTER
seventeen

We raced north, Hatch breaking every speed limit
we passed. Thankfully the roads were quiet, since it was
a couple of hours from the after-school rush. At least
something was going our way.

I was frantic. My heart felt like it was going to burst.
Blood pulsed in my temples. My fingers felt numb.

Tessa's gone. Tessa's gone. Tessa's gone.

I concentrated on Rhiannah. On keeping her comfortable. I trusted that Luda would find the Sarcos. I had to
trust. And I had to focus on doing my job. On looking
after Rhiannah.

That's what Tessa would do.

Tessa's gone. Tessa's gone. Tessa's gone.

She'd be okay. She had to be. I couldn't lose her.

'Are you alone?' I asked when Charlotte opened the door to her shed.

'Well, yes but, firstly, "hello" would be nice and, secondly, why do you need to know?' Charlotte looked past me to Rhiannah, who was unconscious again and being carried by Hatch. 'Oh. Uh, is that who I think it is?'

'Hi,' said Hatch. Charlotte's eyes snapped up.

'Hi, Nathan,' she said tightly. And I remembered. Hatch had been there the night Jenna was killed.

'You okay?' Hatch said.

Charlotte nodded. 'Fine,' she said icily. Then something inside her thawed. 'Look, I never said thank you for looking after me that night. You were really good to me. I appreciate it.'

'You can say thanks by letting us in,' Hatch said, grunting under the weight of Rhiannah's body.

Rhiannah's eyes jerked open. She looked at Charlotte and blinked a few times. She scrunched her eyes up tightly and then opened them really wide, as if she wasn't sure if what she was seeing was a dream or reality. 'No,' she said finally. 'No, I'm not going in there. I'm not going in there with *her*. She's . . . *his* . . . Hatch, put me down.

Put me down now. I'm leaving. Why would you bring me here?'

'You're going in,' said Hatch. 'You don't have a choice. There's nowhere else to go.'

'Yes, of course. Come in,' murmured Charlotte. She sounded shell-shocked. I couldn't blame her. It's not every day you open the door to your hideout to find two missing persons – one injured – a skinny ambo and a scary-looking metal-head on your doorstep.

As I walked past I saw that Charlotte's eyes were red-rimmed and puffy. She'd been crying again. 'Are you okay?' I asked tentatively.

'Not the time, Cat,' she snapped and turned to watch Hatch.

He waddled as quickly as he could over to the maroon velvet couch. 'Nathan! Not on that! It's from France and it's really . . .' But he'd already laid Rhiannah down flat on her back. '. . . *expensive*,' Charlotte finished tiredly.

Rhiannah, of course, immediately tried to get back up. 'I'm not staying here!' she said again as poor Hatch fought to keep her pinned down. For someone who looked so sick, the girl had a hell of a lot of fight in her.

'Would you mind telling me what's going on?' Charlotte said.

'Um, you know how we talked about secrets?' I said tentatively. Charlotte nodded, her forehead creased.

'Well, can we just . . . Look, Rhiannah needs help. She might die if –'

Charlotte's face went white. She nodded. 'We need to stop her dying,' she said quietly.

'Yes,' I said.

Charlotte cleared her throat and breathed out heavily. She shook herself. 'Okay.' She walked over to Rhiannah. 'Look, can you please calm down? You're just making the mess on the chaise longue much worse. And I like that chaise longue.' Rhiannah stopped struggling for a moment and looked up at Charlotte like she'd lost her marbles. 'Now, listen. You can trust me. I promise. Cat and Delphi have been here already and I've kept their secret. I won't tell anyone you're here unless you want me to. And you're obviously hurt. I won't ask how. I can get you anything you need.' She turned to Hatch. 'What does she need?'

'Some antiseptic. Bandages. Probably some antibiotics for her infections. Definitely some painkillers –'

'And arnica,' Delphi added. 'For the bruising. It's naturopathic but it really works.'

'I can do that,' said Charlotte. 'I'm not sure about the arnica, but the rest I can get.'

'No,' said Rhiannah, shaking her head violently. 'No, no, no. I won't have it. I won't!'

'Oh, shut up, will you! I'm trying to help!' Charlotte growled.

Rhiannah's next words were caught in her mouth. She said nothing for a moment, just stared at Charlotte dumbly. Then her head lolled sideways and a trickle of vomit oozed from her mouth, right onto Charlotte's expensive couch. I felt Charlotte wince from a metre away.

'Oh, God. She's out again,' said Hatch. 'Charlotte, can you go and get us those supplies?'

'Of course,' Charlotte said, a determined look on her face. 'Easy. They're all wrapped around my little finger up there. I won't be long but, in the meantime, does she need anything else I might have here? Water? Food?'

'Yeah. If you could get us some water, that'd be great,' said Hatch, squeezing Rhiannah's hand and tapping lightly on her face. 'And something sweet, to get her blood sugar up?'

'Sweet I can do,' said Charlotte, nodding. 'I have Turkish delight . . .' A shadow passed over her face. 'No,' she said quietly. 'No Turkish delight. But I don't have anything else . . .'

'Turkish delight will be fine,' Hatch said quickly.

'But –' Charlotte protested.

'If it's all you have, then it will be fine.' Hatch's voice was firm.

'Okay,' Charlotte said quietly.

'Hurry, Charlotte,' said Hatch. Charlotte went to her fridge and pulled out a floral cake tin.

'Can I have some too?' I asked. Something told me I'd need all the energy I could get for what was to come. 'Please?' I added, remembering my manners.

'No!' Charlotte cried. She must have noticed the stunned expression on my face because she added quickly, 'We should keep it all for Rhiannah. She'll probably need it.'

'Okay,' I said.

'But anything else . . .' Charlotte gave me a small, strained smile. 'Help yourself to whatever you like.' Charlotte backed towards the door. 'I'll be back in a moment.' She pulled open the door and disappeared.

'I'm just going to sneak back out to the ute,' said Hatch. 'I need to get in touch with my station. Let 'em know I might not be making my shift.'

'Okay, Hatch,' I said. 'Don't be long.' *We need to get out of here,* I added silently. *Tessa's gone.* I turned back to Rhiannah. I tapped her face. 'Rhiannah,' I said. 'Rin.'

'Come on. Wake up,' Delphi sing-songed.

'Maybe if she smells this she'll wake up.' I held a squishy square of Turkish delight under her nose. Sure enough Rhiannah's eyes – and mouth – opened wide. I poked the Turkish delight in. Rhiannah chewed hungrily and swallowed.

'More,' she murmured, so I gave her another piece. 'What is it? It smells . . . familiar.'

'Charlotte's Turkish delight,' I said. Rhiannah's eyes narrowed. She looked like she was trying to remember something. But then a fresh wave of pain rolled over her and her face screwed up. 'It's okay, roomie,' I said. 'Charlotte's gone to get us some things to make you well again. You'll be better in no time.'

'I don't want to be here,' Rhiannah protested as I passed her another sugary cube. She stared at me intently, as if she was trying to tell me something but couldn't put it into words. 'I *don't*,' she hissed.

'I know,' I said. 'But it's only for a little while, okay?'

Rhiannah nodded slowly. 'Okay,' she said uncertainly. 'Don't leave me, roomie.'

'I won't.'

Tessa's gone.

Delphi stood up from the chair she'd been sitting on, picking the dried mud from her boots, and moved over to where I was huddled beside Rhiannah. 'Do you remember anything about what happened to you, after the fight? After the Diemens took you?' she asked. '*Was* it them who did this to you?'

'I don't –' Rhiannah cleared her throat. When she spoke again her voice was tired. Slurred. The words melted into each other. 'I don't remember much . . . I think they must have drugged me because all I can remember is really little

bits – like flashes of being awake and then . . . I was back
to dreaming again. I remember they took me to this big
house and I was trying to escape the whole time – we were
in a big black car – and I kept trying to punch and kick at
the Diemens . . . but they were just too strong and then
one of them put this – this *handkerchief* over my nose.
After that I felt sleepy. Like . . . now. And like I didn't want
to struggle any more. Then we were at – at a little house
and they carried me in and they gave me food and clean
clothes and then they gave me a hot drink. And then I fell
. . . asleep and after that I only remember *bits*.' Rhiannah
grimaced. 'This *hurts*.'

I reached out and stroked her forehead, ignoring
the evil glare from Delphi. Rhiannah was my roomie.
And she was hurt. I didn't care about Delphi's glares.
I didn't care about Thyla and Sarco. Suddenly, powerfully,
I knew I never would again. It didn't matter. Not when
people were hurt and dying. *Not when Tessa was gone.*
'Why are you being so . . . so nice to me?' Rhiannah
croaked.

'Gods only know,' Delphi muttered.

'*Delph*,' I said warningly.

'I'm just saying,' she grumbled.

'Well, don't. Please.' I turned back to Rhiannah. 'We're
helping you because you need help. End of story.
We're not evil, you know. Us Thylas. We're nice people.'

'Well, so are us Sarcos,' Rhiannah said. Her eyes were hazy and unfocused. 'I know you probably think we're . . . that we're *violent* and aggressive and –'

'Stupid,' Delphi interrupted.

'Delphi, will you please just *stop* it?' I begged.

'Maybe the Diemens aren't so bad after all,' Delphi said, ignoring me. 'They gave you clean clothes. They gave you food and drink . . . Maybe they just wanted to help you.'

'Delphi, the Diemens *are* bad,' I said. 'Look what they've done to Rhiannah. And they bathe in human blood. And have you forgotten one was trying to kill you on the boat? Before I ripped his throat out?'

'Maybe he wasn't trying to kill me.' Delphi's chin jutted out defiantly. 'Maybe he was just trying to talk to me. To tell me something. A message. From someone . . .' Delphi's face crumpled for a moment. She cleared her throat and the angry, stubborn expression returned. 'We've never *seen* the Diemens bathe in blood. We *have* seen the Sarcos murder our kin. Maybe they murder humans, too.'

'No,' Rhiannah protested, her eyes darting from side to side. 'They wouldn't *do* that. My own people wouldn't. They're loyal. They'd never betray . . . I used to think this treaty was wrong. But then I met Tessa. And you saved me . . .' Rhiannah's face scrunched up. When she spoke again it was whispered. 'I'm pretty sure I nearly died back then. When you nearly die you realise most things aren't . . . important. Hate isn't important. Friendship is. Duty is. Love is.' Rhiannah broke off, her chin wobbling. Talking was causing her pain. 'We don't murder girls,' she whispered. 'And I'm so sorry my kin ever hurt you.'

'Sshhh,' I whispered. 'It hurts, doesn't it? It'll be okay.'

'My clan would never . . .' Her voice trailed off and her eyes slowly closed.

The door to Charlotte's hideout opened and Hatch entered. He looked worried. 'Um, I think I might have been followed here,' he said.

'Charlotte?' I asked. 'She could have been coming –' Before I could finish my sentence the door to the shed burst open. It wasn't Charlotte standing in the doorway. It was a tall skinny girl with skin the colour of Milo, huge eyes and cropped curly black hair that was streaked with gold.

Erin.

CHapter
eiGHteen

'RHIANNAH?' ERIN'S HAND FLEW TO HER MOUTH. HER eyes were red and they had swollen bags beneath them, and she was thinner than last time I saw her. She'd always been wiry but in an athletic way. Now I could see bones beginning to press at her skin. She looked sick. And really sad.

'Who the hell are you?' Delphi grabbed Erin's arm. Erin shook her off and glared at her like she was an annoying insect.

'I'm sorry.' Charlotte appeared at the doorway, puffing. 'I saw her coming but I wasn't quick enough.' Nobody acknowledged her. We were all trying to figure out what to do about Erin.

'Rhiannah! I can't believe it.' She knelt down at

Rhiannah's side. 'I thought after they found Laurel's body that you must be –'

'They found Laurel's body?' Rhiannah whispered, her eyes sparkling.

'Yeah,' Erin said bluntly. 'Shit, hey?' Her jaw was tense. She was fighting to keep herself together. To be strong. 'But what happened to you?'

Rhiannah wiped at her eyes. 'I got . . . beat up,' she said simply. 'Down at – at the docks. Bastards were just spoiling for a fight. Wrong place . . . wrong time.'

Erin shook her head. 'I can't believe it. What absolute –'

'You know this girl?' Delphi interrupted.

'Rhiannah and I both do, Delph,' I said. 'She's . . .' I searched for the right word. The one I found wasn't quite true but it'd have to do. 'She's a friend.' Delphi raised an eyebrow. She needed more information. 'She's Laurel's friend. The girl who died. And I know Erin from . . . She goes to Cascade Falls.'

Erin looked over at me like she hadn't even noticed I was there before. Like she was seeing me for the first time. And *recognising* me. She gasped. 'Geez! Cat? Cat, right? It *is* you? Cat Connolly? Is this the Missing Person's convention? Where've *you* been?'

'Um, I just needed to get away,' I said, blushing. It was a stupid excuse and it was only a millionth of the real truth. But it was all I had. Well, it was all I could tell Erin.

Thankfully, she gave me a small smile and nodded like she knew exactly what I meant. 'Gotcha,' she said.

It seemed there were a lot of people around here who understood about keeping secrets.

'So you're all great mates. Awesome. But you need to go now,' Delphi growled, looking at Erin.

'Seriously! Who *are* you?' Erin rounded on Delphi. 'A time traveller from 1975? Were you just at a Sex Pistols concert? Seriously, don't you know punk's dead?'

'Oi!' Delphi cried. 'I am so not punk. I'm metal, bitch!'

'What? Like My Chemical Romance?'

Delphi's nostrils flared. 'They. Are. Not. Metal. You dumb –'

'Okay, okay!' I said, stepping between Erin and Delphi before things got ugly. 'Delphi, calm the hell down, okay? And Erin, I'm sorry but you do need to leave. Okay?' We really didn't need this. Not now. We needed to fix Rhiannah and get out of here.

'What's going on?' Erin looked from me to Delphi, her eyes narrowed and suspicious.

'I'm sorry to interrupt you girls,' said Hatch, 'but Charlotte's actually brought us some supplies. I need to attend to Rhiannah.'

'I got what I could,' said Charlotte. The guilty look had gone from her face and been replaced by her usual haughty air. 'I had to invent a story about having a horrendous migraine and needing Nurofen. Luckily, the nurse was busy so she just gave me the keys and told me to get the pills myself. I hid what I could in my pockets, but before I could get everything on your list she came in to get some antiseptic and —'

'It's okay,' said Hatch. 'You did well. Rhiannah, do you mind if I take a look at you?'

Rhiannah shook her head. Her eyes were fully closed now. 'No, Hatcher. But . . . if the others . . . especially Erin and Charlotte . . . if they could just go over there for a bit? You know. Just until you've . . .'

Delphi and I knew why Rhiannah wanted privacy. The Thylas have long stripes on our backs to mark our species. The Sarcos have a mottled black and white pattern all along their backs to mark theirs. Rhiannah didn't want Erin and Charlotte to see her markings.

'I have to go to class anyway,' Charlotte said. 'Are you coming, Erin?'

Erin shook her head fiercely. 'Not until you tell me what's happening. There's weird stuff going on. I know. My nan saw it in her visions. And I've seen stuff myself. What happened to Laurel is part of it. Tell me. Tell me now or I'll scream.'

Charlotte's face was white. 'Go,' I said to her. 'Go to class. It's fine. Erin's just a bit upset. We can take it from here.'

'I want to know this too,' she said.

'It's nothing to do with you,' I said, more sharply than I intended to. 'Just go to the school, okay?' I said more gently. 'Be with your friends.'

Charlotte nodded. 'I do need to go to class,' she said. But then she fixed her eyes on me. 'I want you to tell me though. Later. *Everything*.' Before I could answer, Charlotte had stalked out of the shed.

As the door clicked shut we all turned back to Erin. 'My nan saw it,' she said. Her voice was low and growling. 'After Laurel died she had a vision. About magic animals and men with no souls. I know you're all part of it.'

I shook my head. 'No, Erin. There are no magic animals. There are no men with no souls.'

'Laurel got killed by men with no souls,' Erin hissed. 'I know it. And there *are* magic animals. The night Laurel was taken one of them got taken too. Nan said she – this animal – was a girl too. A human girl. She has an animal side and a human side. Nan said it's from having two births – a human birth and an animal birth; a birth by a mother and a birth by blood. And she said that there're more of them. The magic animal people.' Erin's eyes drifted over to Rhiannah, who was hissing and growling as Hatch applied the ointment to her wounds.

'But that's crazy,' said Delphi.

'Is it?' said Erin, looking back. My eyes lingered on Rhiannah. On her side. Which, while it was mottled blue and yellow and green from the bruises, didn't have any signs of Sarco markings. Strange. I forced myself to look away and pay attention to Erin. 'Nan's never wrong. And my Dad sees things. In the bush. He says he sees the tiger but it's a big tiger. It's a *human* tiger – a human with the markings of a tiger. My sister Shirl and pretty much everyone else reckon he's crazy. But I don't. Not now. Now after Laurel. I've been *feeling* it. I don't get the visions but I can feel that these magic animals exist. I can sense the tiger. And I can sense there are devils too. Magic devils. The devil's my totem. He's part of me.'

'You feel like the *Tassie devil* is part of you?' Delphi's eyes darted to mine and I saw the muscles of her neck tighten.

'Yes,' Erin said. 'He helps . . .' She suddenly looked very tired.

'Erin?' I reached out and took her arm. She flinched at first but then she sort of melted into my touch. She was exhausted. I led her over to Charlotte's dining table.

'Erin, you know all of this . . . you're just grieving.' I hated myself for saying the words. I hated that I was belittling what Erin was going through. But we couldn't let her believe it. We couldn't let her know what was going on. And – much as I felt horrible for thinking it – we had to get rid of her.

Tessa's gone. Tessa's gone.

Erin's chin wobbled. 'No. Nan always sees the truth. And I've seen stuff too. When I've sneaked out at night. I've seen men dressed in black, staring through the school gates. They give me the willies. And the night Laurel's body got found . . . I'm sure I saw creatures out there in the dark, pacing backwards and forwards like they were . . . I dunno, patrolling or something.'

'What did the creatures look like?' asked Delphi.

Erin opened her mouth to answer but she was cut off by Hatch, who'd moved over to where we were sitting without us even noticing. 'Think I'm about done on Rhiannah. But she'll need to rest up here for the night. Charlotte said it's cool for her to stay, but I think *we* need to get going.'

'Yeah, we better go,' said Delphi. 'Don't you reckon, Cat? We've got stuff to do.'

'Yes,' I agreed, my stomach twisting. We had to work out a way to get Tessa back. If that was even possible. *Oh, please,* I begged the universe. *Let it be possible.*

'Well, somebody needs to stay with Rhiannah,' said Hatch.

And somebody needs to work out what to do with Erin, I thought, looking over at her. She didn't look angry any more. She looked miserable.

'Erin, can you not tell people we were here?' I asked, hoping that her understanding of secrets would go that far.

'Stay with me,' Rhiannah said. 'Stay with me, Erin. We can talk. We can talk about Laurel.'

Erin looked over at Rhiannah. 'Okay,' she said softly. 'That'd be nice.'

'What about school?' I asked. 'They'll wonder where you are.'

'Cat, seriously, the teachers are used to me not being there. Mrs Bush? She's clueless as. And the other girls? They don't really give a toss about us untouchables.'

'Yeah. Trust me, I remember,' I murmured.

Erin looked at her feet. 'It was crap for you, wasn't it, mate?' she said. 'I'm sorry. Me and Laurel should've been better to you. We always tried to be good to kids who were having a rough time of it. We just thought you tried too hard. And your stories were bullshit. Sorry.'

'It's all right,' I said. 'I was a try-hard.'

Erin suddenly looked stronger. She smiled and leaned in. 'You'll figure it out one day, Cat.'

'What?'

'Laurel always used to try to get me to believe it too. That it seems like it matters heaps who other people think you are, but it doesn't. Who you are is what you believe you are. What other people want for your life doesn't matter. You need to live the way you want to live. Nobody else. Do what makes you fired up. Laurel was always telling me that.'

I nodded. 'Thanks, Erin,' I said. Something inside me was buzzing but I shooed it away. Now was Thyla time, not Cat time. Right now, we had to work out how to find Tessa.

'No worries.' Erin looked back over at Rhiannah. 'And I'll figure out what happened to Laurel. I know you were all involved. I know Nan's right. I'll figure it out.'

My skin felt tingly. Something told me we hadn't solved the 'Erin' problem yet. But I just had to trust again that Rhiannah would somehow talk her around and convince her that all this talk about 'magic animals' was crazy.

'Thanks for staying, Erin,' I said. 'We'll see you soon.'

'Yeah, you will,' Erin said, without turning back to look at me.

'Bye, Rhiannah,' I called out.

'See ya, roomie,' she said in a soft, tired voice.

As Delphi and I left Charlotte's hideout, Delphi whispered in my ear, 'We're mates with Sarcos now, are we? We've forgotten they're our enemies?'

'Yes, Delphi,' I snapped, too tired to care about offending her. 'We have. Or at least *I* have. And if you don't bloody forget all your stupid prejudices then you're going to be left behind.'

Delphi's eyes widened and then they narrowed. She turned sharply away from me and marched off. But as she did I heard her growling, 'If one of those Sarcos ever came near you, I'd rip their guts out while they were still breathing.'

CHapter

NINeteen

HatcH went to find Luda and the sarcos and sent me and Delphi back to the clearing in case they turned up there.

Delphi looked as exhausted as I felt but I knew I wouldn't be able to sleep. Not until somebody came back with news of Tessa. 'Why don't you take a nap?' I said. 'I'll take the first watch.'

Within minutes Delphi was snoring her little heart out. Her MP3 player was plugged in, blaring her metal. I watched her as she slept, her mouth slightly open and soft, snuffling snores puffing out from her nose. She didn't look so tough when she was sleeping.

I sat for hours in the darkness as it turned to light. I couldn't have slept if I tried so I let Delphi sleep through.

I listened to her soft snoring, to the birds in the forest, to the wind through the trees. Every sound seemed to merge into the same rhythm, the song of the forest. And as time went on I could hear words in the song:

Tessa's gone. Tessa's gone.

'Tessa's gone,' I whispered to myself. 'Please let it not be forever.'

A noise in the bushes made my head jerk up. A swooshing, crunching sound. Someone running. I jumped to my feet. Hatch! Or Luda! Back with news of Tessa and Isaac.

But then I sniffed the air. I couldn't smell Thyla.

I eased my cuff down my arm and breathed in again. It didn't smell like wallaby either. Or possum. In fact it wasn't like anything I had ever smelled before *except* . . . I reached back in my brain to a few days ago; to the day I saw the flash of orange in the bushland. There had been a smell that day too. And there was another time . . . I searched my memory and I realised. On the boat. Amid the smoke and dust, I'd smelled it. Musk and blood and *something else*. Something alien and foreign and *wrong*.

And now I could smell it again.

Then the creature burst into my vision in a flash of orange, like bushfire tearing through the forest. It was moving incredibly quickly. Without thinking I planted my feet, steadying myself and distributing my weight so if the creature did launch itself at me I'd be ready to fight. The orange thing thundered closer. It was big. It was as big as me. Bigger.

And it was human. Or at least it was *part*-human. It was a shapeshifter like me: a 'magic animal'. But it wasn't any 'magic animal' I'd seen before. Not in the real world, anyway.

I had a suspicion I might have seen it in my dreams.

The creature was sleek and muscular. It glowed in the dappled light. It had elongated ears and its eyes were huge and yellow. Its nose was long and pushed upwards. Its body had the mottled burnt orange and brown markings of . . . a *fox*. Yes, it definitely was. A fox. In the middle of the Tasmanian bush. Coming towards me. Quickly. I crouched lower, curling my hands into fists. I steadied my breath and I watched it come closer, closer and then . . .

It stopped.

The creature stopped. Right in front of me. Close enough to hit me, bite me, kick me . . .

But it did none of those things. Instead, it wiped a paw across its brow. Then it held the paw out towards me. 'Hello, Cat.' Its voice was part-bark, part-purr. It had an English accent that sounded a bit like my Nigella Lawson impersonation except lower and more gravelly. More masculine.

'Who are you?' I ignored the paw. 'Where are you from? Why are you *here*? And how do you know my *name*?'

The fox laughed – a weird yipping sound. 'Please, slow down, Cat! I'm not as young as I used to be. I'll start forgetting what you've asked me! One question at a time.'

One question at a time? Just who did this guy think he was, sauntering in here like it was *his* territory? Making *fun* of me? This was *my* clearing. And I wasn't in the mood to be made fun of. I pushed my cuff the rest of the way off my wrist and it clattered on to the ground. I transformed fully. Bones broke, claws grew, teeth lengthened. I could smell everything, see everything, feel everything.

'Tell me your name,' I demanded. The adrenaline pulsing through my veins made me forget about being shy. Or polite.

'Feisty little pup, hmm?' he said. 'Okay, since you asked so nicely, I will tell you. My name is Archibald Matthews. You may call me Archie. And yes, as you deduced, I already know you are Cat.'

'How –'

He rolled his sparkling eyes. 'Do you think I just *stumbled* into your little hidey-hole? Do you think I was out here on a stroll, and merely happened upon you? Hardly! I know who you are, Catherine Connolly. I know that's Delphine Kennedy over there, snoring like an articulated lorry.' He waved his paw at Delphi. 'I know that, *usually*, Isaac Livingston is here, when he's not off being a bobby, and Tessa Connolly (formerly Geeves), is here or at school. I know that's *not* where they are right now. I know it all, Cat. I also know that, very shortly, I am going to take you with me to help you *rescue* Isaac and Tessa. They have got themselves in a bit of a pickle, you see.'

My heart stopped.

'You know where Isaac and Tessa are?' I gasped. Could it be true? And should I believe what this fox was saying?

Could I dare to hope? Could I dare to trust?

'Isaac and Tessa have been taken by the Diemens,' Archie said, nodding. 'I do not approve of this capture, just as I did not approve of, well, anything those monsters have been doing. Which is *why* I moved the bodies to lead you to the Diemen boat.'

'That was *you*?' I gasped. 'You left the bodies out? You made the – the arrow?'

'Yes,' he said, his chest puffing out. 'I made another marker too. Pointing towards the other Diemen hideout. But I only used one girl for that one. I hadn't yet perfected my Thyla-directing technique. You found the girl but not my message.'

The girl . . . *Laurel*. The fox had left her body out for us to find. Slowly, things were starting to make more sense.

'You did very well to follow my directions to the boat, though,' Archie went on. 'Up to a point. You found where the Diemen boat was moored. It would have been nice if you had taken it one step further and actually *found* the Diemen boat. I really thought that wasn't too much of an ask. Especially considering it's a jolly large boat and, since it is the *same* boat – or, should I say, *brigantine* – they have been using since they sailed out here, it does stand out among all the motorboats and yachts.'

The same boat . . . The boat we'd *assumed* was a replica. Oh wow. What idiots we'd been. '*The Diemens wouldn't hide somewhere so obvious,*' Hatch had said. We'd played right into their hands.

'Why should I trust you?' I said, ignoring the smug look on Archie's face.

'Cat.' Archie shook his head and tutted. 'I have *already* proved I can be trusted by returning your friend to you. You have no idea how difficult it was getting the poor little mite all the way from the Diemens' laboratory and onto that boat without being noticed. I do hope you're taking care of her.'

'Taking care of wh–' And then I realised: Rhiannah. That's how she got to be on the boat. This Archie fox thing had put her there. *Oh!* 'That was you too? On the boat. You knocked Hatch out. You . . . How? How did you do that?'

'Well, I had been thinking about how to return her to you for some time but, unlike the other girls, the Diemens seemed quite protective of her. She was *special*. Which is why she was not disposed of so casually and cruelly as the others – though one could argue what they did to her was the cruellest thing of all. However, I knew if I returned her to you . . . well, for one, I didn't wish her to be subjected to such viciousness any more. And I did not wish to wait and see what would happen to her once the Diemens tired of her. And, secondly, I knew if I returned her to you, then you would have to trust me.

'When I heard one of the Diemens say that they had information there were shapeshifters on a yacht close to their brig, and that they were going to go and snatch a few of you for their experiments, I thought "aha"! Here's a way to get the girl out. I had planned to wait with her somewhere, hidden, until the fighting was over, but then one of your men nearly saw me and so I was forced to give him a little, shall we say, injury. To keep him from spotting me and spoiling everything. And then the Diemens were very close and I needed to get away quick smart. Which, obviously, I could not do with a Sarco under my arm. So I did the best I could and secreted her beneath a large and handy top-sail. All in all, events did not go exactly to plan but it was the best opportunity I had to do something when everyone else was more concerned with chasing after Thylas . . .' He cocked his head to one side. 'Well, the Diemens were chasing Thylas. My kin were busy trying to find any food the Diemens might have left lying around in the hideout. The Diemens don't really feed us very well, you know. Bastards.'

'Wait . . . there are more of you? And you're working with the Diemens?'

'Working *for* the Diemens,' Archie explained. He shrugged. 'We're their new muscle. Or, should I say, the *others* are their new muscle. I'm not *anything* of theirs any more. I have defected.'

'You ran away?'

Archie nodded. 'Yes, Cat. I'm a runaway. Just like you.'

I processed this. Could I believe the fox? Was he telling me the truth?

He leaned forward. 'Believe me,' he said.

I glared at him. I wasn't going to believe him just because he told me to. But I would hear him out. If he knew where Tessa was . . . 'So, what do you mean by the others – the other foxes – being the Diemens' "muscle"?'

'Their new thugs. Now they're busy with their experiments, the Diemens have decided to . . . outsource . . . some of their more brutish pastimes. Battles and the like. The Diemens quite enjoy violence, you see, but only of the *elegant* variety.'

'I didn't know *violence* could be elegant.'

'Well, then you haven't met many Diemens. They *lust* after elegant violence, and they are quite wonderful at it, too – the slash of a dagger on a virgin's milk-white face; the prick of a stiletto blade on her breast before they drink from it; the curving gash of a rapier through her flat belly before they hang her up and bleed her –'

'All right! All right! I get it. Elegant violence. I understand!' I cried, my stomach churning.

'Yes, well, *that* sort of violence is the Diemens' stock-in-trade. They revel in it. But I think they were rather tired of the other stuff. The claws and fists caper. Of course, they still wish to be involved in the battles – they can't resist a bit of blood-sport – but they leave the thuggery to my kin. The Diemens only went on that boat of yours because they thought they might have a bit of easy, sadistic fun with you. They won't be so foolish again. Some of them did die during their little attack, didn't they? That'll teach them to leave their muscle-men behind. They thought they'd have you in hand easily.'

Archie shook his head and smiled. 'Silly little Diemens. But enough about them. I led you to the Diemen brigantine. I returned your ally. Surely you must trust me now?'

I just raised my eyebrows at him. He sighed and he seemed to sag a little bit.

'Oh, come on, Cat. We both know you *are* going to come with me, because I have just told you I know where Tessa is and I know you're frantic with worry for her.

I know you aren't just going to stay here when there is the possibility of rescuing her and Isaac. I'm *not* working for the Diemens any more. You must believe me. I will explain more about why I'm here later. But time is running short. Come with me. Trust me. I'll help you find your friends.'

My blood ran cold.

'Come with me. Trust me. I'll help you find your friends.'

Those were the words from my dream. This was all getting too weird.

When I didn't reply, Archie kept talking. 'Please trust me, Cat. I am a good person. And I am trying to help. And I know you're a good person, too.'

'How? How do you know that?'

Archie looked embarrassed. 'Well, I have been watching you, as I said. It's amazing how much you can deduce about a person's true character from what they do when nobody is watching. I see how you look after Delphi. I see how you take time and care in the cooking of food. I see how you chat and tell jokes to the small animals that come to visit you. Actually, that is slightly strange. You know they can't understand you, right?' I glanced down at my feet. Damn it. I knew somebody would catch me doing that one day. Archie went on. 'I see you singing country and western songs to yourself and doing silly little dances that make you look a bit like a leprechaun.' Archie smiled. I wanted a hole to open up in the forest floor.

'I don't look like a leprechaun,' I mumbled.

Archie's eyes softened and he stepped towards me. 'I saw how you saved your friend on the boat, with no thought for your own safety.'

I shrugged. 'I just did what I had to. And, you know, I was only excited to be going on the boat because I thought maybe it was my chance to prove myself. I'm selfish. I'm not brave. You don't know me at all, Archibald Matthews. You can't see inside my head.'

'Ah, well, that's not strictly true,' Archie said. 'I *can* see inside your head. Sort of. You see, I am, well, ever-so-slightly . . . telepathic.' The last part was mumbled. Archie dug about in the dirt with one of his clawed feet.

My jaw dropped. Telepathic? Man, I had seen (and *been*), some crazy stuff in my time, but telepathy? I didn't even know that was possible. 'So, what? You can read my mind? You know what I'm thinking?' I narrowed my eyes. 'Are all of your – your *kind* telepathic? Is it some fox thing?' If so, we Thylas had missed out big time. Why didn't we get superpowers?

'No, I inherited my lovely little gift from my human mother. Shapeshifters don't have the monopoly on powers, Cat. And as for reading your mind? No, see, *that* would actually be a useful skill to have.' There was a bitter smile on the fox's lips. 'My brother, lucky – and, unfortunately, long-deceased – duck that he was –'

'He was a duck?' I asked. 'Like, a duck shapeshifter?'

'No!' Archie said, laughing. 'Do you not have that term in Australia? Lucky duck?'

'Oh.' I felt really stupid. 'Yeah, we do. Go on.'

'My brother could read minds. I can only read *feelings*.' Archie spat the word out as though it tasted bad. 'It's totally jolly useless, most of the time. But it does have *some* benefits. For one thing, I can sense when someone is approaching, and whether they are on my side. For another, I can tell who is good and who isn't. I can tell *you* are good, Cat. And not selfish in the least. Everything you do, you do for someone else. For Delphi, or Tessa, or even . . . your father.'

I felt my cheeks heat up. My fists curled. 'You know nothing about my father,' I growled.

'No,' Archie admitted. 'But I saw you one night, talking to him.' I felt ill. Archie had seen that? I was too embarrassed to reply. 'You were right about daytime patrols,' Archie continued quietly. 'The Diemens may only hunt at night – traditionally – but they have somebody else working for them. I don't know who he is. They never let us Vulpis meet him. But he doesn't seem bound by the usual rules. Your kind need to be patrolling at all times. You can't afford to be complacent. The moment you begin to believe you know everything is the moment everything changes. *You* see things the way others of your kind don't, Cat. Which is why I need you with me now. Your goodness and your bravery are the reasons you will come with me to free Tessa and Isaac.'

I didn't say anything. I didn't need to. Archie knew. I'd decided ages ago, the moment Archie told me he knew where Tessa was. I was going. I had to. I had to save them. I couldn't help feeling slightly excited. I was going to go and save Tessa. Specks of dust didn't go around saving people, did they?

Archie nodded. 'See, I knew you'd come around. Now, will you get yourself organised so we can go?'

'Okay,' I said. 'I just need to get a couple of things and put the campfire out and –'

'Yes, yes, get on with it,' said Archie.

I picked up my cuff from the ground and threw a bucket of water over the fire. Then I walked quietly past Delphi to grab my bag, which lay on the other side of the clearing.

'Don't wake her,' Archie said quietly. 'I want it to be just you and me. I trust you.' I looked up at him. Into his eyes. Something lurched inside me.

I trusted him too.

'So what do I call you?' I asked as I walked back towards him. 'I mean, I'm a Thyla. You're a –'

'A Vulpi.'

I froze. The breath left my lungs. *Vulpi*. That was the word from my dream. That was the word that the Diemens and Charlotte had chanted.

My dreams were becoming real.

Archie inclined his head to one side. 'What, Cat? What's wrong? You've heard the word before, haven't you? You know of us?'

I shook my head. 'No. Not really. I mean, I heard the word before, but only –'

'Only what?'

'Only while I was sleeping.' Archie narrowed his eyes and made a little 'hmm' noise. 'What?' I asked. 'What does *hmm* mean?'

'Have you seen anything else in these dreams of yours?'

I thought back. I'd dreamed of Charlotte cradling Jenna's body. And I'd dreamed of Tessa being taken . . . I'd dreamed of Archie, too. *'Come with me. Trust me. I'll help you find your friends'* . . . I couldn't remember much more. The dreams weren't clear in my head. But parts of them did seem to have trickled into the real world.

'They're hazy,' I said. 'They're like bits and pieces of what's real and what's not. Some things in them were things I couldn't have known. But a lot of it's just junk. Stupid stuff.'

'They will get clearer,' Archie said. 'As you develop your powers.'

'What powers? What are you on about?' I was standing close to him again now, my nostrils filling again with his musky smell.

Archie gave a half-smile. 'Your leader should know all this.'

'Maybe he does but he didn't tell me.'

'Okay, I'll explain quickly while you finish up.' I made a show of packing and tidying but, really, I was giving Archie my full attention. I wanted to hear this. Archie spoke quickly. 'Premonitory dreams are dreams that, in some way, predict future events. Only truly powerful shapeshifters have them. These shapeshifters are known as "premonitors". They are a rare species, and an ancient one. William Inglis himself was a premonitor. It was, in fact, Elizabeth who coined the term "premonitor" in the first place. You are a premonitor. Like William Inglis.'

'William? Elizabeth? I don't know these people!' I threw my hands up in the air.

Archie's face froze. He stopped and turned to me. 'Nobody passed on the stories? You don't have a Book? About our origins?'

I shook my head. '*Our* origins? No, Archie. I don't know any of this. *None* of us know where we came from. Not originally. We just know that we *are*.'

Archie nodded thoughtfully. 'I never imagined,' he murmured. Then he looked up at me, his eyes narrowed. 'And that's enough for you? Just to know that you *are*?'

'Well, it *was*,' I said as we ran off into the forest.

CHapteR
twenty

'is it much further?'

I didn't know exactly where we were going, except that we were moving roughly south-west. We weren't going to Taranna. We were going somewhere else. And we were going quickly. I think Archie was surprised at how quickly I could run. He was having to race to catch up. My paws throbbed. My legs ached. My head felt like there was one of Delphi's bands squeezed inside it, playing their clanging, bashing, growling music at full volume and banging their V-shaped guitars up and down the insides of my skull.

Back at the clearing Delphi was probably still plugged in to her metallic dreams. I hoped she'd wake up to the news that I'd found Tessa.

If Mum was here she'd have told me I was completely mad.

I was running off alone, away from my territory, with someone I barely knew. Who may or may not be telling the truth.

I had so many questions for Archibald Matthews. What had he been talking about before, about 'our origins'?

How much did he know about where we came from?

And why had he come to Tasmania? Why did he work for the Diemens and then run away?

That last question was important. Maybe the most important, at least for the time being. Because it would tell me if I really *could* trust him.

Despite what he'd done for Rhiannah . . . despite his *eyes* . . . I needed to know this answer before I could trust him completely.

So I asked it. 'Why did *you* come to Tasmania? Why did you sign up to serve the Diemens? If you're not – not a bad Vulpi.'

'I'm not a bad Vulpi,' Archie said firmly as he ducked below a tree branch. 'I never served the Blackbloods – that's what we call the Diemens back home. But I was never against them, either. I was always . . . well, something of a free spirit. Always after a new adventure. Back home, Vulpis either work for the Blackbloods or they work with the monarch against them. Very few of us work for neither side. We who do call ourselves "free-walkers". We are pacifists. We don't believe in war.'

'You're not answering me. Why did you come, if you're one of these "free-walkers"?'

'For the "experience",' Archie said, a slight sarcastic tone in his voice. 'I heard about the Blackbloods' recruitment drives one night at the pub, and I thought, well, I always wanted to travel . . .' Archie sped up and leapt over a ditch in the forest floor. I followed, landing much less gracefully than he did. Archie took a moment to catch his breath.

I prodded him in the ribs. 'Come on. We need to keep moving.'

'My, you are a hard taskmaster,' he growled.

'Keep telling the story,' I said as I sped off again. 'It makes the trip go faster.'

'All right, well, I'd heard Australia was a cracking place,' he went on. 'So, I enrolled, and they accepted me. I had no intention of actually working for the bastards. I just tagged along. I thought that, once I was here, I'd just escape and go human for a while – enjoy the sights. But they sent me straight to Lord's hideout and, once I saw the things that were going on there, I couldn't just run away. I'd spent my life avoiding conflict, thinking I was doing the best thing possible by not fighting for either side. But that was until I saw just how evil one of the sides really was. I knew I could be a layabout no longer. I had to do something. Sadly, none of my kin saw things the same way. Even if they did have a moral bone in their bodies to begin with, by the second day we were here, they were all too dosed up on Tyrandioxide to think for themselves.'

'What's Tyrandioxide?' I asked. 'Is it a drug? Something to do with the Solution?'

Archie shook his head. 'It's a drug of sorts but it's not the Solution. And the Diemens *have* just recently developed it, as part of their experiments. But it's a sedative. It stupefies you. It's a mixture of Diemen plasma, sugar and some other ingredients to make it more palatable. It's the Diemen blood that turns the brain to gooseberry fool. I never was much into narcotics so I only pretended to take my dose. The others were not so clever. *Right!*' Archie pulled up suddenly. I kept running. 'Oof!' Archie complained, jerking forwards.

'Sorry!' I cried. 'You just –'

'Stopped awfully suddenly. Yes, I know.'

'Why?' I asked, rubbing the elbow that had collided with Archie's ribs.

'Well, that would be because we are right on the very edge of this wonderful, shapeshifter-concealing forest. If we venture any further we may come into close contact with non-shapeshifting types. As in humans. So, it might be a good idea to de-beast ourselves, as it were. I notice you have a bangle there to aid you. I've seen you fellows using it in the clearing. It's how you control your power, am I right? I myself have a pendant. Shall we humanise?'

I pulled my cuff from my satchel and pushed it on my wrist. I doubled over as nausea bubbled in my belly. As Archie clipped his chain around his neck his eyes squeezed shut and his whole body shuddered. 'Golly gosh fiddlesticks croquet mallet spotted dick guinea fowl shagging rotten stinking pile of badger dung,' he growled.

'Stings a bit, hey?' I said, trying not to laugh. Laughing would've hurt too much.

Archie held out a wide, tanned hand. 'Pleased to meet you in people form, Miss Catherine. It's a much more dashing look for me, wouldn't you agree?' I straightened up and took his hand, my eyes tracing his body from his strong, muscular legs encased in tight stretchy black pants, to his broad, tanned shoulders before finally settling on at his face.

And it was then that I felt the world beneath me fall away.

I did agree with Archie. In 'people form', he was *completely* dashing. Breathtakingly dashing. He might have said he was old (and, being an immortal, he could have been a *thousand* years old for all I knew), but he didn't *look* much older than me. He had flame-red hair and smooth, lightly tanned skin that darkened on his sides and back to burnt orange, and a smile as wide as the Derwent River. And those eyes. They were a strange greenish yellow and glimmering. He was amazing. He was *dangerously* amazing. Looking at Archie in his human form felt . . . *perilous*. I wondered if this was how Tessa felt when she was with Perrin.

Archie raked his hands through his beautifully ruffled hair. The muscles in his arms bulged.

I giggled, feeling my cheeks glow with a not-unpleasant blush. 'Okay,' I said. 'Lead the way, boss.'

'Oh, I do *so* like how that word sounds,' said Archie. 'But a simple "milord" will do in future. Speaking of the future: in the *very short-term* future we will be emerging into a world of humans, where I am quite certain anti-nudity laws are still enforced. To be fair, you are only half-nude. However, you might feel inclined to pop a blouse on, don't you agree? And whatever . . . *women's undergarments* you may require.'

My face felt like it was on fire. I reached into my satchel and quickly pulled my crop top and t-shirt over my head.

Archie smiled as he pulled a thin shirt from his back pocket and did the same. 'Don't be embarrassed, Cat,' he said. 'Please, not on my account. I have been around a long time. I have seen everything. Some *things* are more pleasant to see than others, of course.'

I wondered if Archie thought my *things* were pleasant. Then I gave myself a mental slap for letting myself wonder. And for thinking all those other things about how charming and gorgeous he was. We were on a *mission*. There was no time for thoughts like that. Besides, Archie was a *Vulpi*. Developing a crush on him would be like – like having a crush on a Sarco.

'Are you all right, Cat?' Archie said. 'I can feel you're afraid.'

I nodded. 'I am, a bit,' I said.

He reached out and took my hand again. It felt like electricity was pulsing through it. 'You're afraid of what we are about to do,' he said, nodding. I nodded back, even though it wasn't entirely true. I was a bit apprehensive about what would happen next – whether we'd have to fight Diemens or even Vulpis, whether we'd find Isaac and Tessa alive – but what I was really afraid of was how my heart raced when I looked at his face and how my body shivered when he touched me. 'Cat, I believe you can do this,' Archie said. 'Take a leap. I think you'll find you'll fly.'

Archie squeezed my hand. 'Of course, I could be completely wrong. You might fail spectacularly. But that's all part of the adventure, isn't it?' And with that thought to comfort me, Archie dragged me out of the shadows, and into the light.

CHapter

twenty-one

THE WATER WAS MOTTLED TURQUOISE AND TEAL. THE sky was cloudless and the sun was like a warm blanket around our shoulders. The only sounds were the water splashing against the rocks, seagulls fighting over chips, and children squealing as they waded past their knees into the water.

It was a happy place. A place where kids dug in the sand and young lovers splashed each other in the waves. It was impossible to believe that anything evil could ever happen here.

'Are you *sure* this is the place?' I asked as we trudged across the beach. 'I mean, it's just a holiday town. People come here to boogie board and swim and eat Paddle Pops and stuff. Build sandcastles. Not –'

'Take virgin women back to their lair to murder and bathe in their blood?' Archie said, finishing the sentence I hadn't been quite sure how to complete.

'Well . . .' I murmured, shrugging.

'Tell me, Cat, are you a reader?'

'A what?'

'A *reader*. You know, one who has one's thylacine nose in one's book.'

'You mean do I read lots? Yeah, I did. Not so much now, only when Isaac or Tessa remember to bring me something. I miss it. I used to read all the time. Hardy and the Brontës and –'

'Cat, I'm not asking for a list of your favourite authors,' Archie interrupted. 'I'm sure we can have a long conversation about it and many other things when all of this is over. If we are not deceased, that is. But, for the time being, what I am attempting to ascertain is whether you are familiar with the convention in many novels that *nothing is ever as it seems*.'

'Of course,' I said, thinking of Mr Darcy's rudeness and Mrs Rochester in the attic. Books would be boring if it wasn't for those twists and turns.

'Good,' Archie said, nodding. 'Well, sometimes, life is like that too, Cat. Which is a good thing, really, because wouldn't both reading *and* living be a dreadful bore if everything was exactly as we expected it to be?'

'It might be easier. And less likely to result in *becoming deceased*,' I replied.

'Well. Rather.'

'And besides, we already know where the Diemen hideout is,' I pointed out. 'Taranna.'

Archie waved his hand in my face. 'No, no,' he said. 'The Diemens have several hideouts. They conduct their "public" meetings in the city, or at Lord Mansion. Taranna is where the Diemen brigantine is moored. It's their transportation. And before you ask: no, it is no longer sail-powered and yes, it is fast. This place, Kingston Beach – or, rather, just down that little street over there, towards Bonnet Hill – is where they bring the girls. It is where the Diemens take their tea and plasma.'

'They don't *actually* –' The thought of Diemens stirring blood into their Earl Grey made me feel like I might faint. Or vomit. Or both.

Thankfully, Archie just laughed and shook his head. 'No, Cat, they don't. They're really quite *civilised*, aren't they? Apart from the heart-eating and such.'

'Oh, yeah, apart from *that*.' A thought struck me. 'But Archie, do they *always* take the girls back here to – to eat their hearts? Because Charlotte's friends were killed in the nightclub while she was upstairs.'

'Charlotte Lord? Edward Lord's daughter?'

I nodded.

Archie looked thoughtful. 'The Diemens do prefer to bring the girls here to dispose of them and drain their blood. But often they kill them and eat the hearts first. If they're hungry. It sounds to me as if they were interrupted. Maybe they were warned Charlotte was there and they only had time to eat the hearts and take the other girls that Lord had requested for their experiments.'

Who would have warned them, though?' I said. Just then an eagle screeched in the air above me. In its claws it held a small marsupial.

Like a Diemen with its prey.

I looked around me. A moment ago this place had seemed so innocent. 'Hatch – he's my clan-mate – he searched for the Diemen hideout down here,' I said as we walked along the road. 'He combed the place.'

'Then he missed it,' said Archie bluntly. '*Trust me.* There are Diemens in that there house.'

'Which house?' I asked. All of the houses we were passing were just little holiday shacks. I couldn't see anything resembling a Diemen lair.

'That house,' said Archie, pointing. 'Just there.'

The house he was pointing at was *tiny*. It was a shack, standing in the middle of a scrubby block with a weedy garden of sun-browned grass and gravelly dirt. The house was painted eggshell blue but most of the paint was flaking off. There was a kid's tricycle lying on its side on the front step and a wad of bills poking out of the hole in the rusty letterbox. 'You *still* don't believe me, do you, Cat?' said Archie.

'Obviously,' I exclaimed. 'It's tiny! How could a whole bunch of Diemens fit in there?'

'Right then. Duck down.'

'Duck down?'

'Behind that hedge. Now.' I rolled my eyes and did what I was told. 'Are you ready?'

'I don't know what I'm ready for but I guess I'm ready for it.'

'That's the spirit!' Archie picked up my hand and kissed it. And then he grabbed a peach-sized rock from the ground and lobbed it at the shack.

He kissed me. I mean it *was* only on the hand but he *kissed* me. I could feel the spot where his lips had touched me, tingling like sunburn before it starts to hurt.

He kissed me and then he *threw a flipping enormous rock at the blue shack he just told me was the Diemen hideout.* 'Why the hell did you –?' I began but before I could finish, the door of the shack burst open and three guys the size of wrestlers strode out onto the deck. Their hands were on the bronze chains around their tree-trunk-thick necks, ready to pull the pendants off. 'Crap,' I said, my hand tightening around Archie's. 'They're Vulpis, aren't they?'

'The King's finest. Well, the *Lord's* anyway.'

'They're big.'

'Yes. Yes, they are. Largeness is the number one selection criterion for potential Diemen Muscle. And those brutes have it in spades. Pity they don't have the mental muscle to accompany it. That's Charles, Horace and Englebert.'

'Wait, did you say the last ones are called *Horace* and *Englebert*?' I could feel a really badly timed laugh tickling on the back of my throat.

'Yes. What is funny about that?' asked Archie, his face so deadpan I couldn't tell if he was being serious or not.

Charles, Horace and *Englebert* stood on the deck for a few moments more, looking around. 'Perhaps a possum?' I heard one of them say. His voice was much higher than I expected it to be. It sounded wrong coming out of his mouth. He should have sounded like one of the thugs from a Guy Ritchie movie.

'Sneaky little bastards,' one of the others said. His voice was lower and gruffer.

'Don't you observe that Tasmanian vermin are so much more *verminous* than our vermin at home?' I heard the last one say as the three of them wandered back inside.

'Next time we hear them, let's try to catch them,' the gruff one said. 'I'm bleeding hungry. I could do with a meal of possum.'

'I could do with a meal of donkey,' the one with the Beckham voice sighed. 'Come on in, boys. There are no Thylas around here.'

'Can't we go out for a kebab?' I heard another say as the door clicked shut.

I turned to Archie, eyes wide. He shrugged. 'Believe me now?'

CHAPTER

twenty-two

THEY WERE UNDERGROUND. THEY WEREN'T ALL SQUASHED up in the cottage like evil sardines. Underneath that teeny tiny cottage was a mansion full of Vulpis and Diemens.

And Tessa.

Archie and I were crouched behind the bush, waiting for the Diemens to leave. 'How do you know they'll go?' I asked.

'They always travel back towards the city at this time of day,' Archie said. 'I believe they meet with their informant there. They make the Vulpis stand guard while they speak with him.'

'The informant who warned them about Charlotte Lord being at the nightclub?' I asked, remembering my earlier question.

'I am assuming so,' Archie said.

'It's strange,' I said. 'The Diemens *used* to meet with Isaac. But I thought they'd given up on working with humans.'

'Perhaps it's not a human,' Archie said. 'But then, Isaac never was either. Perhaps the difference is this time the Diemens *know* the person they are working with is not human.'

A shiver ran up my spine. The sun was starting to dim and the air was cooling but it wasn't the chill making me shiver. A shapeshifter informant? Could it really be true?

It wasn't just the idea of the Diemens' shapeshifter ally making me feel anxious. It was starting to really sink in that I was here. At the Diemen lair. With a creature I barely knew who might be very handsome but could also possibly be leading me into a very nasty trap.

I know I'd trusted him before but now I was here . . .

'You're starting to mistrust me,' Archie said. 'I can feel it.'

'Why did you only bring *me* here?' I asked. 'Why not Delphi? Why didn't we go and find Luda or Hatch? Why only me?'

'Because I *trust you*,' Archie said simply. 'I knew you wouldn't fight me as soon as look at me. I knew you'd hear me out.'

'Making a lot of assumptions, aren't you, mister?' I said, feeling my tension melt slightly.

'I know what I'm doing,' Archie said, simply. 'I've been around a long time.'

'I still don't understand why you'd come over here if you knew that the Diemens were evil. If you knew they stole hearts and bathed in –'

'I know it might be difficult for you to believe,' Archie said seriously, 'but to me the Blackbloods always seemed something like a fairy tale. Because I never encountered them in England, I only thought of them as storybook creatures . . . like we do with *pirates,* I suppose. We think they're fun-loving fellows who love parrots and singing jaunty songs and saying "yo-ho-ho". We never imagine them as alcoholic, money-hungry rapists and murderers, do we? And so it was with me and the Blackbloods. I never imagined their true horror. As soon as I saw it I knew I had to fight against it.'

'So you were never . . . friendly . . . with the Diemens? They never took you into their chambers and offered you cups of virgin-blood tea?'

Archie gagged. 'Must you put that image in my mind?' He shook his head. 'No, Cat. The Diemens barely speak to us at all, except to give us our orders. Or to say "Cheerio" before they *dispose* of us. We're just slaves. The Diemens like having slaves.'

We sat together for a while, not saying anything, just watching the door. The Diemens didn't come out. I started to get itchy feet. 'Maybe we should just break in?' I said.

'Right. You really think we could fight heaven-only-knows how many Diemens and Vulpis all by ourselves, on their turf?' Archie shook his head. 'No, we wait.'

'Fine then. If we have to wait I need you to tell me more stories. Tell me about what you meant before. About us all coming from the same origins. How do you know that?'

'My, my, aren't we getting demanding?' Archie said, looking at me cheekily. 'All right then. Well, as to how I know all this, unlike your lot, we Vulpis have a very refined, skulk-based education system, covering all facets of shapeshifter existence.' He must have noticed the confused look on my face because he clarified. 'Skulks are what we Vulpis call clans or tribes. Every skulk has a leader. He teaches us all we need to know to be a Vulpi. We learn where we came from. Where we *all* came from. We are none of us alone, Cat. We all come from a common beginning. And it is not just Thylas and Vulpis and Sarcos. We have cousins in the Americas and India and New Zealand. There are bird people in New Zealand, did you know? Not ducks, before you ask.' He raised an eyebrow and I poked my tongue out at him before I could stop myself. Archie just laughed and went on. 'Very mature,' he said, smiling. 'The *Moai* they're called. I have heard they are marvellous creatures. Like strange, tattoo-faced angels. They are descended from the moa, which was a huge flightless bird. But the Moai have evolved. They can fly.' I tried to imagine what it'd be like to be a flying shapeshifter. It sounded awesome.

'Are there many of us?' I asked. 'Around the world? There aren't many Thylas left. Isaac's really picky about who he turns.'

'He might need to get over that,' Archie said. 'But to answer your question, I'm not really certain. We shapeshifters don't converse much across species and continents.'

'I wonder if the other shapeshifters know about where they came from?' I said.

'About Queen Elizabeth?'

'Hang on. *Queen* Elizabeth? Like Prince William's granny?' I asked.

'Oh, I'm sure the Queen would love to know she is known as "William's granny",' Archie said, laughing. 'But I'm not talking about the current queen, Cat. Not Elizabeth the Second, though the Vulpis still serve her. Much to the chagrin of her precious corgis. No, we are Elizabeth the Second's foxes *now*. We have been Henry's and Edward's foxes. When your country was developing, we were Victoria's foxes. Our creator, though, was Elizabeth the *First*. You really don't know anything, do you? I promise I will tell you everything. In fact, when this is over, I have something I will *show* you. Not now, though. Look – it's time for us to make our move.' Archie pointed over at the little blue cottage where, sure enough, the door had just opened and a line of men all dressed in black was filing outside.

It was easy to tell the Vulpis from the Diemens. The Vulpis were bigger and tougher. They walked out first, glancing around and sniffing the air to check for potential enemies or threats to their employers' safety. There were maybe ten of them in all and the smallest would have been over six foot. 'Is that all of them?' I whispered.

'I think so.'

'You *think* so? There could still be more in there?'

Archie looked at me grimly. 'There were many more of us when we came out here, but a few have already perished. Those Diemens don't take kindly to being disobeyed.'

'The Diemens killed them? Is that what you meant before, about saying "Cheerio" and then –'

'Well, sometimes they say "Cheerio". Other times, "Farewell, dear servant". As I said, they're such civilised fellows.' Archie shook his head. 'I might not agree with the career choices of some of my kin,' he said. 'It doesn't stop me feeling . . . disquieted when they are murdered by those horrid men.'

My eyes flicked over to the Diemens. They were smaller, thinner and paler. They wore huge dark glasses. They oozed evil out into the atmosphere; I felt it waft over towards me. It smelled like sulphur and metal. 'Is that all of *them*?' I asked Archie.

'Probably. They come and go, so I am not certain how many there are, exactly,' Archie said.

'I can't see Lord there.'

'Lord is rarely there. Lord is only there for major meetings, strategy summits, and to take his *baths*. He has a family and a business to run as well as being the embodiment of evil.'

'So you don't think he might be *under* there? You can't use your telepathy thing to find out?'

Archie shook his head. 'The Diemens might as well be holding me in their arms – beastly thought – and I wouldn't feel a thing. Because *they* don't feel a thing. That's what makes it so easy for them to do what they do.'

'That makes me feel better,' I mumbled.

Archie grabbed my arm. 'Whether there *are* more Diemens in there or not, we have to go now. If we *don't* go now, we may not get another opportunity. For all we know, your friends are dead already, but the sooner we go, the greater the chance that they won't be and that we can save them.'

So many thoughts galloped through me. I was terrified, exhilarated, lost and found and small and big. I wanted my mother. I wanted to be curled in her arms, being read stories with happy endings. I wanted to be kissed again by Archie, properly this time. I wanted to run into that house and fight whatever was there. I wanted to run away.

But more than anything I wanted to save Tessa.

Tessa's gone, Tessa's gone, Tessa's gone. The voice echoed in my head.

And I will find her.

CHαpteR
twenty-tHRee

ARCHIE WAS FEARLESS. HE WALKED UP TO THE FRONT door of the Diemen hidcout like it was an ordinary house and he was just popping over for a cuppa. He didn't creep or dart. He strode right across the road and along the concrete path, climbed the three front steps and strutted right up to the door. I followed his lead. I even tried to strut but I don't think I did a very good job of it. It's hard to strut when your knees are wobbling like jelly.

I wasn't scared before. Now I was.

When we got to the door Archie paused. I looked at him sideways. I tried to say something with my eyes, along the lines of *'Do you have a plan for how we'll get inside? Because otherwise we are a little bit screwed'*.

'Don't worry,' he whispered. 'We Vulpis are like Boy Scouts. We always come prepared.' He reached into the leather satchel and pulled out a small silver key. 'Tada!' he whispered.

'They gave you a *key*?' I gasped.

'Of course not,' he replied, looking at me like *I* was the mad one. Then he turned away from me and concentrated on pushing the key quietly into the lock.

Inside it was pitch dark. The only light came from the muted beam of sun that crept in with us when we opened the door. As soon as we shut it the light ran away, like it was scared to be there too. I pulled my cuff to the tips of my fingers. Slowly, my night vision started to work and the room brightened. And what I found in front of me was . . . unexpected.

In the front room of the Diemen hideout there were no antique claw-foot baths filled with human blood or scary weapons hanging from the walls. There were no torture chairs or scold's bridles or racks or iron maidens or whips or any of the other horrible devices I'd imagined I'd find in a Diemen lair. There were no gruesome paintings of death and destruction on the walls. There were no goblets lying around with dark red dregs congealing in their bottoms. In fact, the room wasn't one little bit like I'd imagined it would be.

'It looks unremarkable, doesn't it?' Archie asked. 'Just a commonplace little shack.'

'Apart from the posh furniture,' I agreed, pointing at the rosewood table and the gold Art Deco lamps. 'And –' I gestured around at the windowless walls.

'And the wax food,' added Archie, pointing towards the kitchenette. I followed his eyes. On the kitchen bench was a bowl of fresh fruit and a stick of crusty bread. My stomach growled.

'It's really fake?' I asked, trying to hide the disappointment in my voice.

Archie nodded. 'The Diemens don't require food. Well, not food as *we* know it.'

Oh yeah. Suddenly I didn't feel hungry any more.

Archie pointed again. 'None of those books have ever been opened, and see, there's no television, or CD player, or even a telephone. And come and look at this.' Archie walked over to a rug in the middle of the unvarnished wood floor. It looked like the one on the floor of Charlotte's shed. I knew *now* that the creatures on it – the ones being speared – must be Vulpis.

I looked up at Archie, wondering if he had the same nasty feeling I had: that the picture on the rug was not just a made-up scene but one from history. His face gave nothing away.

'Remember, nothing is as it seems,' he whispered. Then he bent down and tugged at the corner of the Vulpi mat. It jerked back towards him, revealing a huge trapdoor with a round brass handle in the middle. Archie indicated with his head. 'Are you ready to visit the *real* Diemen hideout?' he asked.

'Is Tessa down there?' I asked.

Archie nodded. 'And your leader too. They will be especially excited to have caught him. He'll be a lovely prize to present to Lord and his senior henchmen.'

'That's not going to happen,' I said firmly. 'I'm ready.'

Archie pulled the trapdoor open, grunting.

'Alley-oop!' he said, giving me a little push in the direction of the dark void beneath.

'What have the Diemens got against light globes?' I whispered as we climbed gingerly down into the blackness. My Thyla eyes saw Archie hold a finger to his lips. My heart stopped. What had he seen? I couldn't see anything in front of me but more steps going down, down, down as if they were leading all the way to hell.

Archie leaned in close. 'There's someone down there,' he whispered. 'I can feel them.'

'So not a Diemen?' I asked. 'You couldn't feel them if it was a Diemen, right?'

He shook his head. 'Not a Diemen, but not a *victim* either. They don't feel scared or sad or hurt. They feel like they have just done something quite rotten. They feel like they have just hurt somebody else. And they don't feel shame for it.'

'Oh. Great. So they're not a Diemen but we should still be afraid of them?'

'Precisely. Well. Onwards and downwards.'

And so we kept on. I counted the steps as we went: twenty, then thirty, then forty. Then finally, at the forty-fifth step, I saw the bottom. I saw ground. And I saw . . .

Bile rose in my throat. My heart was screaming. 'Oh, crap,' I whispered.

I felt Archie's grip on my hand tighten. 'I know,' he said. I turned to him, my mouth open in complete shock. The sound that escaped my throat was the squeak of a frightened baby possum. 'Come on, big tough Thyla,' he said gently. 'You know you can do this. You've come this far.' I nodded mutely. Archie squeezed my hand and led me gently down the last few steps, where torches lit up the most terrifying room I had ever seen.

The room was like an abattoir or a butcher's shop except, on the row after row of metal spikes that lined the huge dark-walled space around us, there were no pig carcasses or skinned sheep. There were *girls*. Girls who were obviously only recently dead. Girls who still looked *alive* except for the big gashes across their necks and stomachs, which drizzled wine-red blood into metal collecting chambers. They were *crucified* and they were being bled dry. 'Why don't they hide them?' I whispered, feeling tears prickle at my eyes and acid burn in my throat again. 'Why are they here? It's horrible.'

'I know,' said Archie. 'It was horrible for me having to move the bodies out to the bush for you to find. Any sane person would find all this horrible. Trust me, even many of my more brutish, meat-headed kin were reduced to snivelling infants the first time we were led down here. I, in fact, discreetly vomited. But Cat, the Diemens are evil. They do not feel things as we do. The *Diemens* think this is beautiful. To them this is some sort of horrid art. This is like their gallery. Their *grand foyer*. It tickles their fiendish fancies.'

'They aren't . . . experimenting on these ones?' I said. 'They aren't using the Solution on them?'

Archie shook his head. 'No. These are just food. The Diemens still need to eat. They keep the experiments in a separate laboratory. That's where they took Rhiannah. I'm not certain where it is located. I was only able to rescue her when they transported her on the brigantine. The girls the Diemens take to the laboratory are, from what I can gather, much more . . . how do I say this without sounding like a dreadful misogynist? They are quite *attractive*, visually. The Diemens seem to have a certain *type* they're after for their experiments. These girls don't match that type, so they are simply . . . consumed.'

I forced myself to look again, and more closely this time, at the girls on the walls. Archie was right. They just looked ordinary. Not ugly but not freakishly supermodel beautiful either. I looked around from face to face, feeling a small relief creep into me as I did. None of them had Tessa's muscular legs or her sandy-coloured bob. Tessa wasn't there. So maybe there was hope. I took a step further into the room. Archie's hand shot out, holding me back. 'What?' I hissed. 'Do you feel something?'

He nodded. 'Fear.'

'Mine?'

'No. I know what you feel like. This is *different*. This is fear of *us*.'

'They know we're here?' I gasped, feeling my breath catch.

'Yes,' said Archie, tensely. 'They know we're here.'

cHapter
twenty-four

'HOW ARE YOU at KICKING DOWN DOORS?' ARcHie whispered.

'Who do you think I am?' I hissed. 'Chuck Norris?'

Archie grinned. 'I may not be Chuck Norris either. But I *am* Archie Matthews. And if I do say so myself I could give Mr Norris a run for his money in the "ultimate tough fellow" stakes!' Archie paused for a moment. 'Or at least that's what I like to tell myself before I attempt something reckless and highly dangerous. Fake it till you make it!' Archie took a couple of steps back. And then he launched himself feet-first at the massive door.

It wasn't the most polished of entrances. Or the most intimidating. Archie fell first and I stumbled after him. I tripped over his foot. We ended up in a clumsy pile on the floor, Thyla and Vulpi limbs spilling here, there and everywhere. Somehow he ended up on top of me.

For a moment I didn't know where I ended and he began.

The moment was over when I looked up to see a long serrated knife dangling above my head. A drop of blood fell from it and landed with a splat on my nose. It was warm. It smelled like sulphur and steel. I wiped it away quickly and when I looked down at my hand I saw that the blood was black. Diemen blood. I looked up at the person holding the knife. 'Hello, Cat,' she said.

'Tessa!' I whispered, tears stinging my eyes. She was alive. Tessa was *alive*.

She *was* also pointing a knife at me, though. I gulped. 'Tessa, you can put that down now. It's only me!'

'Oh, the knife is not for you.' Tessa's amber eyes flashed furiously. 'It's for your little friend there.'

'This is Archie,' I said. I looked up at his face and saw he was looking at me too. His Adam's Apple bobbed up and down as he swallowed.

'Am I interrupting something?' Tessa snapped.

Archie pulled a face at me and sprang to his feet, holding out a clawed hand. 'Archibald Matthews. Ever so pleased to meet you. Well, formally, at any rate.'

Tessa ignored him. 'He is a *Vulpi*,' she said through gritted teeth.

Archie pulled his hand away from Tessa and held it out to me. He hoisted me up. Tessa moved slowly forward, pointing the knife at him. As she did so she walked into a thin shaft of light being given off by a flickering torch. It was only then that I noticed how bad she looked. She looked like Rhiannah when we found her on the boat, only Tessa's injuries were new. Her eyes were black and puffy. Her lip was split and still bleeding and she was cradling an arm – the one that wasn't wielding a knife – close to her chest.

'Tessa, are you okay?' I asked, my voice trembling. 'On the boat, what happen–'

'They took us. The Diemens. We came back to the boat and we saw them coming. We fought them. They took us. They took us here, to meet their little friends. Your companion is one of them. He is a Vulpi,' Tessa growled again. 'He is a traitor. They all are. The Vulpis work for the Diemens. He is evil. He is –'

'*He* is the cat's father.' Archie clipped his chain around his neck, changing back into human form with a series of grimaces and curses about mushy peas and squirrels. 'And *he* just helped to save your life.'

'Oh, I think you'll find we did that all by ourselves,' Tessa said, pressing the knife against his throat.

'Tessa, don't,' I cried. 'We can trust him. Believe me.'

Tessa looked at me through narrowed eyes. 'You trust him?'

'*Yes,*' I insisted.

Tessa nodded curtly and lowered the knife. 'The other Diemens are still upstairs,' she said tensely.

'We just saw them leave,' I replied.

'Oh, it's "we" now, is it?' Tessa hissed. 'You and the *henchman?* I'm trusting Cat's judgement about you, Vulpi, but you're still –'

'I'll thank you not to talk to me like that,' Archie interrupted calmly. 'I've gone through rather a lot of trouble to rescue you.'

'Nobody asked you to!' Tessa snapped.

'Well, then, perhaps I should not have bothered,' Archie growled.

'Archie!' I cried. 'Tessa's my best friend. Tessa, Archie's a good guy and I –'

'*All* of you are behaving like puppies and kits,' said a voice from the corner. It was gravelly and rough, and more weak and thready than usual but it was still unmistakably Isaac.

I raced over, forgetting every bad thought I'd ever had about him. 'Isaac! Are you all right?' I asked, bending over his hunched body.

'And here was I thinking you didn't care.' Isaac tried to push himself up from the ground. 'Ah, damn,' he groaned as his attempts failed and he crumpled back against the wall.

'What did they do to you?' A lump rose in my throat. I hated seeing him like this.

'Oh, pretty much everything,' he said. 'Apart from, you know, the killing bit. But they might have done worse than killing. If Tessa hadn't pulled a ninja on *that* fellow.' Isaac nodded at the body of an ex-Diemen, sprawled on the floor not far from where we were sitting. His skin was already beginning to sizzle and turn black – the first step in Diemen decomposition. After that it's a pretty rapid downhill slide into black sludge.

'It was not . . .' Tessa looked embarrassed. 'He thought I was unconscious. I pretended. He was careless. He left his knife unattended.' Tessa held up the dagger. 'You were the one who killed the Vulpis. That was more difficult. I am sorry I wasn't more use. If I had been, you might not be injured so *badly*. Isaac, if you had not been here, I would be dead.'

'That's why you pups call me "boss",' Isaac said, forcing a smile.

'I am ashamed,' Tessa whispered.

'Nonsense,' said Isaac gruffly. 'You killed two Vulpis. That one and . . .' He pointed. 'That one. You're just being modest to make me feel better.'

I looked over at the two Vulpis Isaac had pointed at. I squinted my eyes. I couldn't be sure – they were decomposing pretty quickly – but it looked like one of them had its claws embedded in the throat of the other. It looked like they'd somehow killed each other by accident. I turned to Tessa, waiting for her to confirm what had happened.

'You're right, Isaac,' she said. 'I did kill them. We did it together. We are a wonderful team.' I looked back at the Vulpis. They were now almost completely decomposed. I shook my head. I must have imagined what I saw. Tessa said she killed them so she must have. 'I hope they were not your *friends*,' she said to Archie. Her voice was heavy with sarcasm.

'Hardly,' Archie snapped.

'Vulpi,' Isaac called out to him.

'It's Archie, thank you,' he replied, marching over.

'Spiffing name,' said Isaac, mocking his accent.

'Yeah, right, cobber,' Archie shot back in a spot-on impersonation of Isaac's Aussie drawl.

Isaac laughed. It looked like the effort of it nearly did him in. How were we ever going to get him out of here? 'Archie,' he said. 'You'll excuse me for not getting up and shaking your hand, but some of your kin have done some pretty nasty things to me.'

'They're good at that,' Archie sighed.

'How do I know you won't do the same?' Isaac asked bluntly.

'I can feel that you already trust me,' Archie said. As if it was the most reasonable thing in the world.

'You can feel *what*?'

'I'll explain later if that's all right with you,' said Archie. 'We're rather pressed for time down here. The Diemens might come back once they realise the fellows you offed aren't following them. And I'm afraid I can't feel *those* lovely chaps coming.'

'Will somebody explain what he's talking about?' asked Isaac, looking from Tessa to me.

'Don't ask me,' said Tessa.

'Listen, I know I have something of an accent, but I am still speaking English, aren't I?' asked Archie. 'They say you Australians are laid-back, but now is not the time to crack open a stubbie and laze around the *barbie*. We need to go. The Diemens could be back at any moment and –' None of us needed Archie's powers to hear the bang of a door closing upstairs. 'Luckily they're noisy little terrors,' Archie said. His voice sounded light-hearted. His agitated expression showed he was anything but.

'How do we escape?' Tessa looked at Archie, her eyes wide and fearful. 'I don't know if I can deal with seeing those horrible creatures again just now. Especially not if Lord is with them. He is the worst. He is –'

'The nastiest of all nasty pasties. I know, Tessa. Luckily, I got the grand tour of Diemen Central before I scarpered, so I know that there's a secret passageway right behind where our man Isaac is taking a kip.'

'Thank Mother Earth for that,' said Isaac, his voice becoming weaker by the minute.

'Don't thank her yet,' said Archie. 'I'm afraid I didn't stay quite long enough to get to the part where they told us where the key was.'

'Well, don't worry about that,' said Tessa as she limped over. 'I did learn several useful skills from the Flash Mob ladies at the Female Factory. Lock-picking was probably the most socially acceptable of them. Cat, can you help Isaac to his feet?'

'I'm right, I'm right,' he grouched, pulling himself slowly up off the ground. It looked painful. Archie cringed and I realised he could *feel* Isaac's pain. I shuddered as I thought of the agony he must have experienced when he was inside this horrible torture house if he could feel the torment of everyone inside it. Isaac staggered. Archie jumped forward and offered him his shoulder to lean on. Isaac put his arm around Archie's neck and nodded his thanks unsmilingly. That was okay, though. Archie could feel his gratitude. Tessa crouched down in the space Isaac had left. She pulled her cuff to the tips of her fingers and used one claw of her half-transformed hand to fiddle with the lock.

'Well, that's novel,' Archie said admiringly.

'At the Female Factory I had to make do with hairpins,' said Tessa as she wiggled her finger in the lock. 'This is much better.'

'Are you nearly there?' I asked anxiously. It couldn't be long before the Diemens and Vulpis came downstairs to find out what had happened to their brothers.

Echoing my thoughts, Archie said, 'Terribly sorry to rush you, Tessa, but I *can* actually feel the Vulpis. They are not very far away.'

'It's okay, I have almost –' And it was then that I heard the door at the top of the stairs click open. 'Got it,' Tessa finished, pulling the trap door open with her good arm.

'Jolly good. Off we trot,' said Archie briskly, as footsteps began clomping down the stairs.

I burst out laughing. Now I had Tessa back I could laugh again. Archie looked at me, amused. Tessa shook her head. Isaac glowered. 'I'll go first,' I said quickly, climbing into the hole. Tessa followed me and Isaac and Archie brought up the rear. Archie closed the trapdoor quickly and quietly with the hand that wasn't being used to support Isaac.

And we ran.

CHAPTER
twenty-five

I DON'T KNOW IF THEY FOLLOWED US. WE DIDN'T LOOK back. We just ran and ran and ran through the tunnel. Even Isaac, with all of his injuries, packed the pain away inside him and sprinted for his life. When we reached the end of the tunnel we climbed up another ladder and pushed our way out into the light.

We were in some sort of cave by the beach. I could see the sand and sky at the cave mouth and hear seagulls and the lapping of the sea.

'Can you hold him?' asked Archie, jerking his head at Isaac, who was puffing and wheezing and grimacing with the exertion of his race down the tunnel.

'I'm fine,' he said, pulling his arm away and slumping down against the cave wall with his hand at his chest. 'It's getting better.'

I looked back down at the trapdoor. The Diemens had used some sea grass to conceal it but it would take more than that to stop them pushing their way out. Tessa was thinking the same thing.

'Here, shall we fix this against the entrance?' she said, trying one-handed to push a large rock over the trapdoor. I helped her and together we managed to shove the rock into position.

'Well, that should hold them off for a good minute or so,' said Archie. 'We need to hot-foot it out of here.'

'How are we going to do that?' I asked, looking at Isaac, who was moaning in pain.

'The same way any party of respectable gentlefolk would.' Archie grinned naughtily. 'We shall *sail*.'

'We're going to hire a boat?' I asked.

'Obviously not. Young Tessa here is not the only one who's picked up a criminal skill or two in their very long life.'

And so, minutes later, Tessa, Isaac and I were sitting in a speedboat named *Britney* ('Anyone who calls their boat *Britney* deserves to have it stolen,' Archie declared. 'What say we rename it *Juggernaut*? That's a much finer name!'), as Archie steered us away from Kingston Beach and towards home.

For a moment my heart was light as we sailed. I felt as if everything had been righted. Rhiannah was back.

Tessa and Isaac were back. And I'd played a part in both of those things.

But my relief was only temporary. I knew it wasn't all over. There was still the Solution to think about and, really, nothing would ever be over until Lord was dead. But for now at least, it seemed like things were good.

As we motored through the waves, Tessa leaned over and whispered in my ear, 'Thank you. For saving us. It was very brave. You should be proud.'

'Are *you* proud?' I asked.

'Yes,' Tessa said, inclining her head. 'But that should not be the most important thing.'

'I know,' I said. 'Still, it means a lot to me that you are.'

'Perhaps you should not value my opinion so highly,' Tessa muttered.

'What? What do you mean by that?'

'Perhaps . . .' Tessa looked away from me. 'Perhaps I am not as worthy of your esteem as you imagine me to be. Perhaps I am not the person you think I am.' She sighed. '*I* don't even know who I am,' she whispered.

'That's not true, Tess,' I protested. 'You do know who you are. Even after all you've been through, you know who you are. Even when you lost your memory you still knew. You always knew you were Tessa.'

Tessa raised her eyebrows and breathed out shakily. 'I am *trying* to be,' she said. 'Recently, I have been trying especially hard. And failing, I believe.' Tessa's eyes flicked over to Isaac, who was sprawled on a seat further up the boat, his eyes drifting open and closed. The odd grunt and cough told us he was okay.

'What do you mean?' I asked, looking back at Tessa. 'You're fine now, aren't you? You seem like the old Tessa again.'

'You really think so?' Tessa looked at me with shining eyes, then back down at her injured arm, flexing her wrist to test if it had healed. She lowered her voice. 'I try to appear so,' she said. 'And perhaps I am very good at pretending everything is well. You have no idea how much time I spend telling myself: *You are brave. You do not cry!* It comes from my childhood. Growing up in a prison, it was not the done thing to show weakness. I was always watched. By the guards. By the Flash Mob. I had to pretend, you see? Just as you did. I can be just as weak as anyone else, Cat! And I – I need someone I can show my weakness to. Of course, he tells me to "harden up", but he is only joking. He does not mind when I am sad and . . .'

Tessa trailed off, obviously worried she was letting too much slip. She cleared her throat. 'Cat, can you keep a secret?' I nodded, my heart thudding. Was this it? Was she going to tell me about Perrin? 'Well, I may seem like I am completely better, but many of my memories have *not* returned. I simply pretend they have. And although

I executed myself well in that battle on the mountain, since then I have rather lost faith in myself. On the boat it was my incompetence that led to Isaac and me being taken. He tried to help me. I failed him. I don't know what has happened to me. The thought of fighting makes me anxious and I fear Isaac will trust me less if he knows I am not yet . . . *whole*. Perhaps I do not deserve his trust at all.'

'Why did you lose faith?' I asked.

'I do not honestly know,' Tessa said. 'That first night my instinct took over. I just launched straight in. Since then I have had time to think. And to doubt. And this past day, in that horrible dungeon, it has only made me doubt myself more.'

'What happened back there?' I asked. 'What did the Diemens do to you?'

Tessa shivered. 'They drugged us. We woke in darkness and all around was the smell of roses. There was food on the floor for us. We did not eat it. We sat and we waited. When the Diemens returned, they told us they would make us like *them*. That they would use the Solution to make us just as "glorious" as they were. Isaac told them we would never submit. That was when they . . . tortured us. I do not wish to speak of that. They did such horrible things. And then they left. They said they would be back in an hour and they expected us to have changed our minds, because they would be bringing us to see Lord. When they returned, we pretended to be asleep. You know the rest.'

Tessa looked up at me, her face stricken. She was struggling against tears. 'Cat, I have been through so much in my life. My childhood at the Female Factory was very harsh. I have seen many battles, lost many kin, but *this* struggle is the hardest I have faced. I feel I am losing myself.'

'You need to tell Isaac,' I said gently. 'He'll be able to help you.'

'I know,' Tessa sighed, looking out to the horizon. 'I suppose I am waiting for the right moment. As I said, it is difficult for me to show I am vulnerable. Especially to Isaac.' When Tessa turned back at me, she was smiling stiffly. 'I am so very proud of you, Cat. I am still trying to figure out, well, *everything*, and I am much older than you are. You seem to be finding your answers so much more quickly and gracefully than I am.'

I swallowed. I didn't quite know how to process what she was saying. Tessa wanted to be like *me*?

I fiddled with my cuff as I tried to figure out what to say next. Tessa waited patiently while I found the words. I cleared my throat. 'Tess, just before I became a Thyla I found something out that I *thought* was the answer to everything. But I'm starting to think now . . . there's no big answer to everything. Just lots of little answers and lots of little questions. That discovery – it changed me. And I can't go back. I think I just have to realise the path continues. I guess maybe you need to know that too. You've been through so much. Hundreds of years of *so much*! First growing up in the prison then all those years in the bush . . . then losing your memory and going to Cascade Falls . . . This is just a bumpy bit on the path but the path will get smooth again. It has to. The path has to go on. I think –' And suddenly it struck me. The last part I whispered, to myself as much as Tessa. 'I think that's the one thing Dad didn't realise. The path goes on.'

For a while, Tessa and I said nothing. We just looked out at the ocean, thinking about the unknowable hugeness of it. And us. And everything.

'Do you *really* trust him?' Tessa asked finally, looking up at Archie.

'Yeah, I do.'

'Then I trust him, too,' she said, smiling at me. 'I trust you, so I trust him.'

'You trust me?' I said.

'You are mine,' Tessa said softly. 'My own blood. My own heart. Of course I trust you.'

CHAPTER

twenty-six

aꜰᴛᴇʀ a ᴡʜɪʟᴇ, ᴛᴇssa ᴍᴏᴠᴇᴅ away ᴛᴏ sɪᴛ ᴡɪᴛʜ ɪsaac. He grumbled while she checked his slowly healing injuries and then they just sat together not saying much, lost in their own worlds.

'Cat?' Archie called after a few minutes. 'You look bored back there. Come up here. I have something for you to read.'

I moved unsteadily to where he was standing, steering the boat. 'What is it?' I asked.

'Do you remember I said I had something to show you that would explain more about our origins?' I nodded, excitement bubbling in my belly. 'Well, I didn't have a chance to take much with me when I escaped from the Diemens. I left the hideout on the pretence of popping

down to the shop to buy a takeaway curry for us Vulpis
while the Diemens were out. It would have looked rather
suspicious if I'd left with suitcases, or even a – what do
they call it these days? A *man* bag. My notes on the Vulpi
history form rather a large book, so it would have been
difficult to conceal it. But as I was preparing to leave, I did
manage to tear out a few pages, which I hid on my person.
I'd like very much for you to read them.'

'Yes, please,' I whispered. Archie reached into the
pocket of his trousers and pulled out a wad of paper,
folded into a square.

'It's only my poorly copied notes,' he said, looking at
me almost shyly. 'We each make our own copies, from
what our leaders tell us. This is mine. I'm sure there are
many better versions.'

'I'm sure it's great,' I said. Archie and I locked eyes and
for a second it felt like he was seeing into my soul. I didn't
mind. I wanted him to keep looking. And tell me what he
found there.

'Go,' he said. 'Read it.'

When I got back to my seat I unfolded the paper.
Archie's handwriting was messier than I'd thought it
would be. But then I guessed he would have been younger
when he wrote this. He would probably have been about
the age he *looked* now – around eighteen. All young guys
have crap handwriting, don't they? It didn't matter. His

words were so much more important than the way he wrote them.

They were momentous.

> *The shapeshifters were born of alchemy; the same alchemy that aimed to turn base metals into gold. For Queen Elizabeth, however, alchemy was a fascination that extended far beyond the creation of gold. She had her own personal alchemist. His name was William Inglis – a Scotsman. He was a great man, brave and clever. It was his idea to create the Vulpis.*

I glanced up at Archie and saw he was sneaking a look at me too. He pulled an embarrassed face and looked back at the water.

> *It was a turbulent time in our country's history. Elizabeth knew she would need something very special up her sleeve to fight all those who wished to invade her land. Her other advisors could not give her an answer that satisfied her so she turned to William. He told her of a discovery he had made in his laboratory – a way to manipulate . . .*

Here there was a line crossed out and a little asterisk. I looked down to the other asterisk at the bottom of the page. *'what we now know as DNA, but Inglis thought of it as the human soul.'* It was weird thinking that Archie had grown up in a time when nobody knew what DNA was. That was unthinkable to me. I kept reading.

He had been working on one of his alchemical experiments with his assistant – Alexander – in a barn outside. Just as Inglis arrived at a crucial point in the mixing of his chemicals, a fox burst into the barn. It startled Alexander, who broke a beaker and cut his hand. The chemicals from the beaker seeped into his blood. Before Inglis could stop it, the fox had bounded over, and began to lick Alexander's wounds.

Sadly, Alexander was so frightened by the fox that he tried to run away from it. In doing so, he stumbled and fell, crashing into a wall from which a long, sharp scythe was hanging. The scythe punctured Alexander's belly, wounding him fatally. Before he died, however, Inglis witnessed a curious change in his apprentice. His nose lengthened, his legs bent back, he grew fangs. He was a Vulpi. Inglis took his findings to Elizabeth. He told her what had happened to Alexander and asked for permission to repeat the experiment. He believed that the combination of fox and human souls could create a super-race, one powerful enough to defeat the Spanish armada. He was correct. The Vulpis were the first of the shapeshifters. Over the coming centuries, many more shapeshifters would be born, with different features but with the same blood flowing within them. After the first was turned, the power was passed on through the bite. But that first shapeshifter blood was still always within them. The same wondrous alchemy was always within their souls.

My hands trembled as I turned the page. The next piece of paper looked slightly newer and the handwriting was a tiny bit neater.

Today we learned of the shapeshifters in the colony known as Van Diemen's Land, a tiny island far away on the other side of this Earth. It seems marvellous to me that there are shapeshifters just like me so very far away. It takes many, many months to get to Van Diemen's Land by sea.

Van Diemen's Land is a penal colony. Convicts from our land are sent there for crimes both petty and severe. It thrills me, this idea! A whole island brimming with wonderfully wicked people! So much more interesting than our own island of Toffs and Dolls. We are sending all the interesting people away! Our skulk leader tells us that, like other monarchs before her, right back to Elizabeth, Victoria is dispatching alchemists to each of her colonies to create an army for her in her new domains. She sent three to Australia. Once there, the alchemists are repeating Inglis's initial experiment on the native creatures, creating new species of shapeshifter. 'Send me with them,' I cry! What an adventure that would be. I feel stifled here in this small skulk, always being instructed by our skulk-leaders what I must do and how; being told I am destined for a life in servitude to that deathly dull queen of ours. I don't want that life. I want to be where the convicts are. I want to meet the Thylas!

That was where the messy handwriting ended, with a splodge of ink and a smear of something that looked like Worcestershire sauce.

I felt full of so much new knowledge. The world seemed a bit brighter all of a sudden.

As we swished through the waves on our way to the shore, again I thought about what the young Archie had written. We shapeshifters had been created for greatness. I thought about where we were now, fighting the Diemens; trying to save the young girls. I hoped Elizabeth would have been proud of us. I thought she probably would. But then I thought about what Tessa had said, about other people being proud of you not being what was most important.

'*I'm* proud of us,' I whispered.

I closed my eyes then and I thought about the newer pages, the pages Archie had written about Van Diemens Land. How the idea of our island thrilled him. How he longed to meet the Thylas.

I imagined myself a convict girl like Tessa. I imagined us meeting in a dark alley in Wapping, down near the docks of Hobart. I'd be Catherine and he'd be Archibald and we'd run away together like Bonnie and Clyde.

Of course, wherever we went there'd still be Blackbloods hiding in the shadows.

I opened my eyes again and looked over at Archie. There were no Blackbloods here now. There was just me and him and my friends, safe and well. And so much sky and water and happiness.

CHAPTER
twenty-seven

IT WAS TESSA WHO SAW THEM FIRST. WE HEARD HER scream echoing through the bush and we knew: something at our clearing was horribly, horribly wrong.

We'd docked *Juggernaut* near Salamanca. It was dark now and since it was a Friday night half of Hobart was stuffed into the restaurants and pubs down by the water. But it was also cold so, with the exception of the usual crowd outside Knopwoods, most people were inside.

They didn't see us leave the boat.

They didn't see Archie steal the car ('You're returning that in the morning,' Isaac had said, in policeman mode. 'And if you rub me up the wrong way I'm still giving you a ticket').

They didn't see him driving badly towards the mountain.

When we left the car, as far up the mountain as we could get, Tessa and Archie went ahead while I limped behind, doing my best to support Isaac. He kept protesting that he'd healed enough to walk by himself but it was obvious that if I let go he'd fall down in a heap. He *was* healing but only slowly. Broken bones always take longer to repair than other physical traumas. I prayed to whoever was up there and listening that Hatch or Delphi were at the clearing so there'd at least be someone to make his pain less.

I needed them to be there. What I wanted more than anything was to cook us all a meal, and for Isaac to be well enough to eat it. I'd know he was fully healed if he told me everything that was wrong with it. Me? I didn't care what we ate. The thought of a day-old cold potato made my stomach groan with longing.

'Hungry?' Isaac said, hearing the cacophony that was going on in my belly.

'How about I rustle up a meal when we get back?' I said. Isaac looked at me dubiously. 'What? I actually like cooking. I could do with some better *ingredients* but I don't mind being the Thyla cook. I think I'm quite good at it!' It felt weird, complimenting myself instead of waiting for someone else to do it – but good too.

'Well, wonders will never cease,' Isaac said. He didn't sound as sarcastic as he usually did. In fact he sounded almost *impressed*. 'Let's see if we can get you some provisions. What do you need? Spices? I know! Chocolate! You could make us dessert! I'm quite partial to a good hedgehog slice.'

'Tomorrow night: hedgehog slice. Check!' I said. 'Tonight we might have to make do with boiled potato, though. You could pretend it's a hedgehog slice! I'm guessing we're going to have to head out again soon, aren't we?'

Isaac nodded. 'We can't stop our patrols,' he said, wheezing slightly. 'We can never stop looking for Lord, especially not now.'

It was then that we heard it.

'Tessa!' The word caught in my throat. Tessa was screaming. Tessa was in *danger*.

'Leave me here. Put me down on that log.' Isaac's 'boss voice' was back. 'Go. Find out what's wrong.' I lowered him gently onto the fallen tree and sprinted ahead to the clearing. And what I saw in my home, in my small safe circle, made a shudder pulse through my body like an earthquake. In my home where hours earlier there had been only rocks and sleeping bags and birds hopping through the grass, there were now broken bones and torn skin and crumpled, beaten bodies. At least three Sarcos were there, starting to decompose.

And in the middle of it all was Delphi, covered in glistening blood. 'I did it for you.' Her eyes were wild. 'I thought they took you. I thought the Sarcos kidnapped you.'

I made myself speak. 'What the . . . How on Earth did you manage to kill them all?' My voice cracked. So many bodies. How had this happened?

'They were human,' Delphi said, looking at her feet. 'I was Thyla. I was quicker than they were. I – I surprised them. I just . . . got so angry. I lost control.' Her eyes flicked feverishly towards the edge of the clearing. Mine followed.

Tessa was there, crouched over one of the bodies, rocking backwards and forwards. 'My love, my love, my love,' she murmured.

It was Perrin. Perrin was injured. Badly. Blood was gushing from a huge, gaping wound on his chest. Tessa had taken off her shirt and was pressing it against the gash. I looked at Delphi. 'Stay,' I said. She nodded mutely. I raced over to Tessa, blood pulsing in my ears.

'He's healing,' she whispered. 'But not quickly enough.' Tessa looked up at me, tears spilling down her cheek in silken rivulets. 'Don't judge me,' she said, through gritted teeth.

I shook my head. 'I don't, Tessa. I knew already.'

'You knew?'

'I saw you. At Cascade Falls. I'm sorry. I was just –'

'It does not matter.' Tessa looked down again at Perrin's pallid face. 'It means a lot that you're not angry,' she whispered. 'I know it is very wrong, but I love him. I love him so much it is as if he is a *part* of me. What can I do? Cat, what can I do to fix him?'

I felt a presence at my side. 'I thought they took you.' Delphi was standing behind me. I didn't turn around. I didn't want to look at her. 'I thought –'

'Why would you *do* this?' I hissed. Every muscle in my body was tense. My hands were curled into fists.

'I thought it must've been the Sarcos all along. I woke up and you were gone and they were here and, well, Hatch said he saw a creature on the boat and I thought –'

'You didn't *think*,' I interrupted, whipping around to face her. 'You didn't think at all.'

'I thought I'd lost you. Cat, I love you. I love you,' Delphi whispered. 'I thought they killed you –'

'You didn't *ask* them why they were here?' I cried.

'They said something about Luda and Cascade Falls. I thought they'd killed you and Luda and they were going to Cascade Falls to –'

'What? Kill all the girls too? No, Delphi. That's what the *Diemens* do.'

'You don't *know* that, Cat! The Sarcos are murderers!'

'I *do* know!' I growled. 'We've just been there. To the Diemen lair. We've *seen* the girls hanging from the walls with their throats cut and their thighs ripped apart. It's the Diemens, Delphi. It always was the Diemens. Why won't you believe?'

'Because my father was one of them,' Delphi whispered.

My blood froze. *'What?'*

'Cat, help!' Tessa cried. Perrin's eyes were rolling back in his head.

'How do I help him?' I demanded, looking up at Delphi.

'Ahhh . . . a compress . . . I have . . . I have one.'

'Where? In your pack?' She nodded meekly. 'Give it to me.'

Delphi walked over to her backpack and returned with a damp, sweet-smelling cushion. 'And these. Make him swallow these. Two of them.' She held out a blue bottle full of pills that smelled of herbs. I passed Tessa the compress and I shook the pills into my hand, reaching for a water bottle to help Perrin swallow them.

For an unknowable length of time Tessa and I waited. Tessa rocked him in her arms, her tears spilling down onto his wounds. Then slowly Perrin's face turned from grey to his usual chalky white. His eyes stopped rolling.

Tessa looked underneath the compress. Perrin's wound was closing up. The blood was drying. 'My love?' Tessa whispered, her hands pressing against his cheeks. Perrin made a croaking sound. His eyes opened and then fluttered closed again. 'You are going to be just fine,' Tessa said, kissing him on the forehead. 'I fixed you. You will be all right, my darling.'

I stood up and began to walk away. I needed to get Isaac. He would know what to do next. Why hadn't he come already?

I must have stood too quickly. The clearing began to swim and swirl and swing about in front of my eyes. I was exhausted. I'd spent the whole day running and had nothing to eat. I felt like I was going to faint or vomit. The images of the other Sarco bodies – broken and bent and decomposing already – flashed in front of my eyes. I knew some of their faces. Harriet wasn't there, thankfully, but the others I recognised. I knew them. They'd been there at Beagle's goodbye. They were my new allies. 'Oh, no,' I moaned. I'd been in shock before but now it felt all too real.

Delphi had killed them. The Sarcos. The treaty was in danger. We needed the treaty. We had to work together to fight the Diemens.

And Delphi's *father* . . . *Delphi's father was* . . . My knees gave way.

'It's your fault.'

'No, I didn't do anything!'

'You let it happen!' the Sarco growled.

The dream and the real world were merging again.

Suddenly there was an arm around my waist, holding me upright. 'Come on, Cat.' Archie's voice was soft. 'Let's get you sitting down. It's been a big day.'

Tears splashed down my face to the ground, mingling with the blood. 'How did this happen?' I croaked.

'There are not always reasons for things,' said Archie. 'Life is chaos. If you start looking for reasons behind everything, you'll go mad.'

'Can I have a hug?' I whispered. Archie nodded wordlessly and took me in his arms.

I was dimly aware of Delphi's presence nearby. Watching us. Just feeling her eyes made my body burn. No matter how much Delphi's wildness had troubled me I never would have believed she was capable of this. Just thinking about it made me want to sink further into Archie's arms and stay there forever, my head buried and my eyes turned away from the world. But I couldn't do that. I had to keep going. 'I just want to check Tessa and Perrin are okay.' I lifted my head off Archie's shoulder. 'Stay there,' I growled at Delphi. 'Don't you move.'

'I'm sorry,' she whimpered. 'I love you.'

My heart stopped. I shook my head. 'No, Delphi. If you loved me you would never have done this.' Somewhere in my distant memory those words opened a door. Inside that door I saw my mum, sitting on the floor of our kitchen in Campbell Town. *'If he loved me he wouldn't have done it,'* she'd whispered. *'He can't have loved us at all.'*

I was small in this memory. Too small, you would have thought, to remember. But I did. And I remembered too, what I thought as I watched my mother cry: *'I wasn't enough. He left because I wasn't enough.'*

I shook my head. I shook the memory away. I had to keep going.

Archie helped me over to Tessa. 'Are you worried about the treaty?' he asked as we walked.

'You knew about that?'

'I watched the clearing. I saw Isaac and the Sarco leader speaking. They talked about hundreds of years of fighting and the importance of a new solidarity in the face of the Diemen's increasing threat. I could tell they were not chums. But I knew they were on the same side and I was glad. You fellows need as many people on your side as you can muster now.' He looked down at me. 'I had a feeling there was something between these two,' he whispered. 'I saw them together. I felt something. She loved him.'

'Loves,' I corrected. Perrin was starting to sit up. He was going to be okay. And I was glad. Tessa was my best

friend. And Perrin was her love. Without him she'd be missing part of her soul. And I loved Tessa's soul. I wanted it to be complete.

Archie and I watched them for a moment. Not saying anything. Just breathing together, watching Tessa and Perrin and marvelling in their love. 'I think you can't choose who you love,' I said softly.

'True love, I suppose, looks past the colour of one's fur,' Archie replied.

'Cat?' I turned around. Isaac was standing behind us. He was looking stronger now, like his bones were more stable. But he was still much frailer and more vulnerable than usual. Luda was by his side. She was sweating slightly and breathing heavily but she managed to still look elegant.

'Did you see?' I asked, my voice cracking. 'Did you see what she did? The Sarcos –'

Isaac nodded. 'I saw. I know. But we need to go. Luda has brought a message from Rha.'

'I am sorry I was so late coming back,' Luda said. There were tears in her eyes. 'I was with the other Sarcos. I sent the messengers here while I finished speaking with Rha but . . . I should have come myself. I should have come straight back. I could have prevented –'

'Does he know?' I interrupted. 'Rha? About what's happened?'

'I came back here with Harriet. I have sent her back to tell Rha,' Luda said.

'But we have to *forget* what has happened, for now at least,' Isaac said. 'Luda tells me that the Sarcos have discovered information about the Diemens' plans.'

'The Diemens are going to Cascade Falls tonight,' Luda added.

I shook my head. 'Why would they go back there? They know we watch the school.'

Luda grimaced. 'Rha thinks they have someone on the inside. Someone who'll provide them with prey.'

'Archie said the same thing,' I said. I glanced over at Archie, who was sitting down on a log and staring into the forest. He looked as exhausted as I felt. I turned back to Isaac. 'Isaac, we have to get there. There are so many girls there! And Rhiannah's still there too! We have to go *now*.' I took in Isaac's grey, clammy skin, his bloodshot eyes. 'But are you *okay* to go? Are you healed?'

'I've healed,' he said. 'Finally. But someone needs to stay here and look after the camp. Guarding the territory is a very important job, you know.'

'Oh, right,' I sighed. 'It's okay. I'll just stay here and –'

'No, I want you to go. I think I'll stay here and guard for a while. I'm not at my best and I need food. I could have sworn I saw Tessa stash a packet of waffles somewhere around here.' Isaac's lips jerked upwards into a rare smile. 'I'll wait here until Hatch gets back. I'm putting you in charge of the expedition. What I've seen today has shown me I can trust you to do this. You and Luda go first. The Sarcos will meet you there.'

'You don't want Luda to lead?' I asked, glancing at her. She gave me a small smile.

'No,' Isaac said. 'I think you can do this. And Luda will be there too, for backup. Hatch and Tessa and I won't be far away and the Sarcos are on their way there too. By the time you get to Cascade Falls you'll have an army at your command.'

A few days ago those words would have terrified me. I was desperate to be involved and included but being in *charge?* I would have told myself I couldn't do it. Now I just nodded and said, 'Okay.' And then I thought of something. It might be shooting myself in the foot but I needed to tell him. If Isaac was going to trust me he needed to do it while knowing all the facts. And besides, I was proud of what I'd done. 'Isaac, I left the clearing the other day,' I said. 'I went to Cascade Falls. I decided by myself that we should do day patrols as well as night ones. Do you still trust me? Do you still think I can lead this mission?'

Isaac looked thoughtful for a moment. My heart thudded. 'I think you were right,' Isaac said slowly.

'I think day patrols are something we should've started long ago. Yes, I still trust you. Yes, I want you to lead this mission. I'll follow behind as soon as Hatch comes back. He can take over the guard.'

'What about Delphi?' I asked, following his eyes. I couldn't see her.

Isaac shook his head. 'She's gone.'

'Gone? Where?' I cried, squinting to see through the darkness and the trees.

'Into the forest. Away. I saw her running.'

'And you didn't try to stop her? But Isaac, she killed –'

'I think she did it to protect you.'

'That doesn't make it all right!' My heart thumped. 'And it's not fair. It's not fair on me for people to do horrible things and say they're doing it for my sake!'

I thought of the letter again. I thought of the blood in the hay.

'No,' Isaac said, his voice strangely tender. 'You're right. It's not fair.'

'Why did you let her go?' I whispered.

'Cat, Delphi will *never* be one of us again,' Isaac said. 'She will never be part of our clan again. She will never be close to *you* again. That's her punishment. I think losing you might well be the worst thing in the world for Delphi.'

'She'll never be one of us again?' I felt suddenly hollow inside. Empty. 'It's my fault,' I whispered. 'I let her love me.' And that love had caused this terrible thing.

'You did this . . .

It's your fault . . .

You let it happen!'

'It's not your fault, Cat,' Isaac said gently. 'You can't control how Delphi felt about you. If anything, I should have done more. I knew what harm she was capable of. I let her stay with us. I never thought it would lead to something like this.'

'Did you know about her father?' I asked. 'That he's –'

Isaac nodded. 'He *was* a Diemen. He's dead now. Killed by a Sarco.'

Suddenly, so much made sense.

But it still didn't make it okay.

'She told Beagle,' Isaac went on. 'Most children of Diemens don't know their father's secret. Delphi was unlucky. She witnessed one of her father's kills. It was one of her friends; her girlfriend. Delphi tried to kill him. He called the police. He said Delphi had killed the girl as well, after a lover's tiff. The things a parent does can mess you up for life.' Isaac looked at me meaningfully and I wondered how much Mum had told him about Dad. 'If you let them.' Isaac put his arm gently on my shoulder. 'Delphi was never as strong as you are, Cat. She may have acted like she was, but she was afraid. I could see it in her eyes.'

'It's easy to be strong when you've got claws and fangs,' I said.

'It's not being a Thyla that makes us who we are,' said Isaac. 'It's who we are that makes the Thylas we are. And I *do* know you're strong. Your mother has told me.'

'My – my mum said I'm strong?' I whispered.

'And brave and funny and smart.' Isaac looked away from me as he said it, as if he found complimenting me difficult. 'She said the other kids in Campbell Town used to give you an awfully hard time for being her kid but you always walked past them with your head held high. She could see how difficult it was for you but you never gave up. You kept on being funny and positive . . . She said she was always amazed she'd created you. Such a complex, wonderful, tough little creature.' Isaac cleared his throat.

'Why did she never tell *me* that?' My voice caught in my throat. It came out of me broken.

'She thought you needed to figure it out for yourself,' Isaac said. His voice was gentle.

'So did *he*,' I said quietly. And I wondered if Mum had wanted him to figure out *his* place in the world too. I wondered if she thought *he* was brave and good but never told him. Or if she did tell both of us in her own way every day. And we just didn't see it. I wondered if he would have figured himself out if he'd just taken the time to. Maybe he was waiting for someone to tell him who he was. I looked back up at Isaac. 'I don't know if I've figured it out yet. I don't know if I've found myself. But I'm on the path.'

Isaac rolled his eyes. 'Did you swallow a Quote a Day calendar or something?' he said, his usual gruffness returning. 'Sentimental mottos won't do you much good when you're fighting Diemens. They don't give a rat's behind if you've "found yourself".'

'No, you're right,' I replied. 'The only thing the Diemens want to do to me is kick my arse. Lucky for me I plan on kicking *their* arses harder. I'll head off now.' As I turned to go a new thought occurred to me. 'Isaac . . . Um, I know this doesn't sound very mission-leaderish but how am I going to get there before they do? They've got a pretty big head start.'

'You're fast,' Isaac said. 'When you're Thyla you're even faster. The Sarcos and Diemens will be travelling in human form.'

'But we'll be seen. I mean, it's fine to be Thyla in the bush but out in the suburbs?'

'Take back streets and lanes. There are only two of you. And it's a Friday night. If any human does see you, he'll just think he had one too many beers at the pub.'

'There are *three* of us,' said Archie, coming up behind me. 'I'm going, too. And I am superb at sneaking and skulking. It's what we foxes do best!'

I smiled at him gratefully. 'You really want to come with us?' I asked.

'Most certainly,' he said, smiling back. 'I'm not letting you two young ladies go out into the big wide Diemen-infested world alone.'

I felt like my heart would explode.

'What a gentleman,' said Luda, blushing in a way that made her look even prettier. And made me want to bare my fangs. I was surprised at how strongly the jealousy had hit me. But then so many new emotions had taken me over since I'd met Archie. What was one more?

And thankfully Archie never stopped looking at me.

'Okay, you lot,' Isaac grouched. 'Get out of here. You've got Diemens to kill. Try not to kill any more Sarcos, though. Please. We need this treaty.'

'Please, *please* fight *with* the Sarcos.' Tessa looked over at us. Her voice was small and sad.

'I will,' I promised.

Perrin was sitting up fully now. I looked at Isaac. He didn't seem angry. Maybe Tessa had underestimated Isaac. Maybe he didn't need her to be perfect. 'Thank you,' said Tessa. 'I will be there soon.' She stroked Perrin's hair. 'Perrin will be healed soon, also, and he can join us when he is ready.'

'Listen to you, little girl,' Perrin said croakily. 'Making all my decisions for me.' He smiled wryly at Archie. 'I'm totally whipped.'

'Yes, these womenfolk do have a habit of wrapping us around their little fingers, given half a chance,' said Archie.

'And after the fight, you can see your sister,' I said.

Perrin's eyes opened wider. 'Rhiannah? She's back? You found her?'

'Archie did,' I said proudly. 'And we've been nursing her. She's safe and she'll be well soon.'

'Thank you, Archie,' Perrin said, and I thought I saw a glimmer of tears in his dark eyes. 'Thank you, Cat.'

'No worries,' I said.

'All in a day's work,' said Archie. 'Now, come on, Cat,' he said, turning to me. 'And Luda. Pleasure to meet you, by the way. Let's go and save the world.'

CHapter

twenty-eight

ARCHIE MAY HAVE BEEN EXAGGERATING WHEN HE SAID we were off to save the world. But as we raced down the mountain towards South Hobart it definitely felt like we were on our way to do something amazing. And terrifying. I wondered if the other Thylas still felt scared when they were on their way to battle.

I wondered if I was doubly scared now because of where we were going.

Cascade Falls. My old school. It might not have been the happiest of places for me but it was still a part of my history. And it was still filled with girls who were my age, who dressed like me and talked like me. Who might even like some of the same music or books as I did. There might be other girls called Catherine or girls with red hair.

There were almost definitely lots of girls who still hadn't found themselves, who deserved to have a long path in front of them and lots of questions to ask and answers to find within themselves.

Rhiannah was there, still recovering in Charlotte's shed.

Erin was there, still grieving for Laurel.

And Charlotte herself. Charlotte who wasn't my friend yet and might never be but who I knew a lot better now. I knew she could hurt and that she could cry. I knew she could be trusted with secrets. I knew she was a lot more like me than I'd ever imagined she could be.

All of those girls were like me in one way or another and I didn't want any of them to finish tonight with even a scratch on their bodies. It was my job to make sure of that.

I pushed Delphi from my mind. I shoved aside the images of those decomposing Sarcos. I even forced away *his* face. The letter. All of my questions and answers. I had to. I had to focus on *now*.

'Are you okay?' Archie asked as we ran. 'You are unusually quiet. And your face looks a bit . . . scary.'

'I'm focused,' I replied.

'I'm frightened,' Archie said. I was so shocked I nearly ran into a tree.

'You?' I said. I stopped running for a moment. Archie stopped too. He nodded.

'I have betrayed the Diemens *and* my kin. I will be a target. They will want to kill me. And . . . I'm not quite ready to die.' He looked at me meaningfully. 'Not now.'

This was my moment. I was standing in the forest with a breathtaking man who sounded like Mr Darcy and who was looking at me *meaningfully*. A man who believed in me. And who had probably never even heard of V8s.

So why did I want to keep running?

Because we needed to get to Cascade Falls. We needed to stop the Diemens. Isaac was right. Finding myself could wait for another day. 'We need to keep going,' I said gently.

'Yes, we do,' Luda agreed. She ran past us. I'd almost forgotten she was there. When I was with Archie it felt like I was in a bubble.

A bubble that was about to be burst by so many silver fangs and Vulpi claws.

'Okay,' said Archie, speeding up. 'We can't let Luda beat us, can we?'

'Definitely not,' I said as we passed her again. I couldn't help poking my tongue out at her. It was worth it to see the stunned expression on her prim and proper face.

We ran in silence until we reached the very edge of the forest. This was the point where our journey would start to get tricky. We were about to leave the safety and camouflage of the trees and venture out into the human world. 'So, how do we do this, Mr Fox?' Luda asked.

'Ever heard of the expression "Fake it till you make it?"' asked Archie.

'You said it right before you kicked the door down,' I said. Archie nodded.

'So we just go out there and *pretend* we look ordinary?' Luda asked.

'No,' Archie asked, grinning wickedly. 'We don't pretend it. We *believe* it.'

Despite Archie's advice, I felt very much like I had a neon sign on my head saying 'Big, stripy, fangy monster' as I ran along Cascade Road. Luckily, since it was late, the only person we bumped into was a guy stumbling home from the Cascade Hotel singing a Kylie Minogue song to himself.

'Good evening,' Archie called as we jogged past.

'Salutations,' he replied, tipping his Cascade Pale Ale bucket hat at us and staggering off into the night without so much as a hint of a double-take.

'Archie!' I gasped when we were safely away. 'That could have been disastrous.'

'Are you crazy, fox?' Luda said at the same time.

'No, I am not crazy,' Archie said. 'Only mildly eccentric. But yes, we were quite lucky. He was pickled as a herring.'

We kept walking. I hummed the Kylie song to myself and chuckled at the coincidence. 'Better the Devil You Know.' *Or tiger or fox,* I whispered to myself.

'What is that drivel you're humming?' Archie asked.

'Kylie Minogue,' I said. 'Now stop paying attention to my humming and concentrate on the mission!'

Archie rolled his eyes. 'Whatever you say, Miss Cat. You're the boss.' We shared a smile and for a moment it felt like we were the only two people in the whole dark world. Then we rounded the very last corner on our journey and found ourselves staring up at the tall sandstone walls that surrounded Cascade Falls. 'Your former alma mater,' Luda said. Goosebumps raised on my arms. My old school. Now I was running towards it, not away. 'What would you like us to do now, mission leader?'

I'd almost forgotten. 'Boss.' 'Mission leader.' I was in charge.

'I think you should go around the back way,' I told Luda. 'Through the sports oval. I reckon that's the way the Sarcos'll come in. Archie and I will go this way and check on the main building first.'

Luda gave a tiny curtsey. 'As you wish, Cat.'

She raced off into the night. Archie and I really were alone.

'Are you ready to go in?' he asked, reaching over and squeezing my hand.

'As I'll ever be,' I said, shrugging.

Archie smiled at me. 'Shaking in your boots?'

I laughed. He could see straight through me. But I liked it. 'Yup.'

'That's the spirit!'

'After all, what could possibly go wrong? Apart from, you know, death and destruction.' I rolled my eyes. 'Why can't we be one of those *other* monsters – the ones who can't die unless you shoot them with silver bullets or stick garlic in their face?' I moaned.

'I hate to break it to you, Cat, but vampires and werewolves don't exist in the real world. In the real world, we all must die. Even *stars* die, eventually. And, when it comes down to it, human or shapeshifter, Vulpi or Thyla, we are all made of stardust.'

'Really? Stardust,' I murmured. 'We're *all* just specks of dust.'

'And we are all the brightest of lights,' Archie said.

I smiled to myself. I'd never known that before. About stars. It didn't really make the idea of death less scary but it did make me realise all over again the significance of what we were about to do. If *we* were made of stars then so were the girls we were here to protect. Somehow that made it seem even more important. Those girls were my sisters.

Even if half of them had hated my guts.

'We should go in,' I said.

Archie nodded. We each took a few steps back, preparing to jump.

'Cat?' A voice from behind made me freeze. It was a voice I knew. Very well. My nose was flooded with the scent of lavender.

I turned slowly around.

CHAPTER
twenty-nine

my mum was standing there.

My mum was looking at me.

She was looking at me as a *Thyla*.

But she didn't seem surprised. She didn't look scared. She looked how I felt.

Overwhelmed.

Her pale, freckled hand was pressed against her mouth. It was shaking.

'Mum,' I whispered as tears spilled from my eyes. I couldn't help it. I wanted to be a big tough Thyla – a big tough *girl* – but I hadn't seen my mum in so long and here she was. Standing in front of me.

'Come here, Cat,' she whispered.

'But I'm . . .' I looked down at my bare, striped torso.

'I don't care,' she said, wiping at her own tears. 'I absolutely don't care. Come here, honey.'

I nodded and raced forward into her arms. 'Oh, Mum,' I said. She kissed me on my forehead, on my cheek. She held me so tightly I thought I might suffocate. But I didn't care. I didn't want her to let go. 'How long have you been standing there?' I asked.

'Only a little while,' she replied. Lucky Isaac wasn't there. He would have been furious I hadn't smelled her. Usually I *would* have been able to scent a human so close but I was so transfixed by Archie I hadn't noticed *anything*. And Archie had looked as surprised as I did, so maybe . . . Maybe he'd been transfixed too.

Mum leaned back out to look at me. Her face was shiny and wet but a huge smile played on her mouth. 'Oh, my darling,' she whispered. She reached out to touch my face, like she wanted to make sure I was real. I did the same, cupping her cheek in my paw. She didn't even flinch at the claws. She just pulled me towards her again. 'I'm so glad. So . . . oh, I don't even know what to say. I am just so grateful. So grateful.'

'Me too,' I whispered.

Behind me Archie cleared his throat. Mum and I turned around. 'I know you need to get inside,' she said. 'But they're not here yet.' She must have noticed the confused look on my face. 'The Sarcos,' she explained. 'And the Vulpis. And the Diemens.'

'How –'

Mum's voice was gentle. 'Honey, I know quite a bit about your world. Vinnie tried to protect me but I needed to know. I think I've finally convinced him I can handle it but it's taken . . . a bit of work! You might think I'm just your mum but I'm actually very good at my job. Since the night I found out about Vinnie and Tessa, I've been investigating. I know about the Diemens. I know about Ted Lord. Turns out he's not such a top bloke after all. I was even thinking of pulling Tessa from the school or at least making sure she was nowhere near Lord's daughter. But Charlotte knows nothing about what's going on. She's just a girl. Like you.' She shook her head gently. 'Even though you look very different from the girl I last saw.'

My heart was pounding. The world was starting to spin. 'You know everything?' I whispered. 'You knew –'

Mum shook her head. 'No, honey. I didn't know you were involved. I didn't know you were a Thyla. Vinnie didn't tell me. I suppose I should be mad at him – and I probably will be later – but for now? Oh, I'm just so happy to see you. In whatever form you're in.' Mum cast her eyes over me. She didn't look scared at *all*. She must be used to the idea of Thylas now. 'Probably best I find out now. It could have been a bit distracting if I'd run into you inside.'

'You're going inside?' I gasped. 'But, Mum. It's dangerous!'

'It's my job,' she said. She wiped again at her tears with the sleeve of her navy blue police jumper. 'God knows, though, I'm not exactly in the mood for work right now.'

'Me neither,' I admitted. 'Reckon we can we chuck a sickie?'

Mum laughed. 'If only. Would Vinnie make us get a doctor's certificate?'

Archie chuckled. 'You and your daughter have the same sense of humour,' he said. Then he held out his hand, which still had its Vulpi claws. 'I'm Archie, by the way.'

'Nice to meet you.' Mum took the hand with only a tiny hesitation. 'Foxes,' she murmured. 'Now, that is a bit of a surprise.'

'We *should* get inside,' I said. 'Archie and I were just preparing to jump.'

'You could walk in with me,' said Mum. 'I have a key-pass.' She pulled a plastic card out of her top pocket and waved it over the detector on the gate. The detector beeped and the gates opened up. The three of us walked through. 'I can't believe this is happening,' Mum whispered. Her grip on my arm was so tight my paw tingled. But I didn't care. 'It's just – it's so good to see you. I can't even begin to describe how –'

'I know,' I said. 'But . . . Mum, I sort of wish this was happening some other time. In some other place. I wish you weren't here *now*.'

'Honey, you can't keep me safe. That's not your responsibility. I'm trying to teach Vinnie that, too. He wanted to keep me away from all of . . . this. But then all of the girls started to go missing and he couldn't keep it from me any longer.'

I remembered the corpses lining the Diemen lair. *Not missing, Mum. Butchered.* 'How many have actually, um, gone missing now?' I asked.

'Heavens, it must be about thirty now,' Mum said, sighing, 'That we know of. Mostly street kids. No parents. No jobs. No education. It's sad, but many of them were already dead, as far as society – and the authorities – were concerned, years ago. So Vinnie and I have been able to keep it hushed up.'

No wonder Isaac had been so stressed and grumpy lately – having to deal with the increased police workload and his Thyla duties must be nearly doing him in. 'Until last week, only a couple of girls – like Laurel – had come from good homes and attended school. Last week, though, a group of girls disappeared from one of the other private schools. No bodies have been found. It's possible they've all run away together and that's the line we're taking. But no note was found. It's all a bit of a mess, Cat. The numbers seem to be going up and up and we don't know why.' *The Solution*, I thought. It had to be. But just how that fitted in with the Diemens taking more girls . . . that I didn't know yet.

Mum gave me a small smile. 'But I am glad I know about all of this now. I'm glad I can help Vinnie sort it out. I hate the thought that he was doing it for so long on his own. But he has me now. And he's starting to trust me more. He called me here tonight, so that's progress. Apparently I'm meant to be directing the girls while the Thylas . . .' She paused. 'While *you* fight the Diemens. Wow, I never thought I'd be saying that to my daughter.' Mum's hand on mine was shaking. 'But I suppose now we have to work together on this, don't we? We're a team again.'

I smiled back at her. 'Yeah, we are,' I said. 'And we do need to work together. I need to know what you know. Do you –' I searched for the right words. 'Do you have any leads, Mum? About the disappearances? I mean, we know it's Diemens but Archie and Vinnie think they might have help.'

'Oh, honey.' Mum ran her hand through her hair. 'Right, I need to be "professional police lady" now, don't I? Yes, I have a few leads. There have been some eyewitness accounts. Sightings of the girls talking to a young man with long blond hair. Oh, and I have to remember to tell Vinnie, I also had the hospital ring up to say that one of their vehicles had been stolen, and that they thought it might have been taken by one of their ex-employees, a man who was fired after a domestic abuse claim. A few of the eyewitnesses claim to have seen an ambulance driving around Cascade Falls too, and the other schools.'

I felt the veins in my neck tighten. A man with long blond hair. A stolen ambulance . . . I tried to ignore the horrible, twisting, plummeting feeling in my gut.

'What's wrong, Cat?' asked Archie.

I tried to speak. My mouth opened. A noise rattled up from the back of my throat. I wasn't quite sure yet what word it would become and I never got a chance to find out. Archie's body tensed beside me. On my other side I heard Mum's hand pull the gun from her holster and click off the safety catch. In front of me, about two hundred metres away, I saw a flash of black and white. A Sarco. And then another. And then a mob of them, galloping over the hockey field towards Cascade Falls.

It was starting.

Chapter

thirty

'I'm going to go and talk to them,' said Archie.

'No!' I cried, grabbing his elbow. My mind flashed to the image of Tessa cradling Perrin in her arms. 'No. You can't go alone.'

'I'll go,' Mum said. 'Since I am the adult here and a law-enforcement official –'

'No offence intended, Mrs Connolly, but I am rather a lot older than I look – by about two hundred years.'

Mum rubbed her forehead. 'Oh, right. The immortality thing. Still getting used to that.'

'Besides,' Archie went on, 'I think you two will be needed inside for when the Diemens come. Is that okay, Cat?'

I nodded. 'Okay. Good luck, Archie.'

'Oh, I hardly think I shall need that.' I noticed his voice was trembling slightly. 'A dash of confidence, my natural charm and charisma . . . I think I should be just fine. Bye, Miss Cat.' Archie sprinted off into the night in the direction of the Sarco mob, clipping his chain around his neck as he did so. I'm pretty sure I heard the words 'lager', 'Stonehenge' and 'Winston Churchill' floating through the air as he ran away. My heart flipped. I willed him to return to me. I knew I'd only just met him. I was completely aware of how crazy my feelings for him were. But they were *there* and they were *strong* and . . . I couldn't lose him.

'Are you okay, honey?'

I looked over at Mum. 'I'm really sorry,' I began. Because I didn't know what else to say.

She shook her head. 'No, Cat. No apologies. You're here. You're safe. You're loved. And there's a school of girls over there that need protecting. We'll talk more, but we'll do it later.' I nodded. Mum leaned in. 'And I have to say, your boyfriend is dishy. Or should I say, *foxy*.'

'Bad joke, Mum. And he's not my –' Mum looked at me, one eyebrow raised. 'Yet,' I said, stifling a smile.

Mum reached out and I fell into her arms. She kissed my forehead. I wanted to stay there forever but Mum pulled away. 'Excellent. Now, I wouldn't usually say this to a minor, let alone my own daughter, but I think you might be needing this in there.' Mum reached into her second holster and tossed a small gun in my direction. I instinctively swerved as she threw the gun towards me. It clattered on the ground beside me. 'Mum,' I whispered, wishing away the tears that were welling in my eyes. 'That's . . . it's a gun, Mum. I can't.'

Mum's forehead creased. 'You can't? But why?' And then I saw it flash over her face. The realisation. She knew. She knew that *I* knew. 'How –'

'I found the letter,' I said simply. 'And, you know, I was *there*. I found him. I saw him.'

'I never realised you remembered,' Mum said, her voice trembling slightly.

'I didn't. Not really. Until I found the letter. Then it all came back.'

'You read that? Oh, Cat.' Mum nodded slowly. Her eyes were glimmering. 'Okay. Okay, Cat. I'm so –'

'Hey,' I said, reaching out and taking her hand. 'We'll talk more later?'

Mum wiped at her cheeks. 'Yes. Yes. And the gun –' She gestured with her head. 'I know, Cat. I know it will be hard. It was hard for me, the first few times I had to use one, after . . . but Cat, it wasn't a gun that killed your father. He did it himself.'

The words fluttered around in the air and then fell to the ground. *He did it himself.*

'Okay,' I said. 'I guess I can't be Thyla once I'm in there with the girls. But you'll need to teach me. I've never touched one of those . . . things before.'

'Time for a crash course, sweetie.' Mum bent over to pick up the gun. Her eyes locked on mine. 'Just think of it as a machine. Think of it in its component parts. Think of it clinically and logically. Okay?' I nodded. 'It's just a machine and you're in complete control of it. Do you understand?'

'I think so.'

'Okay. So, she's fully loaded. Just flick that little lever – that's the safety – and point and shoot. Usually, I'd say aim for the leg, but on these Diemen mothers, I give you full permission to aim centre-scalp.'

'Mum, did you just call the Diemens "mothers"?' I asked, my eyebrows flying upwards. My mum never swore. 'That's bad-arse.'

'Yes, well, if you weren't here, I might have added another word there, too.' Mum shot me an embarrassed grin. 'But I have to set a good example for my only daughter. By the way, don't say "bad-arse". It's *uncouth*.'

'Thanks for that, Mum,' I said. 'But . . . I'm not really very sheltered any more, you know?'

'Just humour me, Cat,' Mum said, smiling. 'I haven't

been able to *shelter* you from anything for a couple of years now.'

'Okay,' I said, trying not to cry again.

'Are you ready to do this?' Mum asked.

'Yeah, Mum. I'm pretty tough now, you know,' I said.

'I never doubted it,' said Mum. 'I always knew how tough you were.'

'Isaac said that. I never knew.'

'Oh, Cat.' Mum's face crumpled. 'I really wish I'd done things differently. I wish I'd told you the truth. I shouldn't have asked everyone in Campbell Town to keep the secret from you. I wish I'd told you all the time just how wonderful you are but I always thought . . . I was wrong, okay? Parents get stuff wrong. I guess I just thought, after what happened with your dad, I thought you'd need to develop a thick skin. I should have told you, every day, how proud I was of you.'

'It's okay,' I said. 'I've learned how to be proud of myself. And the stuff with Dad? The secrets? It's okay, Mum. I get keeping secrets now. And I get that you were grieving and – and you did what you thought was right at the time. I'm not mad at you.'

Mum nodded. 'Brave *and* wise.' She paused for a moment. 'Cat, I think I might need some of your bravery. I'm scared as hell. Hold my hand?'

I didn't protest. I didn't even hesitate. I just took her leather-gloved hand carefully in my clawed one and said, 'Let's go.'

CHapter
thirty-one

as we walked up to the front entrance of cascade
Falls, Mum whispered to me, 'I think now might be the
time to go human, honey.'

'Okay,' I said. I found my cuff and pushed it on. 'Oh,
holy –' I growled. And then the word Mum had omitted a
few minutes before slipped out. 'Sorry, Mum,' I said once
the gut-churning pain had subsided.

'It's okay, Cat,' she said as I pulled my shirt over my
head. 'Vinnie's told me all about how much it hurts for
you guys to change.'

'Only the change *back*.' I grimaced at the final after-
shocks. 'Changing *there* is incredible. This is hell.'

'Poor possum,' Mum whispered, kissing me on the
head.

We were now right up at the heavy wooden doors at the front of the school building. 'What, do we just knock?' I asked. I wasn't used to 'just knocking'. I was used to sneaking and ambushing and hiding and breaking and entering. Knocking seemed like a really strange idea.

'Humans do tend to knock,' said Mum. 'If they're on the right side of the law, anyway.'

As Mum raised the brass doorknocker I looked up at the stained-glass windows that flanked the building's entrance. There were stylised angels and birds and animals. Among the possums and wallabies and bandicoots, in the largest panel, there was a Tassie devil and a tiger. 'Hi, guys,' I mouthed as I waited. 'Wish us luck.'

Suddenly the door flew open and my head jerked back down. Standing in the doorway, backlit, white hair streaming down over her shoulders and glowing like a halo, was Charlotte Lord. 'Mrs Connolly and . . . Oh. Dear. Cat? Uh, come in?' Charlotte pulled her white satin dressing gown tightly around herself against the chill of the night air. Mum and I walked past, Charlotte and I sharing a *look* as we did.

'Why are *you* answering the door, Charlotte?' asked Mum as Charlotte closed the door behind us.

'I'm in charge for the night,' Charlotte replied. 'I'm head prefect so, in the event of a staff absence, it's my responsibility. Mrs Bush is up in Launceston for a meeting and Holly – she's the new dorm supervisor – was called out to the hospital, so I'm in charge of the boarding house until she gets back.'

'She was called out to the hospital?' I felt my belly lurch again. 'Did she say what for?'

Charlotte shook her head. 'She said she wasn't sure yet, but that it was urgent and she'd be back as soon as she could. Why? What's going on? And, um, you're *back*, Cat?' She raised an eyebrow. Her eyes flicked between me and Mum. She was pretending for my benefit. I was grateful.

'Sort of,' I mumbled.

'It's not important right now,' Mum said firmly. 'What *is* important . . . what you need to know is that we're in a bit of a dangerous situation here. It's possible this school might be under threat. We need your help to make sure the other girls are safe.'

'A threat?' Charlotte stiffened. 'What threat?'

'It's not something we can discuss right now,' said Mum.

'Please tell me. I need to know. Who is the threat? Is it – is it something to do with what happened to Jenna and the other girls? Is the murderer going to come here?'

Mum's eyes widened. 'Murderer? Charlotte, we told you that you can't tell, anybody –'

'And I haven't!' Charlotte cried. 'I haven't told a soul. I've held up my side of the bargain. Now you need to tell me what's going on. And don't bullshit me!' Charlotte cried. 'What happened? What's happening now? I deserve to know.'

Mum's voice was tense. 'Charlotte, you're right. You do deserve to know. But time is short here. It's very important that all the girls are in their rooms, with their doors locked. Can you help us with that?'

Charlotte hesitated for a moment before nodding stiffly. 'Okay,' she said. 'I will. But later you'll tell me everything?' She looked at me. 'Both of you?'

Mum and I exchanged a look. 'Charlotte, please,' Mum said.

Charlotte sighed. 'Fine. I should probably tell you I saw Harriet Dennis sneaking out a few minutes ago. I ran downstairs to try to stop her. That's why I was down here. I would have followed her but it's late and with . . . *everything* . . . I was scared to go out in the dark.' Charlotte looked down, her pink cheeks becoming even pinker.

'I think on nights like this being scared of the dark is probably a good thing,' said Mum. 'But one of us should try to find her.'

'Um, Mum? I think Harriet will be okay out there.' I tried to put as much meaning into my facial expressions as I could. As in, *Harriet will be okay out there because she is a Sarco. Since she has claws and fangs and supernatural strength she can probably hold her own against what's coming.*

Thankfully Mum at least understood that I was trying to tell her *something* and trusted me enough to say, 'Okay, Cat. If you're sure. Charlotte, are you fine to go and check that all the girls are in their rooms? Without scaring them too much?'

'I don't know,' said Charlotte. 'I don't know how to stop them panicking.'

'Do it any way you can,' I said. 'Bribe them. Give them treats. Give them . . . Turkish delight! You know what those girls are like with lollies.'

'It's really important that they do what I say?' Charlotte said. '*Really* important?'

'Yes,' I said.

Charlotte turned back to Mum. 'I'll get going now, Sergeant Connolly?'

Mum nodded. 'Good luck, Charlotte.'

'You too,' said Charlotte quietly. She turned and walked away from us up the steep stone staircase that led to the boarding dorms.

'What now?' I said.

'Now, I guess we wait,' said Mum.

'I'm glad you're here with me,' I said shyly.

'Ditto, kiddo,' said Mum. We walked back outside and sat down together on the hard sandstone steps, preparing for whatever was to come for us.

In the sky above a million stars watched over us. Mum pointed. 'Did you make your wish? On the first star?'

I shook my head. 'I haven't done that for years, Mum.'

'I never stopped,' Mum said. 'I always wished you'd come back.'

'Stardust,' I whispered. 'I wonder if they can hear us.'

'What was that?' Mum said.

'Never mind,' I said. I'd spotted a figure moving towards us. 'There's someone coming.'

Mum and I sprang to our feet. Mum held her gun out in front of her and I copied. 'Hold,' she hissed at me. 'Hold.' I nodded.

'Well, I didn't expect a welcoming parade, but I do think that's rather uncalled for, isn't it?'

'Archie!' Relief flooded my body. He was okay. He was okay!

'You can put the guns down, at least for now,' said another voice. And out of the shadows behind Archie came a tall, bulky man with waist-length black hair tied back in a plait. It was Rha, the leader of the Sarcos. 'Save your bullets for the Diemens.'

'So the treaty still stands?' I asked, lowering the gun.

'As far as I'm concerned it does,' said Rha. 'Some of the others are less convinced, but we all agree that we must work together. Especially in light of what we have just discovered.'

'What?' I felt my grip on the gun tighten as my hands tensed. 'What did you discover?'

Another body joined us in the light. Rhiannah. Her eyes were ringed in black and her face was streaked with tears. 'They made me human,' she said.

CHAPTER
thirty-two

THEY HAD STOLEN RHIANNAH'S IMMORTALITY.

'I tried to change,' she said, her eyes glistening. 'I pulled down my cuff. Nothing. It's like my soul's been taken away. They took away who I am.'

We'd moved over to the green field near the main entrance to the school, hiding in the trees like I'd hidden only days before. But this time we *knew* the Diemens were coming.

'Rhiannah, you need to go now. You understand that, don't you?' said Rha. 'Go and hide inside, with the rest of the girls. I know you'll want to be part of this, but –'

'But I'm useless,' Rhiannah said flatly.

'No you're not –' I began, trying desperately to think of some way to comfort her.

Archie cut me off. 'I can feel them,' he said. 'The Vulpis. They're coming.'

'And with them the Diemens,' said Rha.

I looked out over his shoulder into the night. The dew was reflecting the full moon. It looked like fairy dust. The eucalyptus leaves fluttered in the gentle breeze. The only hint of a threat was the faraway screaming of a possum and the masked owl slowly clapping its beak in warning. Then from the far end of the grounds near Charlotte's shed, a tall, thin, dark body emerged and began to run towards us.

Erin.

'Oh, hell. I told her to stay,' said Rhiannah.

'They're *coming*,' Archie said again. 'They're close.'

'Rhiannah!' Erin cried out as she ran towards us. 'Hey, where are you? I saw you running this way. I know something's going on! Rhiannah!'

'Crap!' Rhiannah grabbed me by the arm and pointed but I'd already seen. Silver hair and dark suits, and the glint of the moonlight on their needle-sharp silver fangs. The Diemens were here.

They walked towards us slowly and in a way that seemed completely unnatural – as if they were floating. As if they were ghosts. *Ghouls.* And then I heard them. I saw their mouths open wider into sneering smiles and I heard their voices: voices that sounded like metal files scraping on steel. They were chanting, 'Vulpis. Vulpis. Vulpis.' Just like my dream. The Diemens were calling their servants.

'Erin!' I cried out. 'Run!'

'Vulpis,' the Diemens chanted. 'Vulpis. Vulpis. Vulpis. Vulpis,'

'What the –' Erin stopped and peered in my direction. Then she turned around.

'*Run!*' I screamed at her.

Next to me, Rha was holding Rhiannah back. 'No, Rin,' I heard him say. 'You can't go out there. You can't be part of this now. I need you to run away. Go to the school building. As quickly as you can. Be safe. Your powers are –'

'I can get them *back*!' Rhiannah screamed. 'Give them back to me! *Bite me.*'

'We don't know if it can be done yet,' said Rha. 'We don't know how the bite will affect you after . . . after you have already been changed. It might hurt you. It might kill you.'

Finally, Erin started running. Behind her, the Diemens didn't run. They just kept slowly floating forwards. But then from behind them, in a flash of flame-like limbs, the Vulpis came. They *were* running. Fast. Erin's long legs moved quickly but she didn't have a hope in hell against the Vulpis' supernatural speed. Within a second the Vulpis had made up almost all of the ground Erin had covered. They were nearly on top of her. Erin was screaming.

'We have to help her,' I yelled. I scrabbled franti-
cally for the cuff at my wrist. Now was not the time to
be human. Out of nowhere another body launched itself
at the Vulpis from side-on. I didn't take the time to look
more closely at who it was or think about why they were
here. All I cared about was that momentarily the Vulpis
were distracted.

And in that moment I wrenched off my cuff, leapt
through the space separating me and Erin, grabbed her
roughly around the waist and slung her over my shoulder.
I heard the rumble of Vulpi paws galloping towards me as
I ran to the school building. I didn't stop to look back.

Rha and the other Sarcos were emerging from the trees.
He motioned to them with his hand over his shoulder.
'Go!' he commanded and they raced past me into the open
ground – towards the Vulpis. The air crackled with electricity as they passed. A second later the howl and thud of
battle began to sound. I didn't stop. I ran until I was back
under the cover of the trees. I put Erin down as gently as
I could and then I turned around. Vulpi and Sarco had
melted together in a haze of amber, black and white. Claws
flashed in the moonlight, blood sizzled and flowed. Fangs
found their targets and ripped flesh from bone.

My eyes were distracted from the conflict to a smaller,
quieter scene playing out behind it. The Diemens had
another creature with them. One of them was holding it

by the neck, its head lolling and its body hanging like a floppy rag doll in his arms. I couldn't see the face but I recognised the black jeans and I knew that stubbly, shaven skull. I knew those stripes. A cracked scream broke from my throat. 'Delphi! It's Delphi!'

I jerked forwards.

'No, Cat,' Mum yelled.

I whipped around to face her. 'I'm going,' I growled. 'She saved us. I'm saving her.'

Mum nodded slowly, her face tight. 'Okay. Okay, Cat.'

I shot out into the darkness.

As I approached I saw one of the Diemens pull from his pocket a silver tube with a spiked end. My heart raced. I sped up. That tube was bad. Whatever he was going to use it for was . . . *bad*. It had been on the boat too and they'd nearly got her then. I had to stop them getting her now.

The moonlight glinted off the tube. It was strangely beautiful but horrible because, suddenly, I knew what it was for.

I was so busy looking at the Diemen with the tube, I didn't notice the one with the syringes.

I was about five metres away when he plunged the first one into Delphi's neck. Her body shuddered and turned human. Her stripes faded away. The Diemens thrust another syringe in her arm. Then the man with the silver tube stuck it in Delphi's chest. I saw her blood rain down on the ground.

I stopped, still.

They'd done it.

That tube. The syringe. That was the Solution. They'd used it on Delphi.

'No,' I whispered.

The Diemens didn't seem to notice me standing so close. They were too intent on what they were doing. In two quick, silent leaps, I was there. One of them looked towards me, a shocked expression on his face. 'Hi,' I said. 'I'm Cat. I'm a Thyla and I'm going to kick your shiny arse.'

And then . . .

I did.

I leapt on the first Diemen, grabbed his skull and twisted. A sharp crack told me his spine was snapping.

Before the other Diemen had time to react to his friend's death I was on him too. I opened my mouth wide and bit at his throat with my fangs. Dark blood splattered my face. I didn't bother wiping it away. The Diemen wasn't dead yet and I wanted him to be.

As he looked up at me, dark eyes full of horror, I grabbed the shiny metal tube from his hand and I drove it into his chest.

The Diemen slumped, lifeless, to the ground.

I turned away. I didn't give a crap about the Diemen any more. All I cared about was Delphi.

I crouched down beside her. Her eyes were closed. Her skin was pale. She was shivering.

She was dying.

Or at least, the Delphi I knew was dying. I could see already a silvery tinge on her skin, a metallic sheen to her stubbly hair.

'Delphi,' I whispered. I put my hand on her bare shoulder. 'Delph?'

Her eyes fluttered open. 'Cat?' she croaked. 'Cat, what's happening to me?'

'It's okay, Delph.' I stroked her forehead lightly. 'You'll be okay.'

'Am I . . . did they turn me . . . into one of them?' Delphi was gasping for breath. Blood bubbled in her mouth. It was black. 'I can feel it. I can feel I'm turning into –'

I hesitated for a moment before I said softly, 'No, Delphi. You'll always be one of us. You'll always be a Thyla.'

'Cat . . . I love you,' Delphi said.

'I love you too,' I replied. And I meant it. Not in the way she wanted. But I still meant it.

'I always thought I'd hear from him again,' Delphi whispered. 'My dad. I thought he was good inside, under all of it. I thought he might have told one of the other

Diemens about me before he died. I thought he might have left a message that he loved me.'

'I'm sure he did,' I said. 'I'm sure he loved you very much.'

'Kill me,' Delphi whispered, her voice insistent. 'You have to. I know I'm turning into one of them. Like my dad. I want you to – to kill me. Before it happens.'

'No!' I said firmly. 'No. I won't.'

I knew what Delphi was saying made sense. I knew why she was asking it but . . . I couldn't.

'I have to die. It's better. For you. For . . . everyone.'

I thought of *my* dad. That's what he'd thought too. But it wasn't true.

'No,' I said. 'I'll fix it. We'll fix you. Come back with me . . .'

'No,' Delphi roared. She sat up quickly. Her eyes were full of fire. She leapt to her feet. 'I'll never go back. If I do, I'll hurt . . . I'll kill . . . I have to run away. Forever.'

'No, you don't.'

I looked behind Delphi into the shadows. A Diemen was floating towards us. 'You're coming with me, Newling,' he said. And then he grabbed Delphi by the neck. 'Say ta-ta to your little friend,' he whispered.

'No,' Delphi whimpered. 'No.' And then her face darkened. 'I'll kill you,' she said, fixing her eyes on me. 'And I'll kill her. Erin. She did this. I'll kill both of you.'

And then the old Diemen faded into the dark, pulling the new Diemen with him.

The last thing I heard – a breath, a whisper on the wind – was my name.

'Cat . . .'

They were gone. Swallowed up by the night. The hole they left seemed to glimmer silver. I couldn't look away from it.

I took a moment to breathe, to steady myself. And then I ran back to my mum.

'Cat, what happ–' she began, putting a hand on my shoulder.

'What is going *on*?' Erin yelled, pushing past her. 'You really hurt my ribs! And . . . hey . . . your face is covered in black stuff.'

'Piss off, Erin,' I snapped, jerking my head around so my eyes were meeting hers. I bared my fangs at her. Her eyes stayed calm.

'You're one of them,' she said. 'One of the magic animals.'

'You don't say,' I spat.

Mum moved to Erin's side. She put an arm around her shoulder. 'Cat, she's scared.' There was a note of warning in her voice.

'*She's scared?*' I cried. 'Mum, I just saw my friend get turned into a Diemen!'

'Oh, Cat,' Mum said gently. 'That's horrible. But we need to keep going and Erin –'

'She shouldn't *be* here,' I said. 'She's human. Right now, this *isn't* a place for *humans*.'

'Oh, really?' Mum raised her eyebrows.

'Apart from you,' I sighed. 'But you have a – a gun.'

'I could have a gun.' Erin pushed herself to her feet. 'Diemens. They're the people . . . or *things* that killed Laurel, aren't they? I want to fight them. I want to *kill* them.' I looked over at Mum. I could see she was having a hard time working out what to say. Erin was a minor. She needed protecting. But then so was I. So were half of the Sarcos. 'I can do this,' Erin said. 'I really believe I can. Please. Let me do this. For Laurel.'

Mum shook her head. 'How the hell did I get into this mess?' she said. 'And where the hell is Vinnie? He said he'd be on his way.'

A familiar scent tickled my nostrils. 'I think he might be –' Sure enough, I turned around to see Isaac striding towards me. He looked much better now. At his side was Tessa and next to her, looking as good as new as well, was Perrin. Behind them stood Luda and Harriet. Harriet nodded at me. I nodded back.

'The fight's started,' I said feebly. I was surprised Isaac didn't say 'Duh'. Instead he shook his head and looked out at the battle.

'The Sarcos seem to have the Vulpis in hand,' he said. 'We need to take care of the Diemens.'

'Can I have a gun now, please?' said Erin. 'Come on! I want to kill a Diemen!' You had to admire the girl. She really knew what she wanted and she didn't care who stood in her way.

'Mum, I think we should give her the gun,' I said before Mum – or Isaac – could say anything. 'If she knows how to use one she might be a help.'

'Yes!' Erin darted over to Mum with her hand outstretched. 'Don't worry,' she said. 'I'm *country*. I've shot much bigger than this little tacker before.'

'You can have mine,' I said. 'I hate the things. And I'm going to do this Thyla style.'

Erin looked at me more closely now, her eyes skimming my body from skull to claws. 'You're awesome, Cat,' she breathed. She clicked the safety off on the gun like she was pressing a button on a remote control. 'Nice,' she whispered. And then, in an even quieter voice, I heard her murmur something that sounded very much like *Wolverine*.

On the other side of the school grounds, the Diemens were standing and watching the battle like it was flipping *Macbeth* or something. They didn't seem the least bit interested in joining in. Well, stuff them. They were going to. 'Let's get them,' I growled. 'They're just standing –'

'Wait.' Isaac stretched out his arm in front of his

motley army of Thylas, Vulpis and humans. One of the Diemens had broken from the pack and was floating over to us – a man with hair more platinum than silver and eyes more silver than blue. A man in a navy suit. Edward Lord. The rest of the Diemens turned in unison and floated behind him.

'Well, hello there,' Lord said as he approached. I could smell his breath. It smelled like rust and rotten eggs. 'And what has brought all of you lovely people out here on this crisp winter evening?'

'We could ask you the same question,' said Isaac.

'What a witty *retort*, little tiger pup,' said Lord. He and his Diemens opened their silver-toothed mouths and laughed. It was a cold sound, not at all like human laughter.

Lord snapped his jaw shut with a metallic clang and his followers did the same. He licked his lips with his black tongue. 'Honestly though, I am so glad to see that your spell in our little *chateau* hasn't roughed you up too irretrievably. It would have been rather a boring evening if we'd arrived here to find you on your sickbed or, worse, already dead. You see, we were looking forward to bringing you to that conclusion ourselves and in a manner of *our choosing*.

'We've had our fill of the little spectacle going on over there,' Lord gestured at the Sarcos and Vulpis. He leaned in towards Isaac. 'We're searching for a new entertainment and we thought it might be quite amusing to see what colour your innards are. We've disposed of a few Thylas in our time, but you are their *leader*. Perhaps your blood is of a different hue. We were thinking, for a time, that we might change you into one of us. But then we realised we so much prefer having young ladies as our new charges. And, well, we *don't like you*. So we'll just kill you, I think.'

'Geez, you guys are bastards,' Erin said before anyone else could speak. She might have been talking to some guy who'd stood her up. While the rest of us were dumbfounded this girl didn't seem fazed by anything.

'What an interesting turn of phrase you have there, Miss –?' Lord floated forward with his hand extended.

'It's Erin, and I'm not shaking that thing.' Erin screwed her nose up. 'Never know what I could catch.'

'Erin! Ah, yes, I remember. You're the friend of that young *ginger* girl, aren't you? I remember her screaming your name as we cut her little white belly open!' Erin roared and launched herself at Lord. 'As you wish,' he said unemotionally. He reached out and grabbed Erin by the throat. He raised her into the air as if she was as light as a kitten. Erin dropped her gun as she struggled and gagged. She tried to scream but Lord was holding her throat too tightly. 'What's wrong, little native? I thought this was what you wanted?' Lord cocked his head to one side. 'It's been a long time,' he said menacingly. 'I've almost forgotten what black girl tastes like. Ooh, *yes* . . . I remember. I used to have quite an appetite for your kind, back in the day.' He cocked his head to one side. 'There is something rather familiar about those dark eyes of yours. So pretty . . . Tell me, do you have any sisters?' Lord licked his lips. 'If you're as delicious as you look I could have a new favourite meal.'

Down deep in my stomach a growl began to rumble and a fire began to flame. I leapt forward and, with all my body weight, I shoved Lord to the ground. He released his grip on Erin and she sprawled onto the dirt, scrabbling for her weapon. For a moment I lay on top of Lord, staring right into his empty silver eyes. I was centimetres from his face. He could have bitten me if he wanted to.

Then, with one swift, deft move, he overturned me so I was on my back and it was him on top of me. My heart thudded. He leaned close. Was this it? Was Edward Lord about to kill me?

'Not yet, Catherine Connolly,' he whispered. 'You are too delicious. I'll save you for dessert. You and your little friend.' Lord licked his lips. And then, Charlotte's daddy *disappeared*. One second he was on me, his weight pressing down, his breath cold on my face and then . . .

He was gone. He hadn't run away or leapt away. He'd just become invisible. He'd become air. How the *hell* had he done that?

'Cat!' Mum screamed from behind me. I heard her footsteps racing towards me.

'No, Mum! Get back!' I cried, shaking off the fear I felt at what had just happened.

At the same time Isaac yelled, 'Rachel, no!'

I scrambled to my feet, turned quickly around and pushed Mum aside into the bushes just as three of Lord's men lunged at her. They hit me instead, hard and heavy and I found myself on the ground again. Three shimmering faces loomed over me, looking at me hungrily. I vaguely recognised one of them but I didn't have time to think about where from. 'I've decided I don't like you guys very much,' I growled. Then I kicked one of them as hard as I could right in his tender bits.

'That's the second time you've done that to me,' he groaned. 'You did it to me in the bush that day, too. It. Really. Hurts.'

'Oh, Herbert, stop being such a sissy,' one of the others hissed. 'Just kill the vermin.'

'Not on my watch!' I looked over the shoulders of the men to see Archie winking at me.

And then it was *on*. The Vulpis had run over to join their masters and the Sarcos were on their tail. They flew at each other, kicking and clawing. Archie pounced, taking out the Diemen whose *bits* I'd squished. Tessa hesitated for a moment, looking nervous before shaking herself and lunging at another one, expertly gouging his neck. 'I *can* still do this,' I heard her cry.

'You flipping can, Tessa!' I yelled as I punched another Diemen in the gut. They wanted elegant violence? Too bad. That wasn't how we Thylas rolled. Black blood spurted all over us. Then I heard shots as Erin used her farm-girl talents to shoot one of them in the middle of the skull. More dark, metallic blood oozed from the perfect dollar-coin sized hole in his forehead. 'And *that's* how you take out an evil dude!' Erin exclaimed. '"Little native" my arse.'

I jumped to my feet and launched at the closest Diemen. I let everything go. I forgot about Delphi. I forgot about Tessa. I forgot about Rhiannah and Hatch and Charlotte. I let all my thoughts and memories get sucked out of me and what I replaced them with was Thyla – pure, crackling, sparking, furious Thyla. I kicked the bastard hard in the stomach. He roared with pain but unfortunately it didn't deter him. He lunged at me, his awful mouth wide open. He wanted to bite. To kill.

I wanted it harder.

I slashed through the air with my claws and dug a deep hole in his throat. Blood erupted from the wound onto my arm and my face. The Diemen howled and lurched forward. I took my opportunity. I opened my mouth wide and I bit a chunk from his shoulder. I spat the dark fabric of his jacket onto the ground. Then I delivered my deathblow: a kick with my powerful hind leg, right in the side of his head. I heard a snapping sound as his neck broke and he fell to the ground in a dark heap.

I still couldn't say I enjoyed killing but I tried to think of it now in the way Mum had told me to think of the gun. Except now *I* was the machine.

Far away from the scrum I heard someone scream. I looked over at Archie, who'd just taken down another Diemen. He heard it too. It was coming from inside the school. 'Go,' he yelled. 'We can take this. See what's going on. But just be *careful*, okay?'

'Okay.' I ducked under the slashing blade of a random Diemen who came face to face with Perrin on the other side of me. As I sprinted away from the field back towards the school buildings I heard Perrin enacting some particularly *inelegant* violence on his opponent.

It crunched.

At the top of the stairs that led to the building I turned briefly and looked back at the battle. I wanted to remember this. I knew I'd want to write it down.

I could see that none of my little army had fallen – yet – but the ground was littered with Diemen corpses beginning to smoke and sizzle. Across the field, Sarcos were still battling Vulpis. I could see a mix of black, white and orange bodies on the jade-coloured grass. It was hard to say who was winning over there. I could see Rha and Harriet still kicking and biting and Perrin had left the Diemen battle and was fighting among his kin.

'Go, you guys,' I whispered. I turned around, wrenched open the door of Cascade Falls and dashed inside.

CHAPTER
thirty-three

IT WAS SPOOKILY SILENT INSIDE CASCADE FALLS. THE ONLY sound was my shallow breathing and the faint dripping of blood – my blood mixed with Diemens' – on the polished floorboards. Where had the scream come from? I looked uselessly around me. There was nobody there. The scream must have come from upstairs. From the dorm rooms.

'You heard it too?'

I whirled around, heart hammering. Standing in the foyer was Rhiannah.

'I was hiding in the bushes. I wanted to go in but, you know . . .' Rhiannah trailed off. She didn't need to finish. I could see she was terrified.

'We can go together,' I said. 'I'd be very happy not to do this on my own. Where'd it come from? The scream?'

Rhiannah nodded towards the staircase. 'Up there. The dorms.'

'Let's go then.' We walked silently up the stairs and found ourselves facing the long corridor down the middle of the boarding dorms. 'There's our old room,' Rhiannah whispered. 'Casa Rhiannah Cat. It feels like a million years ago.'

'A billion,' I agreed.

'I'm stuffed.' There were tears in Rhiannah's eyes. 'They've taken away who I am.'

'You're more than a Sarco,' I said, remembering what Isaac had told me. *It's not being a Thyla that makes us who we are.* 'You're still Rhiannah. You're still awesome.'

Rhiannah looked away bashfully. 'Thanks . . . Um, I can't hear anything, can you?'

'No, I can't but –' I was interrupted by a sound – it was only quiet but my Thyla ears made it out. It wasn't a scream. It was more of a strangled squeal and it was coming from a room right down the end of the corridor. Charlotte's room.

'Down there.' Rhiannah pointed.

I nodded. 'Do you want to stay here?' I asked.

Rhiannah shook her head quickly. 'No, I'll come with you. You're right. I'm still Rhiannah. Rhiannah doesn't wuss out.' She flashed me a nervous smile and I smiled back.

We lapsed into silence as we made our way down
the long corridor. As we got closer to Charlotte's room
I could hear that there were at least two girls in there – one
crying and another talking quietly. And there was a male
voice as well; a male voice I recognised. 'That's Hatch,'
I said, feeling like I was going to vomit.

'He's one of your mates, isn't he?' Rhiannah asked. 'A
Thyla? What's he –' A deafening sound cut Rhiannah's
sentence in half. It was the sound of a body hitting a
hard surface and then the crashing, shattering sound of
breaking glass.

Somebody had just gone through a window.

Without taking the time to think about it I leapt
towards the door. I turned the knob but it was locked
from the inside.

'Bugger,' Rhiannah moaned.

'It's okay,' I said. 'I can get in.' I took a few steps
backwards and then raced towards the door. I launched
myself at it as hard as I could, the way Archie had in the
Diemen lair. The impact pulsed through my body and I
felt as if every bone in me was breaking.

But I heard a crack and I felt the wood crumble and
collapse.

Just call me Chuck Norris.

I fell with a thud on the other side of the door,
splinters of wood ripping my flesh. I stood up quickly,

ignoring the searing pain from the gashes on my thighs and forearms. I scrabbled for my cuff. I couldn't frighten whoever was in the room by being Thyla. Behind me I heard Rhiannah climbing over the wreck of the door into the room. 'Charlotte?' I heard her say. 'What happened here?'

I looked over at the corner of the room. Charlotte Lord was curled in a ball, her white dressing gown and even whiter hair soaked with blood. It was dripping to the floor. 'It's my fault!' she screamed.

'What? What's your fault?' I asked.

'He took them. It's my fault. I gave it to them and he took them. He killed her.'

'Who did he kill?' I asked. Charlotte pointed at the window. Gingerly I padded towards it. I tried to avoid the broken glass but I couldn't escape all of it. I felt it cutting my skin, digging itself deep into my flesh.

I looked down at the ground below Charlotte's window. Lying with her head bent sickeningly, almost backwards, was a girl with cropped blonde hair. It was Charlotte's friend Inga. 'He pushed her,' Charlotte said. 'Two friends now. I've failed them. Jenna and now . . . I tried to fight him, and he pushed her out the window.'

'Hatch?' I asked.

Charlotte nodded miserably. 'I thought he was nice,' she whispered.

'Where is he now, Charlotte?' I asked. Charlotte stiff-ened, her eyes huge. I sniffed the air. Antiseptic and sour, milky breath and . . . Turkish delight. Then a cold pressure on my neck told me there was a knife to my throat.

'Hi, Cat,' said Hatch, using his free hand to grab my right arm and wrench it behind my back. 'You know, it's dangerous to interrupt a professional paramedic when he's working.'

I forced my voice to work. 'What exactly is it that you're working *on*, Hatch?'

'Oh, just a little side business. You know ambos make terrible wages. Diemens pay much better. And "Diemen informant" is a much cooler job title than "paramedic". Has a nice ring to it.'

'You're a traitor,' I said through clenched teeth. The fear was melting away. Now I was just flipping angry.

'No, I'm an *entrepreneur*. And a very successful one. I thought after what happened on the boat – you know, I was meant to help the Diemens capture you all but a sharp blow to the head put paid to that – I thought my career might be over but luckily the Diemens knew they were onto a good –'

Hatch's head jerked sideways. 'Hey!' I glanced tenta-tively in the direction of his gaze to see that Rhiannah had been moving over to us, a shard of glass in her hand. 'Don't even think about it,' Hatch growled. He pushed

Rhiannah against the floor. Hard. I heard a crack of bones and a whimper. 'And I think we'll put *these* on.' I felt my wrists being clamped together in handcuffs behind my back.

'You don't have to do that,' I said.

'Oh, I think I do,' he said, pushing me roughly on the shoulder. I fell to the ground. 'Isaac may underestimate you, Cat, but I know just how powerful you are. It's what always attracted me to you. Look at you. So innocent. So *sexy*,' Hatch trailed a finger down my face. 'You'll fit right in to Lord's little harem. And when you're a Diemen, and I am too, we can be what I always imagined we could be.' He leaned in and kissed me lightly on the neck. It felt like someone ripping my throat out. But I didn't flinch. 'You and me, babes. You were the one I really wanted. You just needed time. You'll make a *great* Diemen. We'll take on the world.'

I looked sideways at Rhiannah. She was shaking. I looked back at Hatch, making my eyes soft. I hated myself for doing it but I had no choice. 'Maybe we will,' I said. 'I'm sorry I said you're a traitor. You're right. Isaac does underestimate me. I'm wasted there. And I'm really interested in what it is the Diemens are doing. Tell me about the Solution.'

Hatch looked at me suspiciously. 'You turned me down,' he said. 'Nobody ever turns me down.'

'I always wanted you,' I lied. 'I knew we could be really great together. Really . . . really *powerful*. But I was afraid of that.'

Hatch nodded. 'I suspected something like that. I never thought you could *actually* not want me.' He smiled and leaned in, angling his face and licking his lips. 'And I'm even better now. Better than I was. I've found the real me. Lord's taught me the right path. No kowtowing to some selfish, useless leader who has no idea about our history or our purpose. Isaac might know a lot about Thylas and Sarcos but he knows nothing of what came before. Lord is a *real* leader. He's not content to sit back and watch as the world around him becomes more and more *mediocre*. And it *is*, Cat. People who have money and power are constantly being pulled from their pedestals – even sent to jail – so the "common man" can feel better about himself and his worthless, sponging existence. I was a common man once, Cat. I *created* a new me. The old me was useless.'

'You weren't –'

'I used to get attacked, did you know that?' Hatch cut me off, his voice rising in pitch. 'When I was at work. Drunks, *losers* – they'd attack us when we were trying to *help* them. And then there was Jenny. She was my girlfriend, but she betrayed me. She told our boss we'd never been together and that I'd *assaulted* her. I was defenceless against *her*, too. Until I saw what it's possible to do to a woman who betrays you. The Diemens taught me that. Such *power*. I showed her. I taught her not to mess with me. I showed her and now I'll show all the rest of them.' Hatch gestured madly. 'Trying to help humans is a pointless exercise. Lord's got the right idea.'

'And what's that?' I asked, feeling horribly sure that I already knew the answer.

'Convert or kill.' Hatch smiled again that same evil smile. 'And I've proved my worth to the Diemens now. I've proved I'm every bit as ruthless as they are. That night at the club was my big test and I showed them. I orchestrated it all, you know. It was easy. Hook the friends of the girls up with men so their attention was taken away; isolate the girls, lure them to the basement with the promise of . . . well, *me*. It was easy as pie. If only you –' Hatch jerked his head sideways, glaring at Charlotte – 'hadn't interrupted us, it would have been the perfect kill.' He smiled again. 'Vain little bitch. It was so easy to convince you to leave your friend. Encourage some young moron to go up to you and tell you that you're pretty.' He shook his head. 'You deserve what's coming to you.' He turned back to me. 'And now I've proved my worth, the Solution awaits me. You do understand the Solution, don't you, Cat?'

I shook my head and swallowed. I was still reeling from the knowledge that Hatch had organised the nightclub attack. That it was because of him that Jenna was dead. It seemed so surreal. I thought I knew him. I thought he was my friend; that he was one of us. But he was a traitor and he was . . . evil. I couldn't let it distract me, though. This was my best chance to find out all about the Solution. 'I don't know much about it, Hatch,' I said. 'But I would like to know. What is it, exactly? Why did they need shapeshifters? Why did they take Rhiannah? What did they do to Delphi with that tube?'

'Shapeshifter blood is an essential part of the process,' Hatch said. 'It is what enables us to turn humans into Diemens. We mix the shapeshifter blood with the Solution to give the humans immortality. We use the heart tube to give them . . . other qualities. Qualities specific to Diemens. A certain . . . ruthlessness and focus on the goal. The heart tube replicates the experience of eating the first human heart. It makes a change in the heart of the subject that allows them to become fully Diemen in nature.'

Fully evil, I thought.

'What happened to Rhiannah was . . . regrettable,' Hatch went on. 'The Diemens took away her Sarco powers – which is the essential first step in the process, when working with a shapeshifter subject. To be born again you must first shed your useless former skin. They made her human again. They would then have used the

Solution and the heart tube to make her Diemen. But she was stolen from them before they could. But, you know, Rhiannah, you're halfway there now!' Hatch turned to Rhiannah. 'If you chose to you could let us inject you with the Solution. Then we could use the heart tube on you. Or you could take the more fun option: kill a virgin, eat her heart and bathe in her blood! That changes the heart as well. Do that and, bingo, you can be one of us too!'

A howl burst from Rhiannah's lips. 'No! No, I won't. I won't —'

'Oh, shut up, you pathetic human,' Hatch snapped.

His eyes fixed on mine again. 'And Delphi, hey? They turned her?' I nodded. Hatch smiled maniacally. 'Excellent. Delphi will make a phenomenal Diemen. Maybe the best. She has it in her to be great. Powerful. She's a madwoman, but sometimes it *takes* a madwoman, doesn't it? To shine an incandescent light on the pathetic dullness of the world. To *burn it up*. I would have *had* her a long time ago, except she doesn't swing that way, does she? That's all right. Lord doesn't have to know that. You never know, he might even get her to grow that hair of hers. She could be quite hot with long hair.'

Hatch smiled again. He twirled a finger around one of my curls. 'I like long hair,' he said huskily. 'You'll both be brilliant. But the Diemens are looking beyond shapeshifters now. Remember I said they need shapeshifter blood to give the subject immortality? Well, they've reached the point where they can make the shapeshifter blood synthetically. There aren't many shapeshifters, Cat. There are lots of humans. Enough to eat and enough to convert. The Diemens are onto a *winner*. Your friend Rhiannah – even though she didn't turn out quite right – helped them so much in their knowledge of shapeshifter blood. Thanks, Rhiannah.'

Hatch looked down at Rhiannah, who was cowering in a corner cradling a broken arm that would not heal quickly. He clapped slowly. Sarcastically. Rhiannah looked away. Hatch's eyes were on me again. Hatch mimed holding a syringe in his hand. 'It'll be so easy now: mix shapeshifter blood – real or synthetic – with the Solution, inject the Solution into humans, give their hearts a little *tweak* with our special tube, and pop! Instant Diemen!'

Hatch started pacing, using his knife to scratch at his neck. He didn't seem to notice the thin trail of blood that was trickling down. He'd totally lost it. 'But you know, Cat, all the Diemens started out as shapeshifters. There's a whole history to it: Queen Elizabeth and the first shapeshifters and the first Diemens . . . I'll save that for a little *pillow talk* at another point, though.'

My blood went cold.

'What?' I whispered.

'Oh, yeah. You didn't know? No, of course you didn't. Because Isaac knows stuff-all about anything. But you won't have to worry about him much longer. Not once we're changed. We'll be among the first new Diemens for *five hundred years*. Can you believe how incredible that's going to be, Cat? Man, I can't wait until my first kill as a Diemen. That first *heart*. I've been thinking about what it will *taste* like . . .'

He pressed his mouth against me. His hand reached down to grab my breast. I struggled and tried to break away but I was trapped. 'You know you want it,' he whispered, pulling away briefly. 'Come on. Let me make you incredible.'

'No!' I struggled against him. No more pretending. I'd got what I wanted. *'No,'* I said, more firmly this time.

Hatch put the knife on the ground. He reached into his pocket and pulled out a cube of strong-smelling Turkish delight. 'Triple-strength Tyrandioxide,' he said, smiling. 'One bite of this and you'll be begging me to take you to the Diemen lair.' His other hand started moving lower down my belly, towards the top of my jeans. 'One bite of this and you'll do *anything I want you to*. You're a good little girl, Cat Connolly. A good little policewoman's daughter.' His sick grin made me gag. 'Oh, yeah, I *know* what I want to do to you, Cat. I know *exactly* –' Hatch's eyes suddenly bulged. A strangled scream burst from his lips, followed by a torrent of blood gushing down his chin. He slumped to the ground.

Dead.

Charlotte stood behind him, holding a knife in her delicate hand. Her body was shaking violently. She looked up at me, her eyes brimming with tears. 'I just killed a man,' she said. I nodded. I couldn't think of anything to say. 'I did it so I won't end up like my father.'

Rhiannah raced over and pushed the catch on the handcuffs with the hand of her good arm, freeing me. 'Don't worry,' she said. 'I think it's just a sprain. The crack was just me falling on some glass. I'll be fine.'

'Are you sure?' Rhiannah nodded. I looked from her to Charlotte to Hatch's crumpled body, still leaking blood on Charlotte's plush white carpet. 'Are *you* okay?' I asked Charlotte.

'My dad is a Diemen,' she said, by way of explanation.

'How did you find out?' asked Rhiannah gently.

Charlotte dropped the bloody knife on the floor. She stared at it for a moment. When she looked back up her eyes were glassy and when she spoke again her voice was emotionless. 'I didn't know. Not really. I knew *something* was wrong. I just didn't know what. After what happened here, with you and Ms Hindmarsh and Laurel Simpson, I just . . . I wanted to be at home. With Daddy. I was scared and . . . I baked him some biscuits and I took them over. I didn't realise Daddy was having a – a meeting at our house. That didn't happen very often. Usually, he has meetings at the office. I knocked on the door but he didn't answer . . .'

I stifled a gasp. My dream. It was just like my dream!

'But then I heard them. They were in the boardroom. I could hear Daddy talking, through the door, but his voice sounded *different*. I didn't think much of it, though. I knocked, but they were all talking so they didn't hear it, so I just opened the door and . . .' Tears rolled down Charlotte's face. She didn't seem to notice. 'I looked at my dad and he looked – he didn't look like himself. His skin looked different. His eyes were . . . and all the men around him . . . they looked like . . .' She shuddered.

'I don't know what they looked like. I dropped the biscuits and I ran away. Daddy came after me. He looked normal again and he asked why I'd run, what had scared me. I'd been too frightened to say anything. He laughed at me and said that he and his men were trialling a new kind of light – sort of like UV light, but silver – used for detecting asbestos in the buildings they were working on. "It can make people look a bit funny," he said.' Charlotte looked up at me. 'I wanted to believe him. I convinced myself I was just messed up because of what happened to Ms Hindmarsh and the girls disappearing. But he's one of those *people*. He's a – a Diemen.'

Charlotte wiped a bloody hand across her forehead, leaving a streak of red on her pale skin. 'Oh, God!' She swayed. I reached out and caught her, helping her to the floor. She slumped sideways, her hand drifting down her face to press against her mouth. 'He killed Jenna, didn't he?' she whispered.

'His men did,' I said, nodding.

'Oh, God,' she said again. Her face was contorted with anguish.

'Charlotte, it's okay,' I said, knowing it sounded stupid. As if having a father who was a Diemen could ever be 'okay'. 'You're not like him.'

Charlotte shook her head furiously. 'I am. You don't understand. I killed Inga.'

'What? No! *Hatch* killed Inga,' I said.

'But I helped. The Turkish delight. I gave her Daddy's Turkish delight.'

'Your dad gave you the Turkish delight?' I asked. And then it all came together. Turkish delight – Tyrandioxide. 'Oh no.'

Charlotte nodded miserably. 'That was the other thing. The other thing that made me know something was wrong. Daddy said it was just a new product they were trialling, but I *knew* there was more to it. I didn't eat any myself because, well, I don't really eat lollies but then when you and Delphi came over I thought serving it to you would be a good way to get rid of it. I could see it in your eyes. You looked different. Relaxed. And so then I did eat some myself, to test it, and that's how I felt, too. I stopped giving it to people but you made me with Rhiannah and then tonight . . . I thought I could use it to stop the girls panicking. I knew it was bad but I still gave it to people. See? I am like him. I'm just like him! Inga ate lots of it and she went all giggly and she was staggering and I started getting really worried, but then Nathan came in. I knew he was a paramedic because of that night . . . when Jenna . . . I thought I could trust him. He told me he'd been called here by the police – that your mum had called him. And Inga seemed sick, so I let him in. And then he kept trying to *kiss* Inga, instead of helping her. It was horrible but she was so drugged . . . I told him to stop but he got angry and he pushed her out . . . out . . . If you hadn't come through the door – It's my fault. It's my fault she's dead. I *am* like my father.'

'Did you hear what Hatch said?' asked Rhiannah. 'All it would take is for them to inject me with the Solution and then use that heart tube . . . or for me to eat a heart . . .' She shuddered. 'I'm so close to being a Diemen.'

'We all are,' I said. 'I saw how quickly they transformed Delphi. Two syringes. And then that thing plunged in her chest and she was one of them. And Hatch said *I* would make a perfect Diemen. We're all so close to being evil. But we can all fight it.'

The three of us sat for a few moments in silence. Through the broken window we could hear the sounds of the battle carrying on. 'I should go and help them,' I said, standing up.

'Can't you just stay here? I – I feel safer when you're here.' Charlotte looked down at her feet. She looked so sad. So small. So I did something I never thought I'd do. I hugged her.

'They need me down there,' I said. 'My kin need me.'

'I think the girls here need you, too,' Rhiannah said quietly. 'The others can take this fight. You should stay here and protect the girls.'

'Cat, Nathan took some girls somewhere before he came in to us!' Charlotte said as if she was just remembering. 'Younger girls. I don't know their names. I don't know how he got in. He went straight to the Year Seven rooms.' Charlotte stood up again, shakily. Her blood-drenched dressing gown stuck to her slender legs. 'We need to find them.'

'Okay,' I agreed. 'We'll find the girls. But then I have to go. There are people I love down there.'

'Your mum?' asked Charlotte.

'Yeah. My mum.' I walked towards the door. 'And all the Thylas. They're all my family.'

'The Sarcos were my family too,' said Rhiannah.

'They still are,' I said.

'I don't have any family now,' Charlotte said. 'How can I ever go back there? To Dad? And Mum . . . Mum must know something about what's going on. I have nobody now.'

I held out a hand to Charlotte. 'Your family doesn't have to be your kin. We can be your family too.' Charlotte hesitated for a moment. Her eyes turned icy one more time. I could see her thinking: *untouchable*. And I wondered if she'd ever really think of me as anything else. But now wasn't the time for that. We had to get out of there and find the girls. Charlotte nodded finally and took my hand. Her fingers were freezing.

'We're all family,' Rhiannah said. 'We'll stick together.' She took Charlotte's other hand. Then the three of us climbed over the already-decomposing body of Hatch, gripping on to each other as if otherwise we'd all fall down. We opened Charlotte's door and walked out into the hallway.

We had more people to save.

cHapter
thirty-four

mum was talking to the girls. charlotte and
Rhiannah and I had found them locked in Hatch's
ambulance. By the time we got back to the field the
battle was over but the grass was clear of bodies. Apart
from a few sizzling piles of black sludge. 'Did we win?' I
asked, allowing myself to hope.

'They took Luda,' said Tessa. 'Luda came to help, and
they took her. They were about to stab her with a metal
pipe. I saw pipes like it in their hideout. I think they are
part of the Solution.' Tessa shook her head. 'I pulled one
of them off. The other one took her.'

'They're going to take her and use the Solution
to make her into a Diemen too. Like they did with
Delphi.'

'What?' Isaac hobbled over. I saw dark bruises and gashes all over his legs; they were fading slowly. 'What did you say?'

'They took Delphi,' I said. 'And I know how and why they're doing it. But I'll explain later. Back at camp. We need to start planning. And I have to write in my journal, too.'

'Cat, I don't think now is the time for writing poetry!' Isaac growled.

'No, it's *not*!' I agreed, surprised at how assertive my voice sounded. 'Luckily, I'm not writing *poetry*. I'm going to write all of *this* down. Everything that's happened. We need to start making a history. Especially now. Isaac, you know all about the Thylas and Sarcos but this is bigger than that. This involves all of us. The Diemens used to be shapeshifters. Did you know that? And did you know there are others just like us all around the world? And the Diemens are multiplying now. The Solution – they're using it to make more Diemens. Isaac, something major is about to happen. We need to work out what we're going to do. Together. The Sarcos and the Thylas –'

'And at least one Vulpi.' I turned around to see Archie – in human form, now – standing with his hands on his hips and smiling his huge smile. I felt like I was suddenly standing in a sunbeam in the middle of the darkness.

'Archie!' I cried. It was all I could do not to race forward and throw my arms around him. 'Archie, are you okay?'

'I'm fabulous, Cat,' he said, grimacing. 'Apart from this rather nasty gash on my neck where one of my former kin tried to bite my head off. I was right. They are annoyed with me for betraying them and whatnot. I'm afraid I might have to come and live with you fellows for a while, if that's all right?'

'Of course,' I said. 'I mean, that's all right, isn't it, Isaac?'

Isaac nodded. 'I think at this point I'd say yes to anything, just so I could get home and get to bed. But yes, Archie. We need to build our forces. That much is clear. And I think you've proved worthy to be one of our little ragtag gang. We're probably a bit less *genteel* than what you're used to, but if you can put up with us, well, welcome to the family.'

'What about me?' said a quiet voice. Erin. She was crouched close to the ground, still cradling Mum's handgun. 'I mean, I did good, didn't I? I shot two Diemens. Can I be one of you now? Cat, please?'

I looked over at Isaac. He shook his head. 'Erin, becoming a Thyla is not a decision to be made lightly. It's dangerous. You will never be the same person. Your life will never be ordinary –'

'I don't want my life to be ordinary!' Erin growled, her eyes flashing. 'Don't underestimate me, mate. I've been through a bloody lot. And it's only made me stronger. And more determined. I can do this. I *will* bloody do this. If you don't turn me I'll just fight as a human. You can't stop me. You ask Cat. I'm not that great at being told what to do. Make me one of you or I'll do it on my own.'

Isaac looked at me warily. 'I've made so many mistakes,' he said. His voice was tired. 'Delphi was a mistake. Hatch was – obviously – a huge mistake. I believed him, when he told me he didn't hurt that girl. I believe him . . .' He rubbed at his temples. 'I don't think I can trust my instincts any more.'

'Then trust me,' I said, feeling a surge of a kind of bravery I'd never felt before. 'I believe in Erin. I know she can do this. My dad . . .' I took a deep breath. Here it came. The true story. I didn't know if I was ready to say it but something inside told me – strongly – that Erin was meant to be one of us. And maybe telling my dad's story was the only way to make it happen. 'My dad killed himself,' I said quietly. 'He shot himself. He did it in the hay shed. I was nearly four and I found him. He was a farmer. The farm was struggling. We had lots of debts . . . He just couldn't hack it. I forgot what I'd seen – the blood, the gun. And everyone kept the secret from me. To protect me. I never knew he killed himself until right before I left for Cascade Falls. Everybody just told me he died, not that he committed suicide. I thought he died in a farming accident. But then I found a note in Mum's stuff.

'I was looking for a copy of *To Kill a Mockingbird* because I'd left mine at school. I found one of Mum's diaries and saw a piece of old paper sticking out of it. I pulled it out and read it. I shouldn't have, but – but it was from Dad. And it said he could've managed the farm stuff going wrong but he couldn't deal with wrecking *my* life.' I felt my chin wobble. 'He said that it'd be better for me if he was gone, that if he stayed alive he'd ruin me. He said I needed to know who I really was, in a way he never had. He said that ever since he married Mum he'd always just been Rachel Connolly's husband. She was the bright shining star and he was just a little speck of dust floating in the air, never truly knowing itself. He said he didn't want me to grow up as a speck of dust. He wanted me to be a star. He said he was worried I'd turn out like him if he stuck around.' I wiped a rebellious tear from my cheek. 'I thought he died because of me. And I thought I must have been letting him down. Because I never did know who I was. Reading the note, well, it scared the life out of me. I knew I needed to escape somehow. I didn't want to be *just* Rachel Connolly's daughter. I know Mum's wonderful. But I didn't want being her daughter to be all I was. I didn't want to be a speck of dust.'

I looked around at my clan. They were watching me with pity in their eyes. 'I'm not telling you this so you'll feel sorry for me,' I said. 'I'm telling you this so you'll know that now, for the first time in my life, I feel like I do know me. And I'm not doing this for Dad any more. What Dad did was wrong. He never should have left me. He didn't realise that the path keeps going on and you can make of it what you want to. He thought it was in a straight line. It's not. You make your own life and my life is *this*. I'm committed to the Thylas and even though it's hard and scary sometimes I'm going to stay and help make things better. I know I'm meant to be a Thyla. I believe in us. And I believe in Erin. I believe she has the right to live her life the way she chooses and if she chooses to be a Thyla then we should support her. I became a Thyla by accident. I stayed because of Dad. From now on I'm doing this for me. And for our cause. And I want Erin by my side.' I finished speaking and looked at Isaac, waiting for his decision.

For a moment there was silence. Then finally, Isaac spoke. 'I think we lost another member of our clan tonight. She might return to us – we can only hope – but she may be . . .' his eyes darted to Rhiannah, 'in a different state from when she left us.' I saw Rhiannah look down at her feet, tears welling in her eyes. 'And Delphi is gone too. We need to build up our forces again. I think Erin proved she's a good fighter. Erin, do you have family who will miss you?'

Erin nodded. 'My family's really close. Mum and Dad, and my Auntie Shirley and my Nan Alwyn, they live with us as well. And I've got two sisters. They go to school at Oakburn Grammar in Launceston. But I reckon I need to protect them too. I know they're up in Launnie but . . . That Lord prick asked me if I have any sisters. They could be in danger, you know? And it might sound stupid but I just feel like I'm *meant* to be like you. Something's telling me I've been involved in this from the beginning. This is my fate. I feel it. Let me do this, please? I can –'

Isaac held up his hands. 'Okay!' he said. 'Please stop. I don't think my head can take it.' He turned to me. 'Cat, if she really wants it, and if you're willing to change her . . . I believe in you. I believe in your judgement. I think Erin would be welcome in our pack.'

'Are you sure?' I asked Erin. 'It is a huge decision. This life is . . . not easy. There are so many dangers. And the Diemens are –'

'Bastards. Yeah, I worked that out. They killed my best mate. But if things are going to get harder for you guys – if these Diemens are going to start multiplying or whatever, you'll definitely need more people. You'll need *me*. I know what I'm getting into.'

'Then it's settled,' said Isaac. 'Erin and Archie, consider yourselves officially on the team. Cat, you will need to arrange a time with Erin to do what needs to be done.'

I looked over at Erin. Suddenly, I remembered something she'd said back in Charlotte's mansion shed. *'The devil's my totem.'* I brushed the thought away. It didn't mean anything. It didn't mean Erin would prefer to be a Sarco. She was going to be a Thyla. She'd *chosen* to be a Thyla. That was all there was to it. 'As soon as possible,' she said. I nodded. I'd do it that night. It was my turn to be a creator, just like Tessa was with me.

I looked over to where Tessa were standing, bundled up in Perrin's strong arms. I'd never seen her look so vulnerable. The past few days had totally changed my idea of who Tessa was. She was just as flawed and fallible as the rest of us. It made me love her even more.

Some of the other Sarcos were glowering at them, some were just looking at them with confusion or suspicion. Rha didn't look angry at all. He was standing with Harriet, talking. Occasionally they looked at Tessa and Perrin but neither of them looked mad or upset. Perrin would have gone straight to Rha and confessed. It looked like Rha had understood, just like Isaac had. They'd both seen so much in their long lives. They'd both lost people they loved. They could see how much Perrin and Tessa loved each other. That was enough for them.

Life is short, I thought. *We need to hold on tightly to those we love.*

Rhiannah and Perrin had already had their reunion. I saw them, Perrin's arms wrapped so firmly around his little sister that I wondered how she could breathe, while she cried on his shoulder and told him about how the Diemens had changed her, taken her immortality, made her human again. Perrin wiped the tears from her face and comforted her. I heard him tell her, 'Rhiannah, you'll always be one of us. You'll always be valuable to us. We'll figure this out, okay?'

Rhiannah had nodded, but Perrin's answer was obviously not enough for her. She needed reassurance from Rha, her leader.

Rhiannah walked over to Rha and Harriet. 'I guess it's goodbye for us, then,' she said. 'I mean, I'm not a Sarco any more.'

'Oh, Rin,' Harriet said. Her eyes were shining.

'You're always one of us, Rin,' said Rha. 'But we can't really risk having you come out with us. Now you're human, you'd be less powerful. You'd be –'

'A liability. I know,' said Rhiannah. 'It's okay. I think I'll have my work cut out manning the fort here. Especially now we know what Lord's doing. He's going to keep coming back for more girls. I can help look after them.'

'We'll do it together,' I said, looking first at Rhiannah and then at Erin. 'I'll come back to Cascade. We'll protect the girls together.'

'And me too.' I turned around to see Charlotte standing behind me. She was clean now and dressed in unusually casual clothes – jeans and a t-shirt. Her wounds were swaddled with thick bandages. Mum was with her, holding her hand. 'I'll help too. It's my responsibility. It's my father who's behind all of this. I can help you. It's the least I can do. For you. And for Jenna and Inga.'

'Of course. We'll be a crack team. You, me, Rhiannah and Erin.'

'And me,' said Mum. 'Of course I will do everything I can to help you girls. And you're welcome at my place any time. All of you.' I nodded, feeling my cheeks flame. I'd been running for so long, wanting to find *Cat*. I knew now that Cat had been there all along and that Mum had always seen her. Mum had treated me like an equal tonight, with respect. She didn't want me to be 'Cat Connolly, policewoman's daughter'. She wanted me to be *me*. Maybe I could go home now and be whoever I wanted to be. Myself. It might be nice . . . 'Just to visit though, right Cat?' Mum went on.

'Huh?' I looked up at her, confused.

'I think that's the best idea,' she said. 'You boarding at school again. You need your freedom. And, well, Vinnie and I have decided to move in together, and it might be best if we had some space to, you know . . .'

'You and Isaac are moving in together?' I asked again numbly. When had all of this happened? 'You and Isaac are . . . are . . .' I couldn't even put it into words.

'Yes, we are. Although, after I give him a piece of my mind tonight, that might well change. Or I might just let him suffer a bit. That might be more fun.'

'So you love him?' I asked. I found it almost impossible to believe that someone could love grouchy old Isaac. And that he could love someone back.

'I do,' she said. And then she gave me a wicked smile. 'And I fancy him rotten.'

I gulped. 'Yeah, me staying at Cascade Falls might be the best idea,' I mumbled.

Mum kissed me on the forehead. 'My big girl,' she said. 'I'm *so* proud of you. Even more so now, and I didn't think that was possible.' She turned to Tessa, who'd moved over to us. 'My two big girls. Have you been keeping your journal going, Tessa?'

'Yes,' Tessa said. 'And Cat is keeping one as well.'

'That's great!' said Mum. 'I always thought you'd end up being a writer. You and your books. Keep doing it, won't you? If it's what you really want to do.'

'I will,' I promised as Mum walked away towards Isaac. The look on her face told me he wasn't going to get off lightly over keeping my secret. Mum might be kind and cool-headed most of the time but she had a fiery temper. I was glad Isaac was going to be the one on the receiving end of it tonight, not me.

'You will keep writing?' Tessa asked, dragging my attention away from Mum and Isaac.

'Of course,' I said. I knew how important it was now. Not just for me but for all of us. I'd thought being a Thyla was the one true and solid thing in my life. But there was so much we didn't know of ourselves. We were still searching. Little questions. Little answers. And I was going to write them all down.

chapter
thirty-five

Later that night, erin and charlotte and rhiannah and I sat in the grounds of Cascade Falls, looking out over Hobart. We sat in silence, each lost in our own thoughts.

A mess of packets lay between us. We'd been able to eat at last. It had been *brilliant*.

And now I had food in my belly and my friends safe beside me, I finally let my thoughts in.

I looked out over my city. It wasn't where I was born or raised but it was where I'd first known who I was. It was home now. I thought of all the people down there, going about their usual routines: watching telly, sleeping, reading, eating; some poor souls who were still working, none of them knowing a thing about this whole other world that existed around their city, this world of Thylas and Sarcos and Diemens and Vulpis. I had a feeling that people would learn about us all pretty soon. The Diemens were getting more powerful and taking more girls. And they were multiplying. 'Sleep tight, Hobart,' I whispered. 'Enjoy your ignorance while you've got it.'

My mum was down there with Isaac and Archie, who'd gone home with them so Isaac could find him some clothes and so they could work out a way for him to make his way in the human world of Hobart. Before they went I'd been brave one more time. I tapped Archie on the arm. 'Can I talk to you?' I asked.

'Of course, Cat,' he replied. We walked away a little bit from the others, into the shadows. For a moment, for the first time since I'd met him, I didn't know what I wanted to say. I only knew that I wanted to say *something*. Or *ask* something, like whether he felt the same flutters as I did when we were close. Or if his stomach lurched when we held hands.

If he felt like he was standing in a sunbeam whenever I smiled at him.

'Cracking night, eh?' Archie said before I had a chance to think of what words I could possibly use to express how I felt.

I nodded. 'It was pretty amazing.'

'It will make for a fantastic letter home,' he said.

'Do you still have friends back there?' I said, kicking myself for never taking the time to ask before. 'Or,' I looked away from him into the distance so I didn't have to see his face, 'Someone special?'

Archie snorted. 'Friends, yes. Someone special?' He shook his head. 'Do you really think it would be possible for me to have someone special? When I can read their every emotion?'

'But that could work to your advantage! You know what women want!'

'Touché,' Archie said, smiling. 'I suppose the worst thing is being so very much older. I have seen so much. What could we possibly share? And that is not to mention the horrible reality that I will probably outlive anyone I love by hundreds of years.'

'What about the other Vulpis?' I asked. 'Or other . . . shapeshifters.'

Archie shook his head. 'No, Cat,' he said, his eyes suddenly serious. 'I'm a loner. A free-walker. It's nice to have companions sometimes but anything else is just too hard.'

Archie sensed my sadness. His forehead creased.

'You knew I felt something for you,' I whispered.

'I did,' Archie admitted. 'But, sometimes, when I sense the emotions of someone else, and they are feeling something very similar to what I am, things get . . . muddled.'

'You felt something too?' My heart swelled with hope.

'Of course. I watched you for some time, Cat, before I met you! I saw how funny you are, and how kind, and how *brave.*'

'Stop with the brave!' I protested. 'I'm going to get a bravery complex!'

Archie laughed. 'Shall I tell you, instead, all the other things I saw? I saw your confidence and your humour and your wit. When I was watching you, I saw so much within you that you only needed to acknowledge. I assumed you knew how wonderful you were, but then, you wouldn't be Cat Connolly if you were convinced of your own wonder, would you? What makes you special is that you're just beginning down the path and that's why . . .' Archie cleared his throat. 'Cat, I can't lie to you. I did think, for a brief moment, that you and I might be, well, soulmates, but then I *met* you.'

'Thanks very much!' I cried, my hope deflating. 'What's that supposed to mean? You met me and you realised you were wrong? I'm not so awesome, after all?'

'No, I just realised you are on the cusp of all the things I've already done,' Archie said sadly. He was silent for a moment. 'It was wrong of me to . . . I liked the way it felt, being with you,' he said finally. 'And of course, I think that you are, well, you must know you're very . . . *comely.*' His cheeks were glowing slightly now.

'But if you liked –'

'Just not now, Cat. You're too young. It would be wrong of me. I'm an old man and you're just a baby.'

'I don't care about *wrong!*' My hands flew up. I was really angry now. I'd spent half my life doing what I thought other people wanted me to do. I'd only just started admitting what *I* really wanted and that included Archie and he wouldn't *let* me have him!

'I *do* care,' he said, his voice firm. 'You have hundreds of years to lose your innocence. Once you develop your premonitor talents, you will grow up quickly. You will be a very powerful creature one day, Cat Connolly, but now you are just a girl making her way in the world and that is a wonderful thing. I'm going to have to let you take the rest of that journey by yourself. I'm not going to steal it from you. That's why we can't be together. Not now.'

'Never?' I asked. I saw Mum and Isaac approaching out of the corner of my eye. I crossed my fingers and wished them away.

'Ask me in a hundred years.' I looked up at him, pleading silently for him to change his mind. 'And don't look at me like that. Trust me. It will pass in the flicker of an eye.'

'Do you love me?' I whispered desperately. I knew it had only been days. Not even that, just one day. But in my books, sometimes it happened in hours. And with Archie I think it had happened in an instant.

Archie nodded. 'I think I do.'

'Then –'

Archie shook his head. 'No, Cat.'

'Wait,' I finished. 'Wait for me.'

Archie nodded. 'I will.' He took my hand and kissed it lightly. And then he walked away. I found myself smiling at his retreating back. He would wait for me and I could wait too. I had all the time in the world.

As I looked down on the city that was going to be his home now too, I wondered where he'd go; what sort of life he'd lead here in Tasmania. Somehow I knew that whatever he did, it would be magnificent.

I didn't think he'd go to Valley Grammar. He was too old for that, even if he didn't look it. Tessa wasn't coming back to Cascade Falls either. She'd decided to go back to being a full-time Thyla and Mum had agreed to it. They'd talked about it after the battle. Tessa wanted to be in the bush, learning how to be a Thyla again. She'd admitted to Isaac that her powers weren't fully back. Or her memories. He'd been surprised but he'd understood. He said he admired her for telling the truth. She'd also told him that she intended to spend more time with the Sarcos now. He didn't argue. Tessa's love for Perrin was the link that might bind the Thylas and the Sarcos together. Maybe her alliance with the Sarcos would mean a treaty could really, finally, be secured. I hoped so. I knew that we'd need the Sarcos on our side if we were ever to defeat the Diemens.

And we'd need knowledge. We'd flailed about for centuries with only a tiny hold on what we were and what it meant to *be* what we were. I was determined to change that.

But I also knew, as much as I needed Thyla knowledge, I still had so much to learn about the human world. That's why I was going back to school. I'd still be a Thyla. But I'd be a girl as well. I'd learn calculus and French and history as I learned more about who the shapeshifters were and who we were becoming.

I'd help Erin to find out who she was. I'd guide her on her path to being a Thyla. I would have a chance to give to her what Tessa had given to me.

And together, all of us – Thylas, Sarcos, Vulpis and humans – would figure out what to do next. It was exciting and tremendous and strange, this new future of ours. And I would write it all down.

When I met Delphi again I'd write about that too. I hoped when I met her I'd be able to help her. I hoped when I met her we'd be friends, not enemies. She was my family once. I hoped she could be again. And I hoped what Hatch said wasn't right, that Delphi would not become a brilliant Diemen. I wanted her back with us.

In the meantime, surrounded by the girls who were now part of my odd and wondrous family, I took out my journal again. I looked first at Erin and then at Charlotte and Rhiannah, all lost in their own complicated worlds. Behind me I heard a branch snap and I jerked my head around. At first I thought I might have seen a shadow or a flash of white but I told myself the shadow and the flash were just in my mind. I was still edgy from the battle. I was creating monsters. I told myself to stop. There were enough monsters in the real world without me creating more. I turned back around and picked up my pen.

> *I am Cat. I am a Thyla. I'm sixteen years old. And I'll be sixteen years old forever. I'm in love for the first time and it's beautiful and painful. I'm finally being me and that feels awesome.*
>
> *I live in Tasmania, at Cascade Falls, with my new family. We are shapeshifter people – Thylas, Sarco, Vulpis. We now know how we began and why. And this new knowledge will give us power.*
>
> *We are part-beast and we are part-human. We love and we hurt and we laugh and we cry.*
>
> *Just like the rest of you.*

I put down my pen and looked up at the stars. 'Goodnight, Dad,' I whispered. 'Keep watching me. I'm going to do great things.'

acknowledgements

AS USUAL, I HAVE TO THANK FIRST MY SUPER-AGENT, NAN. Without you, I'd be nowhere and I am grateful for your support, honesty and wisdom every day. Also, to the extra-ordinary people at Random House: how did I get so lucky? Zoe and Kimberley, your guidance, kindness, creativity and gosh-darn cleverness have made this series possible. And to everybody else at RH: thank you for making me part of the Random family. I also have to thank my writing peeps: 'The League of Extraordinary Writers' (Nansi, Ben, Michael, Rhiannon, Jacqueline, Stuart and the queen of bats, Marianne), and my other 'Critterbugs', Jenny and Bec. You all fill my world with so much laughter and joy and I am so grateful for you. Thank you also to my family: Mum, Dad, Leigh K, Laurel, Craig, Lil Bro and all other Lovells, Gordons and Kleins. And, of course, to my Mephy: thank you for your cuddles, and for being my muse and somebody whose fur I can bury my face in and scream when it all gets too hard! And finally, thank you to everyone who picks up this book. You allow me to do what I love, and every word on every page of this novel is written for you.

about the author

kate GORDON GREW UP IN a very booky house, with two librarian parents, in a small town by the sea on the north-west coast of Tasmania.

In 2009, Kate was the recipient of a Varuna writer's fellowship. Her first book, *Three Things About Daisy Blue* – a young adult novel about travel, love, self-acceptance and letting go – was published in the Girlfriend series by Allen & Unwin in 2010.

Now Kate lives with her husband and her very strange cat, Mephy Danger Gordon. Every morning, while Kate writes, Mephy Danger sits behind her on the couch with his tail curled around her neck.

Kate was the recipient of a 2011 Arts Tasmania Assistance to Individuals grant, which means she can now spend more time losing herself in the world of Thylas and Sarcos.

Kate blogs at **www.kategordon.com.au/blog** and you can follow her on Twitter at **www.twitter.com/misscackle**. She sometimes says some funny stuff!

7-11-13